Coma

J.P.Lewis

authorHOUSE®

AuthorHouse™
1663 Liberty Drive
Bloomington, IN 47403
www.authorhouse.com
Phone: 1-800-839-8640

First published by AuthorHouse   06/08/2011

ISBN: 978-1-4567-8302-0 (sc)
ISBN: 978-1-4567-8374-7 (ebk)

Printed in the United States of America

This book is printed on acid-free paper.

Coma

Contents

Part One—
"Charlie"

CHAPTER ONE

Charlie gave a little nostalgic wave as he cycled out through St Edwards Primary School gates for the last time. He was so excited. It had already been an incredible day. He had passed all his exams and would be starting a new venture in September at the Grammar School. But for now, it was the summer holidays and he couldn't wait. His best friend Daniel Hoggatt and he had so many games to play. He had lots of stories in his head and he knew his sister, Marika, would love to hear them and act them up. Daniel was right behind him. Poor Daniel wouldn't be going to his new school next term and he would miss him. There had been a party at the school for all those leaving and tonight he had another party to look forward to. It was his eleventh birthday and he couldn't wait to see his dad again. He loved his dad. He couldn't remember a time when his dad had lived with them as he had split up from his mum when Charlie was just a baby but he was always there for him. He knew that and he loved that about his dad. His mum was okay but she had many hang-ups, which sometimes made her difficult to be around. Dad was always fun and Charlie couldn't think of a better way to kick-start the holidays.

"Shall I come straight to yours Charlie?" Daniel shouted.

"Don't you need to go home first?" Charlie answered.

"Nah. Mum will still be at work," Daniel told him. "She knows I'm coming to your birthday party. We might have time to play a bit of our game before the others arrive."

"Okay," Charlie agreed. "I think we'll have about an hour before everyone else gets there. We might not be able to go to the woods though". Their favourite game was playing soldiers. They had made a camp in the small copse at the back of where Charlie lived and would stage wars with some of the other children who lived in a nearby road. Charlie's sister, Marika, was their Captain. Yes, she was a girl but she was one year older than them so was always bossing them about. They didn't mind. Charlie loved Marika. They were so close. He had other siblings as well but they had a different dad to him and Marika. Their dad was dead. Rebecca was the eldest. She was at University now so they didn't see much of her but she would be there for him tonight. She had ambitions to be a doctor of medicine like his dad. His dad didn't practice though. He also had a law degree and that was his job as far as Charlie knew. His dad's dad was a Judge. He knew that. He had tried his wig on!

Matthew was eighteen and had just finished his A Levels. Charlie knew he would outshine his effort of passing his tests for Grammar School as Matthew was a bit of a swot. He was very ambitious and competitive. He always had to win when the family played cards and usually did. Charlie didn't mind. He hoped Matthew would achieve great things in his life and make them all proud. Then there was Mark. He was so different from his elder brother. He was sport mad and wasn't really into reading much. He was always out playing cricket or horse riding at Granddads Farm. Granddad may have been a Judge but he lived on a working Farm in the country when he wasn't in London. The youngest of the "Apostles" as Charlie's dad had nicknamed his stepsons was fourteen-year old Luke. He was going through that teenage thing right now. He had played soldiers with them a couple of years ago but not anymore. He was more interested in pop music and girls these days. Charlie loved pop music too of course and he could play the piano. He was secretly hoping that he would get a guitar for his birthday.

The boys had cycled double fast. The adrenalin from the excitement of the day had fuelled them and they were just a minute from getting home when it happened. Daniel saw it first even though he was behind Charlie. The car seemed to be going really fast and was coming towards them on their side of the road. Daniel knew they were on the right side of the road. Both he and Charlie had taken their cycle proficiency tests. They even wore the naff cycle helmets which although weren't really cool to wear on their bikes were great to wear when playing their war games.

"Charlie, look out!" Daniel warned as he bounced his bike up onto the pavement to avoid the car. His warning came too late.

CHAPTER TWO

When Ben Casey was told to take leave he felt lost. It had been a nightmare. How could they do this to him? He had given everything to the Regiment. He had obeyed their orders to the last. Now they were denying those orders and hanging him out to dry. What was he supposed to do now? The Army was his family, his life. He had nothing else. His closest friend was in hospital blown up by some disillusioned religious fanatic. Ben and Mac had been invincible. They had met up five years before when he had joined Macs Regiment. Mac had saved his skin so many times and Ben had returned the compliment. Then Mac was sent on some secret mission, Ben knew nothing about, while he, had been sent to Mexico to kill the terrorists. They had got used to having each other around and suddenly to be sent on separate missions didn't bode well. He had heard the news about Mac just before confronting his targets but that hadn't affected his performance. No. They had died as ordered and it wasn't his fault someone photographed the killing and gave it to the Press. The uproar was because they were unarmed but you don't stop to find out with terrorists. The boot of their car was packed with explosives and firearms but that wasn't enough. His CO was behind him of course but the actual people who had ordered the hit couldn't be seen to have done so. It was a deniable operation like so much of their work. "Take some leave, disappear for a month and when it's all died down we can get back to business" his CO had told him. No medal then!

Of course Ben had gone straight to the hospital to see Mac but he knew his friend didn't want him there, any more than he wanted to be there. It just wasn't their style. Mac was going to live. He had been lucky. The bastards had only cut off his legs. Lucky! Ben was doubtful Mac would look at it that way. They were like brothers, peas in a pod, and this would cut him off from his "family" and Ben knew what that was like. He had been estranged from his "real family" permanently, on his eleventh birthday. His mother had stepped in front of his father as Ben fired his dad's own shotgun at him and she took the hit. Ben supposed she was trying to protect her son from potentially ruining his life, not his dad, but he hadn't seen her until it was too late. She died two days later but at least she had finally owned up to what had been going on in that house that was supposed to be home. The neighbours had called the police and Ben had been taken away. He heard that his mother's dying statement had led to his father being arrested too, but he was never told any more. He never saw his old man again thank goodness. He wondered if he would still try and kill him, if he did. He knew if he had the chance now he wouldn't be messing it up. Every man he had killed since, and there had been many of course, had the face of his dad. He told the Courts the truth at his own trial and he didn't know whether they had believed his story. He wasn't called as a witness at a trial for his dad so now he realised he probably got away with it. After that, all he knew was the confines of Juvenile Detention and he witnessed first-hand how cruel some human beings could be. It was a good grounding for some of the inhumane acts he would see later on.

So where could he go? He didn't have a home outside of the Regiment. The only people he knew would be there. Mac as always gave him an idea although he didn't realise it.

When Ben had first joined up eight years before, his brother in arms back then had been Andy Davies, although not at first. Andy was a completely different character from Ben. For a start Andy came from a loving family home and was quite a gentle soul. Not really cut out for the Army. His father was a doctor and lived in a big house with a beautiful garden. Growing up where he had in Wales Ben had never realised such places existed in real life. Ben hadn't felt the need to stick up for Andy early on when their Sergeant Major took an instant dislike to him although he hated injustice. He realised that the SM was probably thinking what he was; that Andy wasn't made of stern enough stuff to survive and maybe it was better to let him down now. So he hadn't befriended Andy and actually kept his distance. But Ben didn't make friends easily back then anyway. It took him a long time to speak to the other cadets let alone let them in. He was a loner. He had had to be, to survive his life up till then. Andy, on the other hand, was a team player and from that point of view had something to teach Ben who had only ever looked after himself. Andy's entire family turned up to watch their final Parade. No one was there for Ben.

Realising Ben's situation Andy and his dad invited him back to their home when they were given a period of leave following passing out. It wasn't until he arrived at their lovely house in Windsor and saw the obvious love and respect between father and son that he became almost in awe of his friend. For that's what he was now, his friend. He wasn't jealous, that wasn't his nature but rather enjoyed the privilege of witnessing it first hand. Had things gone differently the good life might have rubbed off on him and he could have been a much better individual. He knew he wasn't as good as he should be. He was a trained killer after all. He'd inherited that trait because of his old man.

Andy and Ben were posted together and for the following two years their friendship went from strength to strength. There was such a contrast to their upbringing and personalities but it made no difference to them. It probably helped Ben more than Andy. It gave him the education he had missed out on by teaching him there is a decent side to life and when the chips are down you still watch your mates back and he will watch yours. Ben helped Andy to be more Worldly-wise of course and not believe everything he's told. Sadly Andy's naivety proved to be his undoing when a car bomb exploded and blew his legs off. He was only twenty.

So that's how Mac had given Ben the idea.

He hadn't kept in touch with Andy after he was invalided out of the Army, to his shame. Being around someone who had been seriously injured whilst doing their job always had a bad effect on people like Ben. It reminded them of their immortality and that wasn't good when you still had to go out and do the job. He knew Andy wouldn't blame him. That's just how it was.

But that had been five years ago now and it was time.

CHAPTER THREE

As Jonathan Havers left the office his mobile bleeped. He didn't want to look at it. He was excited. He was heading off to his son's eleventh birthday party and he didn't want anything to hold him up. It was the downside to being a "bachelor". The office always thought he could be the one called out when a client had fallen foul of the law because he didn't have a life. But that wasn't true. Jonathan was quite the man about town these days. No one really knew how he had got trapped into such an obviously bad marriage. He was extremely handsome, intelligent, wealthy and eloquent. In fact, some glossy magazine had just printed a feature about him, citing him as the man most women would wish to meet.

But Jonathan wasn't interested in things like that. He was a genuine person and he would never regret having his beautiful daughter, Marika and his loving son, Charlie. Sarah wasn't a bad person, just a mistake. He had probably been a bit naïve when he met her. She was very attractive and quite determined when she put her mind to something. What a strange life she had lived up to that point. Raised in a Vicarage she had rebelled wildly in her teens, run away from home and joined a pop group called The Dixie Chicks. They had been fantastically successful almost immediately with three number one records straight off. Sarah had succumbed to all the usual pitfalls of course. She had been too innocent back then to escape. When the group split she had fallen into complete degradation, a drug addict with several broken relationships behind her. The money began to run out and she was in the depths of despair at only twenty years of age! Then unexpectedly she had met Adam and was "saved"! A devout Catholic Adam converted Sarah back to religion and she cleaned up her act. They married quickly and started a family immediately. She had four children under the age of eight when he died from cancer. Had God let her down?

She started drinking at Adams funeral. No one could blame her for that. But she had an addictive personality and the drinking got heavier. Her Church rallied round for the sake of the children. She was a fragile spirit. She couldn't cope alone. She needed a new mission to focus on. She was still devout so the Church enlisted her to form a Committee to begin raising funds for a new Spire. She met Jonathan at a Garden Party she hosted for the Church Fund. He had just graduated from medical school but was confused about what he wanted to do and was taking some time out. He had travelled to begin with but the money had run out and so had been forced to live at home again on his dad's farm. His father was supposed to attend the party as the local dignitary but had gone down with flu the day before. His mother persuaded him to escort her to the party instead and Sarah was in good form that day. She was in her element. The star attraction, the hostess with the most and Jonathan had been impressed. He loved her children. She suddenly realised that he could be the answer to her prayers and set about snaring him. He was, of course a few years younger, but he had such promise.

After she told him she was pregnant, of course, he had to marry her. It wasn't really an option back then. It certainly wasn't in his plans. He had decided to take up law and had gone back to College to study. His father had been delighted with that and fully supported him but marrying Sarah was not in the reckoning. For a start, she was older and she had four young children. Yet it was a fait accompli.

By the time he graduated from Law School, Marika and her brother had both been born. He had been allowed to choose his daughters name, didn't want another biblical one and she was incredible, he had to admit that. Baby John had also come along a year later and now Sarah had the complete set of Apostles! John soon got called Charlie from his middle name though, to avoid confusion in the house with his dad. But the marriage was struggling. Jonathan tried his best. He adored all six children but Sarah was difficult to live with and he realised he didn't really love her. He suspected he never had. Eventually they agreed to separate for the sake of the children. The rows were having a negative effect on the family home and Jonathan wanted to avoid that at all costs. Sarah agreed it wasn't working out but she was a stronger person now, thanks to him. She stated that she would never give him a divorce but he could live away. Part of the breakdown was her refusal to use any form of birth control due to her faith and her absolute conviction that she didn't want any more children. She refused all surgical intervention as well and so basically they had separate bedrooms. His moving out wasn't really a big deal as since he had got a job at a Law Firm in the City he was hardly ever there anyway. The children missed him most but he always tried to find time to spend with them and never missed anything important in their lives, such as birthdays, sports days, school plays etc. In that way he did better than Sarah who had fallen into a busy life with the Church Committees she attended and the constant Fund raising.

So, this was one of those important days, his son's birthday as well as his last day of school. Should he check his phone? What if it was work? It was hard for him to say no to his boss just now. He was working hard trying to prove himself, what would they think? He had reached his car. If he was going to check his phone he had to do it now before he started driving. He looked and saw with relief the call was from his step-daughter, Rebecca. The relief was short lived.

CHAPTER FOUR

Ben had been incredibly impressed that Dr Davies actually recognised his voice on the telephone and had sounded delighted to hear from him after all this time. That was typical of such a nice family and Ben felt a suitable semblance of guilt. Not usually his style. What was it with this family that could bring out something in him he usually kept buried? He put him in touch with Andy and he was on his way to visit him. A lot had happened it seemed in the five years. Andy was now a successful musician, married, with a baby son. Having false legs hadn't held him back. He lived in Kent. Ben had only been there when travelling to France or for his initial training at the firing range near Hythe but it didn't take him long to find the pretty chocolate box thatched cottage next to the village pond. He smiled when he saw it.

Andy's wife was American and she was also a musician. They both played guitar and had actually sold real records. They were practically famous. She was incredibly welcoming and he was offered a bed for as long as he wanted. He was overwhelmed with the generosity he was shown yet again.

Andy knew something was bothering his friend, otherwise why would he be there. He was not the sort to feel sorry for him-self so it had to be serious. Although they hadn't kept in touch he knew that Ben was going to go far in the Army. He was made of the right stuff but Andy had always sensed that there was a more gentle side to Ben if only things had been different for him when growing up. He knew a bit about his background, just snippets. The fact he never talked about his family gave him a clue. This had something to do with the Army. He probably never took leave normally, not long enough to get right away like this anyway. Had he been thrown out? He wasn't injured physically but there was something. There had been a lot in the Press lately of course about the SAS executions, as they were phrased. Was that Ben? Was he SAS now? He was still so young but Andy knew his friend would aspire to that Regiment for sure. What Andy did know was not to ask. If Ben wanted to talk about it he would in his own time but for now Andy would just let him know he was there for him. That's what being a friend meant, albeit a lapsed friend.

CHAPTER FIVE

When Jonathan reached the Accident and Emergency Department at St Edwards Hospital he saw Sarah was talking to a Doctor and joined them immediately. She looked distressed and his stomach was churning. He wasn't religious like her but if there was a God, please, please, please . . . .

"Oh God Jonathan, it's serious", Sarah turned to her husband for comfort.

"Is he?" Jonathan could hardly bring himself to ask.

"Your son is still alive Mr Havers but his condition is critical, I'm afraid" the doctor informed him. "He has suffered a great many injuries but the most serious is that we believe there is a swelling and possible bleeding in the brain. I have sent for a Consultant and we need your permission to operate as soon as he arrives."

"We have money. We can pay for the very best Doctor," Sarah said needlessly.

"Sarah, I'm sure Charlie is in good hands here and I doubt he can be moved" her husband told her in a voice sounding much calmer than he felt inside. "Of course you have our permission Doctor. We want you to do whatever it takes to save our son, please".

The doctor smiled patiently and left them. Sarah asked for his phone. She had left the house with the police and hadn't stopped to collect her handbag. "I want to call Father Benedict, he needs to be here, in case Charlie needs the last rites", she explained. Jonathan wasn't in the mood for arguing with her and handed the phone over telling her to go outside before she used it. He helped himself to some coffee from the machine and prepared himself for the long and anxious wait that lay ahead. How could this have happened?

Mr and Mrs Hoggatt came to collect Daniel. He hadn't been injured but the paramedics had insisted he attend the hospital too just to be checked over. Daniel appeared from behind some curtains and ran into his parents arms crying. Jonathan watched from a distance unable to comprehend the situation. The Hoggatts hurried off, as if unable to face the Havers, Their son had been spared. He didn't blame them but had hoped for some information, some explanation from Daniel. Perhaps the police would come again. Sarah hadn't come back. She was probably having a cigarette outside, he thought. She was supposed to have given up but he knew she still had the odd sneaky one when the situation called for it. Well, it certainly did now. He almost wished he smoked.

After some time, Father Benedict and Sarah walked back in together. He wasn't able to visit Charlie as the Consultant had arrived and the operation to relieve the pressure on the boys' brain had begun. Jonathan was relieved. He didn't want Charlie receiving the last rites; that seemed obscene to him. His son wasn't going to die. He was eleven years old today. His birthday couldn't possibly be his death day. No. Instead the priest took Sarah off to the hospital Chapel to pray. Jonathan decided he should update Rebecca who was holding the fort with the children at home although he didn't know what he would say, but they would be desperate for some news. He would call his parents too and Sarah's dad. He would just keep busy but still the time would seem endless and the wait unbearable.

The Consultant had wasted no time getting to the Hospital. He was a dedicated man and the patient was just a young boy, like his own son. He scrubbed up and began the operation. The boy was beautiful. He had terrible injuries. Broken bones and trauma to his body wherever you looked but still he was beautiful. Thank Goodness he had been wearing a helmet. That at least had saved his life up to now but there was no telling if he lived what his life would be like from this moment on. Things would never be the same the doctor realised that but for now he could only worry about keeping him alive.

The operation took a long time but had been successful. They had stemmed the bleeding inside and relieved the swelling causing the pressure on the brain but there was a long way to go. For now, Charlie was in a coma.

CHAPTER SIX

January Davies loved her life. She had come to England as an art student, playing guitar to make ends meet. She had grown up on a farm in Tennessee and music was in her blood. All her family played instruments and there was always singing when they got together. She missed them but wouldn't change anything. When she had met Andy it had been love at first sight. He played the guitar better than her, she believed, true Spanish guitar, not electric and his accent was to die for. Actually Ben had a decent voice too. It was Welsh and very lyrical. She wondered if he sang. He hardly spoke. Was he shy? No, out of his depth maybe, but not shy. She understood Andy was playing a waiting game. Move too soon and you could lose but she wanted to move things on a bit quicker. She was pregnant again and wanted time alone with her husband to tell him. She knew it would be joyous but didn't think that would be appropriate with Ben so obviously depressed. So, she urged her husband to take Ben to the Pub and try to bring him out of himself more. If he could just start talking he might not stop and once he had opened up he would feel a lot better. That's what her mamma used to say and she was seldom wrong.

The Pub, as it was affectionately known, was actually a very infamous venue. Situated in their village it was owned by an ex pop star, Rees Darrow, who had been the King of Pop just a couple of decades ago. She and Andy played there regularly and some very famous musicians were often seen jamming. It was the villages' best-kept secret, informal and relaxed and the Celebrities loved it. Ben would be amazed. A few pints of their excellent local brewed Ale and who knew? The two pals walked the short distance to the Pub. Ben was impressed once more at the ease his friend managed to overcome his handicap. He had an obvious limp, his walking did look awkward and if it caused him pain he never complained. He knew Mac would benefit from meeting Andy once he got out of hospital and resolved to do something about that.

The Pub was amazing. Ben wasn't that well up on the list of Who's who in the world of celebrities but even he recognised a lot of the faces sitting around the bar having a quiet drink or two. He felt a little insignificant and decided to hit the bottle to give his self some courage. The whisky chasers were starting to have an effect but Ben wasn't going to open up to Andy. Andy had been to hell and back and never complained. How could he whinge to him about the Family; the Army? Instead he was going to forget all that tonight and have fun and who better than the good looking bird standing at the bar sipping red wine. She was his kind of woman. Olive skinned, very dark long hair, big brown eyes, gorgeous. He made a move while Andy was visiting the little boy's room. Oh yes, he was pretty drunk but he could still make the moves. Jill Juanita Sorenson wasn't impressed. She was a happily married woman. Her husband Dave was a famous guitarist in the best rock and roll band in the world and she would die for him. The young man was nice looking but he was drunk and she wasn't sure what would happen if Dave walked in and caught him chatting her up. It was an awkward situation as she didn't want to cause trouble but she needed to get rid of him. He was trying to charm her and she wanted to be polite but not give him any illusions. Yet the more she shied away, the more he seemed to take that as a challenge and then it happened. Dave walked in and was not happy. There is no doubt in the world there would have been a punch-up had the "angel" not stepped in when she did. Jill knew her husband was tall and strong but she doubted he was a match for this stranger. There was something about him that looked dangerous. As the boys squared up the girl didn't hesitate. Marika had only come in about five minutes before with a girlfriend from the theatre where they both worked. She had spotted Dave Sorenson the minute he walked in. She was a massive fan of his band. She couldn't allow him to get hurt. She acted on instinct. What else could have made her do such a daring thing? She moved in on the agitated stranger.

"Hello darling, when are you going to buy me a drink?" she said to the stranger. Ben was definitely caught off guard for once. He hadn't seen her coming but there she was making him an offer he couldn't refuse. She was gorgeous, dark haired, his type again. Blue eyes, not brown, but so startling blue he could hardly hold that against her. She wasn't giving him the run around, saying she's married, telling him to go away and sober up. No. It was quite the opposite, in fact. Ben had never backed down from a fight in his life but somewhere in the background he suddenly spotted his friend, Andy, looking a bit concerned. This was his local. He played music here, probably depended on it. He couldn't wreck the place. That would be very bad form. Was this his get out? Could he just ignore the Spanish senora now and save face by taking up with this beautiful gate crasher? Of course, that was Marika's plan. Give the man an excuse and he will see sense. If not, he wasn't someone she should be drinking with.

"Of course darling, you're late. What's your poison, the usual?" he asked.

Oh yes that's better she thought. She liked a bit of fore play. "I thought you'd never ask".

And that was how they met.

CHAPTER SEVEN

"When is he going to wake up?"

Sarah had asked that question so many times and to so many people. It was a rhetorical question of course because no one knew the answer. He would wake up when and if he wakes up. No one, it seemed, understood comas. At least no one could explain them to her. It was a good thing apparently. The rest would do him good and give his brain a chance to recuperate from the terrible trauma. In fact, the longer he remained in a coma the better his chances were of a full recovery. The doctors were probably just trying to give comfort because the truth was no one knew, she understood that now but it didn't stop her asking the question again. Keep talking to him she had been told. Well that may sound easy enough but what could she possibly say to an eleven year old boy who wasn't responding. She had run out of conversation a long time ago and the endless bleeping of the machine that was keeping him alive was also driving her to distraction. She didn't think she could do this much longer. Thank Goodness everyone was rallying around.

Father Benedict was a regular caller and they would sit and say prayers next to Charlie's bedside. That helped Sarah a lot, made her feel useful. Jonathan would be there too, every evening, as soon as he could get away from work. He had been there non-stop in the beginning but eventually had had to return to work. He didn't work like he used to though. He thought they could sack him if they wanted to. His son was more important than his job. He wasn't going to be at their beck and call, not now. Maybe when it was over, one way or another, they could have their pound of flesh again but not now. When Sarah had been at her most desperate she had made him a deal. If God spares their son, if he would only wake up, she would let Jonathan go. It would be her sacrifice for her sons' life.

Jonathan's parents were also regular visitors. The Judge could only come at weekends of course but he would spend hours talking to his

Grandson. Jonathan had never had any proper conversations with his dad while he was growing up. His father was too aloof, too busy, too important, and too clever. He had been in awe of his dad. He loved and respected him but was always a bit frightened of him too. He was the man who could cut off your head. Well, no, not exactly, but he had had the imagination of all children. Of course he had always wanted to impress his dad, anything to grab his attention. He shied away from law at first because he was too intimidated of not being so successful. He almost felt jealous of the way his father could talk to Charlie. He didn't talk to him like he was a child but a grown-up and he knew Charlie would love that. His son couldn't wait to grow up but would he ever get the chance?

Jonathan's mother, Joy, was a different character altogether. She was a wonderful mother. He had been an only child so she doted on him but tried hard never to spoil him. She was so competent at all she did, that of course she succeeded in bringing up her son to be a well-rounded caring and loving man. She would visit the hospital whenever no one else could. Rebecca had set up a rota for visitors. She was such an organised child. She felt it was important someone was always there and of course she was right. Charlie mustn't feel he's been abandoned. Marika would be there every minute of every day if they had allowed her. Her distress was apparent. Charlie was her partner in crime. He was her other half and she needed him back.

Daniel came a few times in the beginning. He talked to Charlie about their game. He updated him on the war in the woods but their army was so depleted without their Captain, (Marika had no time for playing any more) and their best fighter. Their best fighter, Charlie, had his own private war it seemed.

What happened to the driver of the car? He/she had driven off from the scene. Daniel had provided a description of the car to the police and a couple walking their dog had thought they spotted a man behind the wheel but the description was vague and there was no car number. All they really had to go on was, it was big and black, and possibly a people carrier with blacked out windows. That's why it had been difficult to see the driver. It would be damaged of course and the police would alert all the garages in the area but for now no one could say. It was an unusual time for a drink driver to be about and the local pubs had no further information. The story had been all over the front page of the newspapers and Luke had kept a scrapbook for Charlie.

Nurse Gwen Booth was impressed with Charlie's fan club. She had very little to do because of it. His sisters and Grandmother were always keen to help wash the boy and keep him comfortable. They were like clucking hens. His mother wasn't so impressive but she seemed to have personal problems dealing with it and the nurse wasn't surprised when her name disappeared from the rota. She still came, from time to time, but usually with the priest. She noticed that after they had said their prayers and left there was a change in Charlie's demeanour. She could have sworn he appeared to give a sigh once and this made her smile. "Bit of a captured audience, aren't you my lad?" she would say to him. "Best wake up then and tell them their prayers worked so can they please desist!" His father, on the other hand, was impressive, very dishy and always cheerful. He used to tell his son hilarious stories about his day, probably made up or exaggerated ridiculously she suspected but he certainly had a way of telling a story. She could imagine they had a wonderful relationship.

His brother, Matthew, wanted to be a doctor and was always asking her questions about her job and the equipment surrounding his brother. He was fascinated by everything about the hospital and was charming. "He's going to break a few hearts that big brother of yours Charlie, mark my words", she would say to her patient after Matthew had interrogated her again. "I expect you will too when you grow up".

CHAPTER EIGHT

When Ben woke up he had no idea where he was or how he had got there. The bed was very warm and there was this beautiful creature's head on the pillow next to his. He tried to focus. It was the girl from the Pub, what was her name? It was something exotic, something that suited her. Marika. Eureka! He smiled. Wow! He felt happy for the first time in what seemed like forever! It was a beautiful room, high ceiling, white walls but not much light. What time was it then? His watch told him 6.52am. She was breathing very gently, sleeping peacefully. He eased out of the bed and found his clothes and moved stealthily across the room without waking her.

It was a basement flat in an old Victorian building somewhere in London, no wonder there wasn't much light in the bedroom. There was plenty outside. The birds had got up some two hours before. The light actually reminded him that he had a hangover. He checked the kitchen out, checked the whole flat out in fact. It didn't take long. There was only one bedroom, a galley type kitchen and an enormous lounge with massive windows up to the street above. He loved it. She had good taste. Well of course! Hadn't she picked him?

Marika woke up just a few minutes after Ben. She was actually smiling she realised. Had she been smiling in her sleep? How embarrassing. She stopped smiling when she saw the empty pillow beside her and the dent in the bed where he had laid. Oh typical, he's done a runner. I only know his name is Ben. Ben what? No idea. Where does he live? No idea. Phone number? No. What does he do for a living? Who knows? Suddenly and inexplicably she felt really sad. She didn't want to let this one get away. Of course she had only stepped in to stop a fight. It had been instinctive. She hated confrontation. She despised fighting. Life's too short. Everyone should make love and not war. She understood war. She wasn't exactly a pacifist, but maybe a bit of an idealist. It just seemed to her it would be a sensible thing to do. Step in, stop the macho hormones flying around the bar and just have a drink and be happy. That's what she had gone there for in the first place. Her girlfriend Sally, (wonder what happened to her Marika thought), had thought the Pub was the perfect place to meet the right man and Marika had just written off another failed relationship. Well, it wasn't exactly a relationship. She had been out with James for about a month but it hadn't worked out. He bored her and that was no good. She knew she could be difficult to handle. It wasn't James' fault but he just wasn't up to the challenge. Ben seemed like he could handle a challenge. But now he had fallen at the first hurdle. How dare he run out on her? Was she angry or sad? A bit of both if she was honest. Not only that but she had a headache. What had they been drinking last night? She didn't know but she remembers singing in the taxi and the driver applauding her as they got out. He said he had loved her voice. Well, didn't he realise that people actually pay to hear her sing, not the other way round. No, in fairness, Ben had been chivalrous enough to pay the cab fare. What happened then? She offered him coffee but realised there was no milk. Her fridge was empty and he mocked her. She was hopeless in the kitchen. That was the penalty for living two streets away from the best coffee house in London. Why bother to make it yourself when Antonio is an expert at Lattes. She pretended to be upset at his mocking and they had a play fight which led to the bedroom and then . . . no, this was one you mustn't let get away Marika.

She was about to get up when she heard the door click and Ben appeared at the bedroom door with a tray of two lattes from Antonios and some fresh croissants and she knew her life was about to change forever.

CHAPTER NINE

"I'm so sorry Major I haven't been to see you all week but we started back at school on Monday and mum won't let me come out in the evenings because of homework", Marika told her brother as she tidied his bedding and re-arranged his latest Get Well cards. "You're such a lazy boy. You've missed the whole of the school holidays lying about here and it was sunny on at least three occasions that I can remember. I haven't been to the Camp in the woods. Since you told me about that man chasing you and Daniel I think the troops have been posted elsewhere. Has Daniel been in this week? He would have started at his new school and probably hates it. I did, when I first started at the big school, remember? I didn't like leaving you behind at St Edwards for a start. Then everyone stares at you in your new uniform. It didn't help that mum sent me to school an hour earlier than any of the other first formers were starting on their first day and they sat me on a chair in the playground until the rest arrived. I had all the older ones taking the mick. I hated her for that. She's such a dummy sometimes, well actually, most times. You've missed your first week at the Grammar School now, you'll be behind the others when you get back but I suppose you'll catch up. I'll help you. I bought a new record today. Our favourite group Spirit have a new one out and it's gone to number one in just one week. No wonder, it's absolutely brilliant and of course I'm besotted with the keyboard-player, as you know. I'll have to copy it for you to listen to. Matthew did terrifically well in his A Levels. Well, we knew he would, didn't we, swot that he is! Mum is beside herself telling all the neighbours and the Church and anyone who can be bothered to listen or can't escape. She's so proud of her children when it suits. She loves all the sympathy she gets over you, of course, lapping it up. You'd think she was the one suffering. You must wake up soon and steal her thunder. Matthew is going off to Uni next month. He has got into Cambridge. Says he doesn't want to steal our Becky's thunder at Oxford. More like, he's scared she'll beat him. Mark, bless him has opted out of school, did he tell you? He said he didn't want to go to Uni so there didn't seem any point staying on for 'A' levels and all that. I don't blame him. Soon as I can I'm out of there too. I can't understand anyone wanting to prolong the agony. I'm going to be an actress did you know that? Of course you did. Remember all the plays we used to put on for Gran at Christmas. She'll be expecting another one this year so you'd better hurry up and get better before then. I shall need your help writing it up and getting our costumes ready. You know how you love sewing. Yeah right! Anyway, Mark is going to help out on Granddads Farm. He's going to go to Agricultural College and learn all about farming, so that someday, he can take it over. Won't that be cool? How does your arm feel? Did you know they reset it? Your leg is coming out of plaster too soon. You should see what daddy wrote on it. It's really funny. Oh do wake up Charlie. It's dead boring without you. I want to ask your opinion about my new boyfriend. His name is Ben and I met him yesterday on the school bus. He's dead cool, a bit older than us. I need you to meet him and tell me what you think. I think you'll like him. He's quite quiet but that's probably a good thing for me isn't it? I can talk for everyone you always say".

"Come on darling, say your good-byes to Charlie, it's time to go", the children's Grandmother said.

"Oh Gran, I need just a bit longer. I haven't finished telling him everything yet!" Marika protested.

"Well, you can tell him next time," Lady Havers told her. "You should save something. We can come back tomorrow".

"He looks a bit better today don't you think Gran?" Marika commented. "Bye Major, this is your Captain signing off for now. See you soon. Love you".

CHAPTER TEN

Five days had gone by before Ben realised he hadn't spoken to Andy to let him know where he was. He should call him and thank him for his hospitality and pick the rest of his kit up. He could buy Andy a farewell drink and promise to keep in touch. This girl had taken over his life. He had never experienced love before, except from his mum and his sister, Gwen, but he chose not to remember all that now, after what happened. Yet, he was sure this must be it. When she wasn't there he couldn't stop thinking about her and when she was he couldn't stop staring at her. She was absolutely beautiful inside and out. They still knew nothing about each other although it seemed like they had talked and talked. Well, she had, anyway. She was incredibly amusing. He knew she was an actress, as she had to go to the theatre every evening to perform. She was in a comedy, not exactly at the West End, but still playing to a house upwards of 500 people. How did she do that? He couldn't imagine. He had been to see her every evening and never got tired of it. He probably knew her lines better than her now. He also knew she couldn't cook. He had never been trained in the art of family cooking but he knew how to fry eggs and make tea and if he had to start a fire to cook on he could do that too of course. He didn't. There was a small stove in the galley and he loved trying to create meals for her. She ate whatever he made and pretended to enjoy it. He loved her for that. It was her flat but he was trying to contribute and she appreciated that. He was living the dream he supposed. Sooner or later reality would have to kick in but for now, well, this would do nicely.

Marika had even surprised herself. She was not known for picking up strange men in bars bringing them home on the first date and keeping them captive. What was going on? When she thought he had done a runner she was devastated but then he came back and wowed her. No man had brought her coffee and fresh croissants in bed before. It was impossibly romantic in her book and yet he seemed an unlikely candidate for that, when she first saw him. It hadn't been love at first sight. He looked "interesting" but she would have gone no further than that. He was obviously full of male testosterone, a he-man who liked to go out and capture the food, bring it back and serve it up to her. She knew he needed to feel he was the provider in this situation. It was her flat, she held the keys but she was very close to handing the spare ones over already. He hadn't moved in exactly. He had no clothes other than what he stood up in and had bought from the market on their first excursion out into the wide world together. That had taken two days. They hadn't left the bedroom until they got so hungry and she knew she was back at work that night. So, they'd gone to the market together and even that was fun. She'd tried on all sorts of hats, she loved to expand her weird wardrobe whenever possible, and chose his clothes. He didn't look impressed, he wanted the jeans and t-shirts exactly the same as the clothes he already owned. She was willing to bet that his kit at Andy's was full of jeans and t-shirts. Yet, he bowed to her judgement and looked great in the new outfits. It took a bit of persuasion but he realised he actually liked the new him.

When he said he wasn't going to the show that night she felt a murmur of disappointment rising in her stomach. Oh no, he's getting bored of me, she thought, though she also couldn't imagine how he had sat through three performances already. Then when he explained he wasn't coming because he was going to see Andy and pick up his kit she felt a rush of excitement. Does this mean?

"I think I owe Andy an explanation. You don't mind do you?" he asked her in that beautiful lyrical Welsh accent she had fallen in love with.

"No, of course not and of course you do. He must think I've eaten you or something by now," she told him.

"Well you nearly did last night", he said cheekily. They both smiled as they remembered the incident.

"Will you pick up your kit?" She liked to use the same words he did when describing his property. It was nicer. Kit. That's not particularly a Welsh term she thought, more an Army term. Was that what he did? He did have an organised mind and a sharp haircut.

"Well, I suppose I should relieve them of it, might be stinking by now". He was desperate not to sound presumptive. What if she thinks that's too much? He can't just bring his stuff in here. It's her flat. He should wait to be asked. So he tried to make a bit of a joke of it.

He's joking about it but I want him to bring it here, she thought. I want him to feel he can stay but what do I do? What if I ask him, will he run a mile? Marika had never felt so unsure of herself. She was walking on glass, trying not to say the wrong thing. How to sound casual so he doesn't feel pressurised. "Well, shall I make some space? Can I expect more jeans and t-shirts?" That's it. Make a joke too. Keep it light hearted. Oh this was ridiculous. She was a direct person who said what she was thinking. Why was she behaving like this? "You are coming back aren't you", she eventually got out trying not to sound as desperate as she felt.

Oh my god, he thought. She actually wants me back. I can't believe this. She's fantastic and she wants me here with her. I'd be an idiot to mess this up. "If you'll have me?" he almost whispered.

They fell into each other's arms and there was no more talking.

CHAPTER ELEVEN

"I started at the Comp this week Charlie. I hate it. None of my friends from St Edwards are there and the uniforms horrible. I wish you were there. You'd have a right laugh at the history teacher. He's got really long hair and thinks he's hip but he wears really tatty jackets and talks with a bit of a lisp. He's terrible. I'm not going to learn anything off of him. He doesn't want to tell us about the war. Keeps going back to the Agricultural Revolution and boring stuff like that. I hate it. Can't wait to leave school and join the Army. My dad says I'll never be big and strong enough to be a soldier but little does he know, eh mate? We took that bunch from Henderson Street last year, just you and me and a girl! Marika doesn't ever come to the woods now. I heard she's got a boyfriend. No one knows where he's from. Not been seen around our neck of the woods before and he travels on her school bus but doesn't have a uniform on. That's what I've heard anyway. Do you think it's true? It's a bit of a mystery. Everybody at the youth clubs talking about it, making up stories and stuff. Could be, he's a bit older than her, maybe not even at school anymore? Dunno. My bike's been playing up again, got to get those gears fixed. Maybe it'll get nicked at school and I can have a new one. The Police took your bike away, what was left of it. Evidence they said. They're probably trying to match the paint on it to the car that hit you. That's what they do. I saw it on The Bill last week. They came to see me again to see if I could remember anything but I can't. I want to. I try to picture the car but I can't. It's a bit of a blank. You'd think I'd been hit on the head, not you. Mum says it's just the shock. Wish I could remember though. I was thinking Charlie. What if it's that man that chased us? Do you remember? You saw him throw something, a sack or something in the pontoon, then I sneezed and he saw us watching him. Well, he saw you. He didn't know I was there, did he? I was down below the bank and you said to me to just run. So we ran back to our bikes and beat it. It was scary. What if it's him? Should I tell the police? I'm scared if I do he might come after me. I want to help the Police catch him for what he did to you but I'm scared. When you get better we could catch him in our trap and take him back to HQ and torture him till he admitted it. When are you going to wake up then? You've been sleeping since the start of the holidays. That was two months ago now. It'll be Christmas soon and you haven't even unwrapped your birthday presents yet. I think you got a guitar from your dad. I saw it wrapped up when I went round to ask when I could visit. I've told Rebecca I can't come much now. Mum and Dad don't like me sitting here all the time but I'm not ready to give up on you yet. If you don't wake up soon though mate, well it's dead boring talking to you and you don't talk back. Can you even hear me?"

Nurse Gwen Booth knew all Charlie's visitors by their names now. "Hello Daniel, are you still here?"

"Can he hear me do you think nurse?" Daniel asked.

"Oh yes he can hear you all right. I'm certain of it," the nurse replied positively.

"How can you be?" Daniel was sceptic.

"Oh, he lets me know in his own way," Nurse Booth answered.

"Do you think he will wake up?" Daniel asked her.

"One day Daniel, one day," she replied.

"But when?" he asked vainly.

"That's something we don't know. But when he's ready he'll wake up and he will remember everything you've said and how good you've been at coming to see him," she said.

"Will he?" Daniel was impressed.

"Is he your best friend Daniel?" she asked him.

"Oh yes, Charlie's the best friend ever and I really miss him," came the tearful response.

"Don't cry little man. Just remember he might not even be here giving us all hope," and with that Nurse Booth gave Daniel a cuddle until he felt better and his mum came to pick him up.

"So Charlie you see how you've upset your best friend now, don't you think it's time" she said to her patient as she tucked his sheets in and made him comfortable. She wouldn't swear to it but she was sure he smiled, just for a second.

CHAPTER TWELVE

"I'm glad you called in dad. I've got some news," Marika told her favourite person in the whole world, well until Ben that was.

"Have you got a live-in lover?" her father asked astutely.

How did he do that? Her dad always could read her like a book but straight to it. It was uncanny. "How did you know?" she asked, surprised.

"Could it be because you're making coffee in your own kitchen? You've actually got milk in the fridge and there are washed up dishes on the draining board. I know you've only got the one bedroom so you haven't taken in a lodger and of course there is that incredibly wide smile on your face!!" Jonathan teased her.

Marika smiled from ear to ear as if to prove his point. "He's amazing dad. I only met him nine days ago but I feel I've known him all my life. I think I'm in love. Am I dad?"

"How would I know?" Jonathan asked. He had yet to experience it for himself.

"Oh yes, I forgot, you've never been in love," she could tease just as well as him.

"Okay, here's the dad bit," Jonathan put his serious face on. "What's he called? Where is he from? What does he do? How much does he earn? Is he a good person? Does he treat you right?"

"Let me see. His name is Ben," she replied.

"Ben? Ben who," Jonathan asked.

"Ah, I don't know yet. I think he's from Wales," Marika told him.

"You think?" Jonathan asked again.

"Well he has a gorgeous Welsh accent. I think he may be in the army," she said.

"What?" her father was a bit shocked. He had never imagined his arty daughter getting mixed up with a man of war.

"Well, I'm just guessing. I don't know for sure. He has money, pays his way, more than. I don't know if he's a good person but he treats me more than right, yes," she continued.

"I thought you said you felt like you've known him all your life. You don't seem to know much about him," Jonathan commented.

"I know. We do talk a lot but I suppose never about those things. I don't like to push him. I think he has a story to tell but I want him to choose the moment he tells me everything," Marika explained.

"How do you know he isn't wanted for murder or something?" her father said.

"You need to meet him dad. We should go out for a drink but you mustn't interview him or anything. If you scare him off I'll never forgive you," his daughter warned him.

"You know me better than that love," Jonathan told her. "Where is he now?"

"He's gone running. He's super fit. Usually goes for miles along the river first thing in the morning then comes back with fresh croissants and coffee from Antonios to wake me up with but, this morning, other things got in the way," she couldn't hide the smile as she remembered what those other things were. "So I sent him off now so I could get you down. How was Hamburg by the way?"

"Does he know I live in the flat above yours?" her father was still curious.

"Not yet," she answered. "You've been away so it didn't come up but dad, you may have to curb calling in here when you feel like it, without, well you know, a bit of warning . . . ."

"How long have I got?" Jonathan asked.

"You should go now," Marika realised. "I'll call you when I've told him and we'll have that drink. He needs to realise he has to pass the dad test if he's staying."

"And is he?" her father asked.

"Hope so dad, hope so," she said.

CHAPTER THIRTEEN

"I think you look a bit brighter today Charlie. All this sleep must be doing you good. I wish I were a better sleeper. I've had a very tense week. Had a woman up before me for manslaughter," the Judge told his Grandson. "She was one of those battered wives and she finally retaliated. Do you know what I mean by battered wife? Her husband used to go out drinking and come back from the Pub at closing time demanding his dinner, which of course, was in the bin. When he didn't get what he wanted he would start to slap her around. Of course, in the morning, when he sobered up, he'd beg for forgiveness. He was sober but her face was still bruised and she wouldn't be able to go to work for the shame. He wouldn't get his beer money and this would cause more rows, of course. The violence would escalate. Sometimes he would rape her just to make a point. Show her he was in charge. It was a never-ending cycle. Your Grandmother will tell me off for telling you all this. You're not supposed to know about such worldly things at your age. I expect you understand what rape is though. Children today seem to know everything or at least they think they do. Your Grandmother would prefer you not to know of course, she thinks children should be allowed to be children and she has a point but I think we should all live outside our bubbles. This wretched woman had children too. Violence is all they know of life. Her son will probably grow up thinking that hitting a woman or anyone of inferior physical standing is fair game. You will grow up knowing nothing of this life. The thought of your father hitting your mother would never occur to you because it would never happen. I expect you've heard them have arguments but you would never be able to put yourself in the shoes of this woman's little boy and why should you. I think it's right to know about these things though. It will make you a more rounded person when you grow up. You won't always assume that people in trouble with the law have brought it on themselves. There is always a reason for actions people take and I want you to know that now, so I'm just going to ignore your Grandmother. Did you realise that a husband can rape his wife? Men like him don't always stop at the wife either. I have known men rape their own children. I don't want to frighten you. Maybe I'm going too far now. Let's go back to the Trial. Of course, even though provoked beyond reason, I cannot condone what she did. Facing violence with violence should not be the answer. She could have left. There are places to go. Sheltered homes they call them. These houses would take her and her children and her husband would not be able to find them. But these women are born victims I believe. They rarely escape. They rarely seek alternatives. It's as if they want to be abused, they can be just as guilty of provoking it, as the perpetrator. Believe it or not Charlie, there are women who get rid of one abuser for another, time and time again. So who really is the victim? What if her husband had grown up in a home like the one he had created? What if he had been just like his son once? What if his father had abused his mother? Do we feel sorry for him? The same for his wife, was her mother abused by her father? Or perhaps her father raped her? Is that how she became a victim? Did she grow up thinking that was a woman's lot in life? These are questions I want you to ponder young Charlie while you're lying there in your cosy bed. There are two sides to a coin but what should the Law do about it? Nothing can be done for the husband now, except for justice. Is it justice if his wife is sent to prison and his children sent to care? What would you do?"

"Hello Granddad," the old man's ramblings were interrupted by another of his Grandsons.

"Luke, what are you doing here?" he asked surprised to see him.

"I've come to see Charlie of course," Luke grinned.

"Don't be cheeky. I mean what are you doing here now? Shouldn't you be at school?" the Judge scalded him.

"No Granddad, it's Saturday," Luke was surprised his Granddad didn't know that.

"When I was at private school we had to do work on a Saturday," the Judge thought quickly.

"We do sometimes but today it's just rugby training and I got out of it by saying I had to come and see my brother," Luke told him honestly.

"I thought you liked rugby Luke," the Judge said.

"No, that's Matthew," Luke answered. "Mark loves cricket and me, I just like girls, Granddad".

He was a cheeky one, this one, but the Judge suspected he would do well in life for it. He was training Charlie for the Law but he was artistic and musical, maybe Luke would be a better bet.

"Tell me about school. Do you like it?" the Judge asked.

"Shouldn't we be talking to Charlie, Granddad?" Luke avoided the question.

"He can hear us. What would you be saying to him anyway?" his Grandfather asked.

"I suppose I would tell him about school and that," Luke admitted. "Yes, I quite like it although some subjects like science don't interest me much. I like History and English best. What did you like at school best Granddad?"

"Oh well that was a long time ago but I suppose I liked the same as you," his Grandfather told him.

"Did you always want to be a Judge?" Luke had lots of questions.

"Not at first. My father was a Politician and I thought I might follow him into Government but then I met your Grandmother and she wasn't keen. She doesn't have a lot of faith in any of our Politicians of today and I must say I think I agree with her. The Law seemed a respectable occupation and I am very glad I chose it now. I think we chose it together. Anyway, you should think about going into Law Luke. You might feel you can make a difference and it can be pretty lucrative you know," the Judge told him.

"That sounds interesting. I like money Granddad," Luke admitted. "I want to have a Porsche when I grow up, a bit of a babe magnet I reckon."

"I'm not quite sure I understand what you're talking about boy but now I'm going to leave you and Charlie to chat and go home. I'll see you tomorrow Charlie, after church, I expect, and you can tell me the answer to what we've been talking about," the Judge said, suddenly feeling very tired.

"Bye Granddad," Luke said. "I think he's losing his memory, Charlie."

CHAPTER FOURTEEN

It was one of those fantastic days you sometimes get in late October, the calm before the storm, blue skies and a weakened sun. It wasn't just the weather that had made it so perfect for Marika though. She had a night off from the theatre so they had got up early and headed for the Kent coast to make the most of a day out together. Ben seemed so relaxed and they walked along the coast for miles just holding hands, sometimes chatting, sometimes silent, but clearly just happy in each other's company. They ate fish and chips and even finished up with an ice cream, real seaside stuff. A walk up Dover pier, visit to the Amusement arcades and maybe even candy floss would have finished it off but they didn't do that. For now they just wanted each other's company and were happy to find a park bench overlooking the English Channel, where they could cuddle up together and kiss.

"Ever been over the other side?" Marika casually asked as they watched the constant flow of ferries in and out of the Dover docks.

"A few times", Ben answered. "What about you?"

"Oh yes, I love France. I have a girlfriend who has a small house in Normandy and I try and visit every year. It's in a fabulous spot, cycling distance to the sea and the Boulangerie. Now the croissants there are to die for," she smiled. "Have you travelled much Ben?"

"Yes. Have you?"

She was having a stab at trying to gain information without appearing too pushy but he wasn't really playing. He had seemed so relaxed, she thought it may be time but had she got it wrong? Would he never open up to her? Maybe if she started to tell him all about herself he would feel more like giving her something. She didn't really care about his history except it was part of him and she cared about every part of him.

"Not that much really. Never seem to have time or opportunity. I remember as a child my dad taking my younger brother and me to Spain for a holiday. I was about ten. We stayed in a hotel with a fabulous pool. It was heaven. I was going to do a bit of travelling, you know, back packing, that sort of thing, when I left drama school, but somehow never got round to it. I was so lucky to fall into work straight away and in my profession you dare not pass up any opportunity of work. That's just foolish. Have you been all over the world then?" she tried again.

"Pretty much", he answered before changing the subject. "How long is your Comedy going to run for?"

He was clever, always answering a question with another straight away. He liked to turn the spotlight straight back onto her. Maybe she was going to have to be more direct again.

"I've got another three months grace before I join the unemployed again but I've got a few auditions lined up next week so you never know. What do you do Ben?"

He actually laughed. It was a great sound because her question had carried a certain amount of trepidation with it. She found herself laughing too with relief. "What? What's so funny?" she asked.

"I wondered if you'd ever get round to asking that one." He was still laughing.

"Well, I wondered if you'd ever get round to telling me," she laughed back.

"I know. I'm sorry," he said a bit more seriously now. "Actually I don't know just now."

"What do you mean?" Marika asked.

"Well, maybe I'm like you, going for auditions," he said mysteriously.

"Not that I've noticed," she said on a roll. "Do you want to know what I think?"

"Go on," he was enjoying this.

"I think you're something to do with the Forces," she said pleased with herself. "Am I right?"

She had actually caught him by surprise again. He hadn't realised he had been that obvious. Where had that one come from? He was impressed. Wait a minute. Has she been speaking to Andy behind his back? "Why do you say that?" he asked suspiciously.

"Woman's intuition" she replied now feeling rather smug. She was right. She could tell by his expression. She was starting to know this guy.

"Describe woman's intuition". He wasn't giving in that easily.

"Okay. Let's think about how we met," she began. "You were spoiling for a fight? You could handle yourself that was obvious."

"Could have just been the drink," he suggested.

"No, you had an air of confidence, not enforced by alcohol," she mused. "You knew, that in a fight, there was no way you would come off worse. Also, there was certain recklessness about it."

"Isn't that contradictory?" he objected. "I mean, you say on one hand, I knew what I was doing but on the other, it was reckless?"

"Oh stop playing and just tell me," she prodded him in his ribs. "Am I right?"

"Have you spoken to Andy?" he asked her.

She laughed then. "I am right!" Ben smiled but still admitted nothing. "No, I haven't spoken to Andy. I don't actually know him. I know he's a musician and plays at the Pub sometimes. So how do you know him?"

"We joined up together," he smiled.

"You see!" She stood up jumping up and down on the promenade. Ben joined her and the moment he had been dreading suddenly turned into something of a joyous moment. How had that happened? It happened because of her. She really was incredible.

"Okay, okay. You're amazing. I bow to you, your majesty," he told her mockingly.

"Am I?" she asked.

"What?"

"Amazing?" she asked, digging for compliments.

"Oh yes," came the emphatic reply she craved.

"Love you". She couldn't help it. It was such an intimate moment somehow. The first time he had told her anything about himself. It was nothing really but it was everything too.

He didn't answer but he took her in his arms and his kiss told her what she wanted to know.

"I want you to meet my dad," she threw in daringly.

CHAPTER FIFTEEN

Daniel Brendan MacManus had had an uncomfortable night. It wasn't the pain. He had been worried. He hadn't heard from Ben for a while and knowing what his friend was like was concerned for his safety. They had a pact, he and Ben. Whenever things really got to them they would ensure they got drunk together and kept each other out of trouble. It had worked up to now. Mac knew that Ben's birthday was one of those days in the year when they needed to get drunk and take care of each other. He had his own date.

This situation with the enforced leave was another. It was typical of Mac. His own situation wasn't anything to laugh about either but by keeping Ben in his thoughts he could somehow put his own plight on the back burner and that suited him. Where would he go? He had no home. He had no family. The Army was his family. Mac wasn't much better off but he did have something else to hold onto, something very precious, his son, Robert. He was looking forward to spending more time with him when he got out of this hospital. When his mother had divorced Mac she had gained custody full time. It was totally unfair. He had been overseas risking his life, as was so often the case, and she had bedded the Army Padre. She said she had been lonely. Well he was lonely too but you didn't cheat on your partner. The problem was, he couldn't blame her really. He was lousy husband material. The truth was, he had never wanted to get married but when she fell pregnant he had no choice. He wondered if he had ever loved her. The marriage had dissolved very quickly. He couldn't regret Robert though. He loved that boy, more than life.

The divorce hadn't exactly been amicable. Mac couldn't understand why she got to keep everything including Robert when he was the wronged person. What's that all about? He was in the Army yes, he had to work yes, but he could have made arrangements for child-care. He had actually wanted to, back then. In hindsight, it probably wouldn't have worked out very well. His own father had hardly spent any time with him when he was growing up in Northern Ireland. He was a police constable and worked really long hours. It didn't stop him loving his dad and cherishing every moment he did see him but he did regret the many school plays and sports days his father had had to miss for work.

It wasn't so bad seeing Robert when he got time off, but then, within no time, Bernice had got remarried and moved to Spain to run a hotel. How was he supposed to spend time with him then, on his precious days off? He had fought against it. It had cost him money in legal fees but in the end, once again, he had to admit defeat. That was when he decided to join the Regiment.

He had never really wanted to join the Army when he was growing up. He wanted to be a teacher. He was quite bright at school did very well at his final exams. He had even won a place at Liverpool University in England. That would have been perfect. He had an Uncle who lived in Liverpool. Uncle Pat was like a second dad. He had never married and had no children of his own but doted on Mac. But it wasn't to be. In the summer period before he was due to leave home for the first time his father had fallen victim to an IRA car bomb. It was fatal. Mac had been devastated and so very angry. He found it difficult to grieve. Anger just kept getting in the way. He was a teenager of course, headstrong and reckless. The day after the funeral, he joined the British Army. He wanted revenge.

His Uncle was doubly devastated it appeared. Mac would learn later, that appearances could be deceptive. Uncle Pat had lost his brother and now his nephew was ruining his life. They had argued fiercely. Mac had been shocked at how much Uncle Pat seemed to care about this. Why didn't he care so much about the bombers? Anyhow, it was too late. He went off to train and he didn't see much of his family for a very long time. He had been lonely and homesick naturally and meeting Bernice, a nanny working in London, but originally from across the water, had cheered him up no end. She probably had her eye on an Army house. Was that fair? He was only twenty when they married and Robert was born four months later and she had her house, whatever.

The day his father had died was his special day for getting drunk with Ben. Mac knew that Ben's birthday was also the day his mother had died and was his special day for getting drunk, with Mac. Of course they would be friends with that in common. He had been with the Regiment almost two years when Ben joined them and he had taken him under his wing. Mac was already a Major and he recognised certain qualities in Ben which, if honed correctly, would see him turn into a brilliant soldier and possibly even gain promotion to his rank, younger than he had. He had been proved right recently when Ben had done just that.

Mac was the bright one, he had been educated but Ben had something else. He had had no education except in survival skills. The two of them were invincible together. Hadn't this latest incident proved that? Mac had lost count of the times he had saved Ben's life and vice versa. He should have known something ominous was about to happen when they were sent on separate missions. If Ben had been with him in Angola he would have stormed the building before the enemy had the chance to arm themselves. His recklessness had often been insightful. Mac had been too cautious. He wasn't with his mate and he wasn't sure about his right hand man out there. He would have done a good job but Mac had hesitated. Sometimes his brain worked overtime. He knew had he been with Ben in Mexico his brain might have warned him something was wrong with the hit. Ironically, hesitation out there would have worked.

The truth was they had been sent on the wrong missions but it was all water under the bridge now. The 'Invincibles' were no more. Mac would never continue in the Army now. Oh yes, they would give him a job in some office but he didn't want that. He could be an Instructor maybe and then his life would have gone full circle, he could be the teacher he always wanted to be. Right now he couldn't face any of it. He didn't want to think about the future. He needed to know Ben was all right. Where is he right now? Is he okay?

CHAPTER SIXTEEN

"How was it for you?" Marika asked.

"Actually, he's a lot like you isn't he?" Ben had been surprised.

"Amazing, you mean?" she was full of it tonight.

"Do you think I met his approval?" Ben asked earnestly.

"Of course you did. My father believes in me. As long as you treat me right and I think he realised exactly what my feelings for you are, this evening, then he will approve," she reassured him.

"What happens now then?" Ben asked.

"What do you mean?" she was intrigued by the question.

"Well, I've met your father and he's given his approval. Doesn't that mean we have to get married or something?" What was he saying? He must be drunk, he thought. No, he'd been careful not to overdo the vino tonight, didn't want to give the wrong impression although Marika had joyfully told her dad exactly how they had met. That was a bit embarrassing but he liked the fact that she had been truthful. She clearly held her dad in the highest esteem and they had an enviable close relationship. He was impressed. He didn't know a father and daughter could have such a wonderful relationship. It wasn't something he had ever witnessed with his sister and his dad. Oh sure, his dad had given his sister affection but it wasn't the sort of affection a daughter would wish for from her dad, particularly not at the age of thirteen. She had proved that by taking her own life. That was on Ben's eleventh birthday. That was the day he had tried to kill his dad. He shuddered.

Marika had shuddered too. Did he just propose to me, she asked herself? Wow! Three weeks ago she had never met this stranger. Now, she was ready to say yes, if he meant it. Was he drunk? No. He had hardly drunk anything, he had been on his best behaviour and of course dad had put him at ease immediately. He's wonderful, my dad. He had that way about him.

When she had first met Ben he was the most wound up person she had ever known. She had no idea what was going on in his life at that time but it wasn't good and yet, now, well . . . She realised she was actually just staring at him open mouthed. She should say something or he might retreat into his shell again. "When a man proposes I expect him to get down on one knee," she joked.

It was exactly the right thing to do of course. Her words snapped him out of his dark thoughts and brought him back to reality with joy. Oh My God. I did say that out loud, he realised. Is this mad? Yes, probably. But Major Casey was famous for being reckless. Suddenly, he wanted this more than anything in his entire life. So he got down on one knee and she said, "Yes please."

"There's just one thing," he whispered in her ear later after they had made love.

"Only one?" she smiled.

"Well, I've met yours, you should meet mine," he joked.

"Your family?" she asked excitedly.

"In a manner of speaking," he replied. "Mac needs to give his approval too."

"Who's Mac? Your brother?" she asked intrigued.

"He's my brother in arms and right now he's pretty poorly. He's in hospital, here in London. I should go and see him," Ben said as much to himself as to Marika.

"Yes, you should," she told him. "And whilst you're making hospital visits there's someone else in my family you need to meet."

"What, in hospital?" Ben asked surprised.

"Yes," was all she said but those beautiful blue eyes, usually so radiant, glazed over, ever so slightly.

CHAPTER SEVENTEEN

"I saw Daniel today Charlie," Marika informed her younger brother. "I went round to his house to give him what for. He wouldn't face me to begin with. Got his mother to answer the door and pretend he wasn't in. So I waited until he showed his face and I got him right between the eyes. Said he'd been too busy to come and see you. I mean—too busy I ask you. What does a twelve year old have on that makes him too busy to visit his best mate in hospital? I was really cross and he was shaking in his boots I can tell you. Teach that little rat. Apparently he likes his new school now and has a new best friend called Peter. Peter has a computer in his bedroom and they play stupid games on it all the time. If he didn't do that he'd have plenty of time to come and see you, wouldn't he? He's such a traitor. I told him he was being thrown out of the Army for treason. He didn't like that. He said his mother wasn't very happy about him coming here. The Police don't even call on him anymore. Seems they haven't got any new leads on the driver of the car. She thought it was time for Daniel to move on. She said you would probably have stopped being friends by now anyway when you both started at different schools but she doesn't know us Havers. We're loyal to the end. I think being betrayed is one thing but when it's your best mate, well, that's another. You need to wake up now Charlie and teach him a lesson. Anyway I think you're better off without him now bruv. Next time I come I might bring my boyfriend. Would you like to meet him? He's okay. Quite a good kisser but don't tell anyone. Same age as our Luke but much more sane! Luke says he had a chat with Granddad and he might be a Barrister now. Thinks he'll get lots of money and drive around in a Porsche. He's so shallow sometimes. I was talking to Nurse Booth earlier. She's really nice, isn't she? I think she's got the hots for dad. She's done all sorts in nursing. Said she used to work in a baby unit before she came here to look after you. She said that it could be quite sad though coz sometimes the babies died and that was really sad.

I asked her why babies would die and she said sometimes they are born too early and they're too small and they just don't make it. You've nearly missed a whole term of school now Charlie. It's Christmas in two weeks and you still haven't opened your birthday presents. What do you want for Christmas? I want some make up. I think mum might buy me some to stop me pinching all hers. I'm in the school play of course, leading part. I have to sing three songs on my own, do a bit of dancing too. It's brilliant. You have to get up and come and see it".

"Time to go now honey," her father said, as he entered the room. He had been in conversation with the Consultant. There was really nothing they could tell him. Charlie was holding his own. All his broken bones had mended nicely and generally he was doing okay. The brain was healing itself they believed but still he remained in the coma. No one really understands comas or what the patient is experiencing. All Jonathan knew was he was glad to have his son still in this world and it no longer mattered how long it took for him to wake up, just as long as he did come back to them one day.

"What did the doctor say?" she asked her father.

"That your brother is holding his own. I'm starting to believe he's going to pull through darling and he'll have a lot to thank you for."

"Of course he will dad. We Havers are made of stern stuff," she said stoically. "Why should he thank me?"

"For keeping him company so often and talking to him and just generally being an all-round fantastic sister," her father told her giving her a cuddle. He was incredibly proud of his family, they had all rallied round brilliantly and it was a testament to the way they all felt about his youngest child. "So, when am I going to meet this boyfriend of yours? What's his name?"

"Ben," she replied. "I don't know dad, would you like to meet him. I mean it's not serious or anything".

"I should hope not. You're far too young for that sort of thing," her father announced, remembering his own mistake.

"Need to play the field a bit, eh dad?" she laughed.

"Need to think about the future and what you're going to do with the rest of your life and certainly not rush into anything you might regret later," he said patiently.

"You mean, like you dad?" she observed.

"Don't be cheeky, but since you mention it, exactly like me. Come on, we need to go now," he said pretending to be cross. She could be far too old for her years sometimes. She enjoyed winding her dad up much too much.

"Bye bruv. See you later alligator"

"Bye son, in a while, crocodile".

CHAPTER EIGHTEEN

"Is that your baby?" George heard a small voice ask, behind her.

She turned round to see a young boy, maybe eight, staring at her. "Yes, it's my daughter Ella," she answered.

"Hello Ella," the boy approached closer. "Why is she in that glass case thing?"

"She's very poorly. The incubator is keeping her alive," George answered. "And just who are you?"

"I'm Robert," he held out his hand and she shook it feeling slightly amused at his confidence. "My dad is poorly too. He's just down the corridor but he's asleep now so I thought I'd have a walk about."

"I see," she nodded. "Where's your mother?"

"Back at the hotel I think," Robert answered. "I left her there to come and see dad,"

"So who are you with?" George was slightly alarmed.

"Oh, I came on my own," the boy answered confidently. "We flew in from Spain today and mum got us booked into a hotel close by. It's got a fountain in the hallway, really cool, but no swimming pool. I have a swimming pool at home. I might take a dip in the fountain. What do you think the hotel would say to that?"

Despite her intense anxiousness and misery she found herself smiling at this boy. "How old are you Robert?"

"I'm seven. How old are you?" he asked cheekily.

"Don't you know you should never ask a lady her age," she told him patiently. "I'm older than you and I don't think you should be here".

"How old is Ella?" He was a dab hand at diverting attention when he thought he was about to be sent away.

"She's three months old," George answered solemnly.

"Wow, she's tiny. What's your name?" he asked the nice lady.

"George," was the unexpected reply.

"That's a boy's name," he said sneeringly.

"Well, my full name is Georgina but most people call me George for short. Do you get called Bobby or Rob?" she explained.

"Sometimes, at school usually," he admitted. "I'd better go now and see if dad is okay."

"I'll come with you," she said, her maternal instinct kicking in. This was no place for a child to be wandering about and she wanted to see if he really did come from the hotel by himself. She had hardly left Ella's side since she was born three months ago but the nurses were on hand and she wouldn't be long, maybe, pick up a coffee while she was at it.

The boy took her by the hand and she warmed to him instantly. He led her along the corridor, down a flight of stairs and into another ward without any hesitation. His father was in a side room on his own and he looked very ill. "This is dad". Robert's voice woke Mac and he couldn't believe his eyes.

"Hi son. You're here?" he whispered. Robert jumped onto his bed with all the exuberance of a seven year old and Mac winced.

"Careful," George warned the boy. Mac suddenly became aware of another person in the room and it wasn't his ex-wife. She didn't have a uniform on either.

"Who's this, son? Have you pulled?" His son laughed. George felt her-self smile and blush at the same time. Robert's dad was pretty dashing if you ignored his ghostly pallor.

"I'm George. I found your son or rather he found me on another ward. He says he came here on his own", she explained.

"What? Where's your mother Robert?" Mac was shocked.

"George has a little baby whose really tiny dad," the boy avoided the question.

"Answer the question son," his father told him sternly.

"I think she's back at the hotel," he answered sheepishly.

"What do you mean? What's going on Robert?" Mac's voice was a little more serious now as he tried to focus, through the drugs.

"We flew in and she wanted to go straight to the hotel. I wanted to come and see you but she says she needs to unpack and wash her hair and stuff to get rid of the flight. She was taking ages so I left and I found you. The taxi man pointed out the hospital to us on the way to the hotel and I memorised the streets just in case," Robert explained as if he was talking about an everyday event but beginning to realise his father wasn't exactly pleased.

George was impressed but recognised his father's distress. "Do you want to borrow my phone here and ring your wife?" she offered, pulling her mobile out of her pocket. "Are phones allowed here?"

He was grateful for her help and she was quite a looker he noticed, (well done son). "Ex-wife," he got in quickly. "I don't think they are. Would you call a nurse for me and maybe they can ring the hotel from reception. Any idea what the hotels called Robert?"

"No, but it's on Southgate Street, from here you turn left and . . ."

George said she would go to Reception herself and find out if they could recognise the hotel. It had a fountain in the foyer she told him. This was certainly a diversion she thought and right now was very welcome. She didn't know how she had got through the last week. It had been the worst week of her entire life without a doubt.

When she returned, the dad was looking a bit brighter she noticed. Obviously the "Robert" treatment was working. He was certainly a tonic, even for her. He had been telling the truth. His mother was in her hotel room having a bath and hadn't even noticed her son had disappeared. She was on her way and George let them know.

"Resourceful chap isn't he?" she said.

"Oh yes. I can't thank you enough, by the way, for your help. My name is Mac," he held his hand out in exactly the same way as his son and she shook it. Of course it was a lot firmer than the boys and for some reason appeared to send shock waves through her body.

"Pleased to meet you," she said politely.

"I'm sorry about your little girl. Robert said she's not well," Mac said.

"Yes and I should really be getting back to her now," she remembered. "Bye Robert."

"Bye George," the boy replied. "Can I come and see Ella again?"

"You'd better ask your father," she said smiling. She looked at him and added sweetly, "Bye".

CHAPTER NINETEEN

"How's it going along bruv?" Matthew asked Charlie. "I'm sorry I haven't seen you for a while. Been tucked away at Uni but I'm home now for Christmas so we can have a nice catch up. Uni's okay and I'm learning loads. Sir David Essex gave us a lecture last week on surgery. He's probably the most eminent doctor in this country and it was absolutely fascinating listening to what he had to say. I've already decided I want to be a Surgeon now and not just some GP. Do you know he has his own Clinic in Harley Street? He has loads of famous people as his patients, including Royalty. That's how he got knighted, I think. What a guy. I was in complete awe of him but I actually spoke to him after the lecture and told him all about you. Guess what? He only goes and says he would be happy to examine you and offer a consultation. I can't wait to tell dad. It's pretty exciting, eh? The great news is that every year he takes on the very best student from across all the Universities in the country and trains them at his Clinic. You get to work there and you're made for life. So, that's what I'm about now. I'm going to work so hard, like you wouldn't believe. I know you think I'm a swot anyway but just think. If I come top in the country I automatically get offered an internship at the best hospital in the world. How cool would that be? I'm even starting to question whether Cambridge is a good enough Uni for me now. Sir David studied at Edinburgh from all accounts and maybe I should think about a move up there at the end of my first year. What do you reckon? I shall certainly be looking into it. Anyway, we've had an exciting term all in all. I should have been back a couple of days ago but we had the police round and weren't allowed to go on holiday until we had all spoken to them. There's a girl in the house where I live on the Campus and she's gone missing. There's a right panic about it. It is a bit of a mystery. I didn't know her very well, just met her once or twice in the communal kitchen. She didn't say much. I got the impression she was a bit pre-occupied. Well, to tell you the truth, I thought she was on drugs or something. You hear bits of gossip and from all accounts she was certainly a party animal. She missed lots of lectures and wasn't doing very well with her work. It turns out she went to Blues, the Nightclub in the City, and was caught on CCTV leaving there on her own at about 2am. Then, there's more camera footage of her walking along Queen Street, which is really close to the Uni, talking on her mobile and looking upset. She's crying even, but then nothing. She's just disappeared and there appear to be no clues although I suspect the police aren't telling us everything. So, I get to be interviewed by this gorgeous looking policewoman, in uniform. I couldn't tell her much of course but they had to speak to anyone who knew her, apparently. Anyhow, I end up asking this policewoman out on a date and she agreed. Her name is Sian. Couldn't do much about it then as I was told I was free to come away for the Christmas holidays but she's given me her phone number and when I get back next term I'm going to call her up and ask her out. So, bruv, what do you think to your brother going out with the law? Maybe she'll handcuff me to her bed. I shouldn't be saying things like that to you, should I? You're still just a boy but I know you, always prefer the company of adults, don't you? You know, you're missing out on a big chunk of your childhood right now and need to get that sorted. Everyone is waiting for you to just wake up and start pestering us again. Anyhow, I'd better go, got some Christmas shopping to take care of, always leave it to the last minute. I see you've got some music there now. I suppose Marika's been recording all her records for you to listen to. What's that band you both like? Are they called Spirit or something? Yeah, they're pretty good. I do like their music but I suspect Marika is just in love with the keyboard player. Well, there you go bruv", Matthew attached some earphones around Charlie's head and turned the MP3 player on. "Enjoy and I'll see you tomorrow".

CHAPTER TWENTY

"Wake up dad" Robert whispered gently in his father's ear. Mac had finally had a more pleasant night and slept well. It was amazing how his son could have such a good effect on him.

"Hello son. Where's your mother?" he asked suspiciously.

"Don't worry dad. She brought me here today but she's gone off shopping or something," his son answered honestly.

"That's okay then," Mac said. He was pleased not to see Bernice in truth.

"Can we play a game dad?" Robert asked.

"Well son, I'm not up to much just now. What about battleships?" Mac suggested.

"Oh yeah, cool". Robert loved having this interaction with his father.

"We need some paper and pens. I think my kit was put in this bedside cupboard here. Have a look and tell me what you see in there," Mac told him. Robert had a rifle through. "Can you find anything?"

"Look dad, here's a mobile". He pulled the phone out of Macs jacket. Robert had always had a fascination with phones even as a baby. "Can I have my own mobile for Christmas dad?"

"Is that what you would like?" Mac asked him surprised that a seven year old should want such a present.

"Yes please," Robert said sweetly.

"What would your mother think?" Mac asked.

"I don't care. She's always on hers, sending texts to her friends and stuff. If I had one dad, I could ring you up and we could talk whenever I wanted, and if I got lost I could call for help and all my friends at school have got one now." He was building up a case. "Can you show me how your phone works dad?"

"Well, I can show you some of its functions, but we're not allowed to make any calls apparently," Mac said.

"Why can't we?" Robert asked.

"I think the sound waves interfere with some of the hospital equipment or something like that," his father explained patiently.

"You mean like that incu, incuba, thingy, that glass case that Ella is in?" Robert tried to remember the name.

"Yes, her incubator." Mac turned his mobile on and noticed immediately that he had three messages. He couldn't remember when he had last used the phone, before he got blown up he supposed. He put the phone to his ear and played the messages hoping one might be from Ben. The first was just some message from his server and he deleted it straight away. The second was equally unimportant but the third made him sit bolt upright, a move he regretted almost instantly, as it hurt so much. The third message was from his sister, Sian. She sounded completely distressed and very distant. He heard about two lines and then got cut off as his battery went. He swore, forgetting his son was in earshot.

"What's wrong dad"? Robert sat bolt upright too.

"My battery's run out, that's all, son. I have a message I need to hear". What he had actually heard already was enough to make him need to hear the rest. He suddenly remembered George had offered him her mobile yesterday in order to phone his ex and he'd noticed that it was the same phone as his. "Do you think George is here today?"

"I don't know dad. Shall I go and see?" Ordinarily he would not be in favour of his seven-year-old son wandering off down the hospital corridors but this was an emergency.

"See, if she can spare me a minute," he suggested to his son.

Robert was delighted. He loved helping his dad and to be given permission to go off wandering, when he fully intended to do so anyway if his dad fell asleep on him, was just brilliant. He found his way to the baby unit in no time and was thrilled to see George sitting there next to her baby, looking somewhat forlorn. Her demeanour changed completely when she saw him. "Hello Robert, should you be here?"

"Hello George, hello Ella." There was something very touching in the way the little boy didn't ignore her baby girl. "Dad sent me actually," he explained.

"Are you sure?" she asked gently.

"Yes, he wants to see you again." Robert had suddenly sensed an opportunity for mischief here. "He hasn't been able to stop talking about you since he saw you yesterday."

George was fascinated but hesitant. Is he telling me the truth? It was a pleasant revelation if it was true. Not that she was looking for a new relationship, not right now. She still hadn't decided what to do about Nick, her husband, and she had more than enough on her plate with Ella. Even so, the stranger had certainly created an impression, his son, even more so. "You are up to something young Robert. You're quite a handful I can tell. Does he really want me to see him or is he just sleeping innocently and you've sneaked off again without telling him?"

"Come and speak to him if you don't believe me," Robert answered. "I promise you he asked me to come and get you." Well, that's sort of the truth the boy told himself. He'd just left out a few details but after all he was only seven and couldn't be relied upon to get everything right. He was really enjoying himself. He liked George a lot and she wouldn't make a bad stepmother he had started to fantasise and he had always wanted a brother or a sister. Ella looked okay.

George decided she could leave her baby daughter long enough to check out his story and so she took him by the hand once again and together they walked back to his father's room. To her surprise, when they got there, he was sitting up in bed and fully awake and he smiled at her. He had been expecting to see her after all. Her stomach gave a little flutter at the realisation that Robert might have been telling the truth. Even if she didn't want a new relationship it still felt good to flirt with this stranger. "Hi," he greeted her. "How is your little girl?"

"Not much change it seems. His Lordship here tells me you wanted to see me. Is that right?" she said trying to sound as casual as possible.

Her question, even though meant to be casual, had an unusual effect on Mac. He found himself a little nervous suddenly. After all she was a very beautiful woman and clearly out of his league but when summoned she had come. He liked that thought although common sense told him she was probably just concerned that Robert had run off again. She probably thinks he's a really bad parent. "Yes, I'm really, really sorry to tear you away from Ella again but I wondered if I could ask you a favour." She responded with a smile that tore at his heart. "You see, I've just found my mobile among my belongings and the battery's flat and there's a message on it which I really need to hear. I was just wondering . . . ."

"Oh yes of course, do you want to borrow mine?" She produced the phone from her pocket and held it out to him.

"Sorry, I wouldn't ask but it's just I noticed yesterday it's actually the same as mine and thought I could probably just swap the battery long enough to hear the rest of the message," he explained unnecessarily. She had given him her phone and her permission to do so but he felt he had to justify getting her to his room. He didn't know, of course, that his own son had got her here under slightly false pretences and she looked at Robert as Mac swapped the batteries around and gave him a knowing stare that said she was going to get him later (and probably tickle him to death). He tried to look completely innocent and once again she found herself smiling and laughing inside. Mac listened to the full message. Sian had simply said; "Hi bro. Please answer the phone. Oh God, where are you? I need you. I'm in such trouble. I need your help. I can't talk now. Call me back soon, it's really urgent." What the hell was going on? He didn't think he ever had to worry about Sian. She had come to England last year and began a two-year Business course at Liverpool College. She was being watched over by Uncle Pat. It just didn't make sense. The message was now five days old and that worried the hell out of Mac.

George suddenly sensed his anxiousness. "Can I help?" she offered kindly.

"I need to use the phone urgently. Can you arrange it for me with a nurse to have a phone I can use in my room?" He looked really anxious and George sensed that wasn't good for him.

"Of course," she said without hesitation and turned to leave straight away.

"What is it dad?" Robert had sensed the concern in his dad's voice too. "Is it work?" He knew his dad was a soldier and not just any soldier either. He was special.

"No son. Don't worry. I just have a few calls I need to make. Would you like to go and get yourself a drink and some chocolate or something?" He didn't want Robert around when he rang Sian back. He had no idea what was going on but for his sister to ring him was in itself a rare event, let alone be asking for his help. He told Robert to look further into his kit bag and help himself to some money.

George had done her stuff. She had got the hospital reception running round and a phone was found and brought to Macs room. She left him to make his calls in private and went to find Robert trying to make his choice from the vending machine. She would keep him occupied for Mac, there was no question, and maybe plug him for some information about his mysterious father.

Mac had tried to ring his sisters mobile but the line was dead. Maybe he was too late. Had something terrible happened to her? He rang Uncle Pat who seemed pleased to hear his voice at first. Uncle Pat was a self-made millionaire. He had left Ireland in his teens and started working at bingo halls around Blackpool. He was an entrepreneur. No one in the family could be sure how he had made his money in the first place but he now owned a Casino and a Night Club in Liverpool. He still had very strong ties with Ireland however and always an opinion to offer during the troubled times. He was a regular visitor to their household but sympathetic to the IRA despite what happened to his brother. He had never married and always looked upon Mac as the son he never had. He used to tell Mac that he would inherit everything one day but Mac wasn't too interested in all that. He loved his Uncle and having lost his father was quite happy for Uncle Pat to stay around on this Earth for many years to come. His Uncle had made no secret of his despair and anger when Mac had joined the Army. He was preparing to pay for Mac to go to the finest College. Pat had believed Mac was the bright one in the family and he wanted to hone him for his own needs. Make him part of the business so that one day when he did inherit it he would know how to keep the MacManus empire going. Mac knew that Sian, only nineteen, had hankered to come to England too. She was ambitious and didn't want to end up like so many of her friends, a housewife with a string of kids. She knew that Uncle Pat was rich and could be her ticket out and had tried to ingratiate her-self with him by offering to go to Business College with a view to taking up the ropes from him at the Casino one day. He seemed to go along with it and had offered to assist her financially while she stayed in Liverpool to study. Uncle Pat gave Mac all the usual blarney but something wasn't right. "Do you know where my sister is Uncle Pat?"

"What do you mean son?" Uncle Pat asked him nervously.

"Well, she's not at Business School is she?" Mac stated.

"How do you know that?" his Uncle asked.

"Is she?" Uncle Pat was being evasive and he wasn't going to give all his cards away.

"Well, you know what youngsters are like today son. Here today and gone tomorrow. Sure, she comes to me last year, practically begging me to help get her set up at college and then what does she do. Spends a year doing whatever and then announces she needs a year out. I mean, I ask you. Isn't that what all the youngsters are doing these days? They start at Uni or college or whatever, they have all these grand ideas but then suddenly, oh, they've worked so hard, they need a year out. I would never have got where I am today son if I'd have taken a year out let me tell you." Although he had moved to Liverpool in his teens his Belfast accent was still surprisingly thick.

"Why did she want a year out?" Mac asked surprised this was the first time he had heard it.

"Like I say, like all these youngsters, to go travelling she calls it. Wants to see a bit of the world before she settles down and all that," his uncle prevaricated.

Well it was beginning to make a bit more sense, Mac thought, though not much. "When did she go?"

"Oh I don't know, last month I think. Heading for Australia, she said and wanting to go to New Zealand too and maybe America. I gave her some numbers of our relatives in America to look up," Uncle Pat told him.

He didn't know why but he wasn't sure his Uncle was telling him the truth. He decided he needed to lay his cards out, however. His time on the phone was running out. "I had a call from her Uncle Pat."

"What?" His Uncle sounded genuinely surprised and a little concerned. "Now what in BeJesus would she be doing calling you? Sure, she knows how busy you are. Is everything all right by the way?"

Mac suddenly realised his Uncle had no idea that he was in hospital and that he wouldn't be walking out of it on his own legs ever again but he didn't want to get into that now. So, on the one hand you had Uncle Pat being typically Irish and a bit vague with the truth and on the other, you had his nephew definitely being more than a bit evasive about what had just happened to him. What a combination. "She sounded like she was in trouble".

"Why, what did she say exactly?" he was much more interested now.

Mac relayed the message and his Uncle was quiet for a second, but only for a second, and then he continued to prevaricate and offer all sorts of ridiculous excuses for her message and said, "Look, don't you go worrying that head of yours about any of this. She's probably run out of money or something. I'll sort it out. I'll get hold of her and I'll let you know later what's going on. She's probably just in an area where there's no signal.

Leave it to me son. I'll sort it out. Will I call you back on your mobile?" He was fishing. He knew Mac wasn't on his mobile right now.

"Can you text me, Uncle Pat?" It was a genuine question. Texting was very much a young person's occupation, he didn't know if his Uncle could manage it

"Oh sure, right you are. I know you can't tell me where you are right now son. Some secret mission again is it? Well, watch yourself. I'll speak to Sian, give her what for and put your mind at rest in the next day or so. You see if I don't." Uncle Pat replied.

"Thanks Uncle Pat, bye," and he hung up not feeling any more comforted that he had before making the call. He still knew nothing about what was going on but what else could he do. He needed to see Ben. He decided it was time and sent a message to his mobile.

CHAPTER TWENTY-ONE

Ben was on his way to the hospital when the text arrived. They often did things that the other was thinking about. It was a psychic connection between two very close friends. He turned up in Mac's room five minutes later. Mac was shocked to see him. "That was quick," he told his friend.

"You rang, my lord," Ben teased. Mac immediately recognised a change in his brother. He was clearly more relaxed and back on track. Had the Army exonerated him finally?

"How did you do that?" Mac asked him.

"I'd like to say I walked into a telephone kiosk, got changed, and flew here but actually I was already on my way to see you," Ben joked.

"About time too," his friend scolded him.

"I know mate. I'm sorry but you know I needed to clear my head and so did you I reckoned. How are you?" Ben asked.

"I've got a job for you if you're free or are you back in the fold?" Mac surprised him.

"Nope, I'm free. CO sends me texts once a week to say, keep the faith and all that, but they haven't summonsed me back yet. So, I'm all yours mate. What's up?" Ben was intrigued.

"I'm surprised. I thought maybe from your sudden cheerfulness you'd been given a reprieve," Mac was fishing.

"Nope again, the Politicians are still chewing it over I guess waiting for the press furore to die down. Has the CO been to see you?" Ben was cagey.

"He put in an appearance a couple of weeks ago apparently but I was non compos-mentis at the time having just had further surgery so I didn't get to speak to him. So how come you're looking so good bro?" Mac was more direct this time.

"You wouldn't believe me if I told you," Ben teased.

"Try me," his best friend said patiently.

"I've met someone Mac and she's well, I don't know how to describe her and do her justice," Ben admitted.

"Oh my God, the boy's in love." Mac was shocked and pleased at the same time. Ben, like him didn't have much time for serious relationships and besides they weren't usually conducive to the job. When they were working the last thing they needed was a distraction. As far as he knew Ben had never had a sweetheart. He preferred to have a string of women in every port to deal with his needs when it suited him. He wasn't husband material, mention commitment and he would run a mile. Well, that was until now. It was such a relief to Mac, who had been genuinely concerned for his friend's welfare while he hadn't been there to support him. He almost forgot about the phone call from his sister.

"Here are your grapes, by the way," Ben handed him a brown paper bag with the stalks of what had been grapes but were now half eaten. It was a standing joke between them of course. This wasn't the first time either of them had been hospitalised. It was an occupational hazard, although past injuries had never been as serious as this time.

"So are you going to tell me her name and how this amazing woman managed to seduce you, you old bugger," Mac persisted.

"Marika. A name as beautiful as the lady herself Mac," Ben said surprising his friend with his romantic overtones.

"God knows what she sees in you then," Mac brought him back to earth.

"Oh sorry to interrupt," George had returned to see if Mac needed any more help and had been pleasantly surprised to see he had company that was cheering him up no end. Not bad either.

Ben noticed his friends eyes transfix on this incredibly beautiful woman who had just walked in on them. She clearly wasn't a nurse. Who was she and more important, what was she to Mac, he wondered? Could his friend have summonsed him at the exact same time he had decided to visit him anyway to tell him about the woman in his life. It wouldn't surprise him. They were so in tune most of the time, why shouldn't they both fall in love for the first time together. Wouldn't that be amazing? They could have a double Wedding. He hadn't got round to mentioning the Wedding yet. Mac would have to be Best Man of course but if he was a Groom as well, well, that was just fine with him. In fact it couldn't be more perfect. He didn't want there to be three in the marriage.

"Ben, this is George. George, meet Ben." He had clocked his mate's smile and knew exactly what he was imagining. It was ridiculous, of course. How could he seriously think that this gorgeous woman would look at someone like him, especially now? He watched his best friend shake the hand of the woman he fancied like mad but dare not do anything about. Please don't say anything embarrassing he thought.

Ben was charm itself and didn't let him down.

"I was just wondering if everything was all right?" she asked Mac.

Oh god yes. She was bringing him back to normality. How had he forgotten about the phone-call? "Oh yes, sorry. I'm not really sure, to tell you the truth" he responded and then to Ben, "You might need to help me with something Ben. I'll tell you later."

"Would you like me to go?" she asked, sensing Mac still had a big problem.

"No, no, you're all right. Where's Robert by the way?" he asked her.

"He's chatting to another boy, down the ward. He's about the same age and has come in with a head injury. The nurse said it would be all right for them to talk and she would keep an eye on him. Do you want me to fetch him?" she said.

"Robert's here?" Ben asked his friend excitedly.

"Yes, the 'ex' kindly brought him over for a few days during the school holidays," he told Ben.

"Wow, that's unusually generous of her," Ben said. He knew how much grief Bernice had caused his friend over custody issues in the past.

"I think she wanted to do her Christmas shopping in London," Mac explained.

Ben gave a knowing look and then turned his attention back to George. "So how did you two meet?" He made it seem like they were a couple and they both blushed.

They were saved from answering as Robert suddenly burst into the room. "Dad, dad, you'll never guess who I've just seen," and then he noticed Ben and jumped into his arms. "Ben," he said joyfully.

Ben swept him up easily and gave him a boy cuddle. "Hiya tiger," he said to him. "Who have you seen?"

"That pop star, the guitar player in Spirit," Robert answered proudly.

"What, Dave Sorenson?" Ben asked. He had also seen him. Not today. It was the day he met Marika, of course, when he had chatted up his wife in the Pub and nearly caused a fight.

"No, the other one," Robert said.

George's hackles had suddenly been raised at this news and she thundered out the room. "Excuse me," she said as she departed without a second look.

All three boys looked at each other. "What's got into her?" Ben asked.

"I have no idea," Mac said but he wanted to.

CHAPTER TWENTY-TWO

A couple of days elapsed before Mac received a text from his Uncle. He realised he still had George's battery in his mobile. She hadn't been back since she had rushed off so mysteriously and Mac hadn't stopped thinking about her and wondering if she was okay. He had sent his little spy off to check her out at the baby unit yesterday but Robert hadn't found her. He read the text and it occurred to him he had been so pre-occupied worrying about George he had completely forgotten about Sian, but at least Ben was on the case. The text was short and sweet: "Spoke to Sian, she's fine, just ran out of money and panicked. She's in Australia. I've sorted it. She says she's sorry for bothering you and won't do it again."

Mac didn't know if the text made him feel better or not. He decided not. Sian would not have left him such a bizarre message just because she had run out of money. She didn't sound panicky but scared. Something was definitely not right. Why would his Uncle lie to him? Was he trying to protect him, perhaps? Why wasn't he able to get through to Sian, but his Uncle had? Australia may be the other side of the world but technology had come a long way. There were too many anomalies and he wasn't happy. Not that he could do much about it right now. The doctor had just been to check him over and he wasn't happy things were mending as they should. The trauma to his lower body had been massive. They may have to operate for a third time. In the meantime he was on morphine for the pain and it was hard to think straight.

"I just came to apologise," George appeared at his doorway, as if in a vision. She really was a stunner. He surprised himself at how pleased he was to see her.

"I don't need an apology from you but I am glad to see you're okay. I . . . er . . . we were worried about you," he didn't want to sound too pushy.

"Where is your little helper?" she asked, noticing Mac was alone.

"Sadly on a plane back to Spain this morning. His mother needed to get back before the Christmas rush so that's it," Mac told her unhappily.

She sensed his loss and understood it only too well. "I'm sorry," she said, with tears in her eyes.

He was touched. "Hey, it's okay. I'm used to it now. Haven't spent Christmas with my son in a long time," he said trying to cheer her up.

She sat down on his bed and the nearness of her stirred his whole being. He wiped the tear from the corner of her eye and the tenderness of his action seemed to break something in her. She leant into him and he cuddled her, unable to believe what was happening but realising something was definitely very wrong in her world. "Does this have something to do with that pop star?" he asked. "What about Ella? Is she okay?"

George seemed unable to contain her emotions any more at the sound of her daughter's name and the tears fell uncontrollably from her beautiful brown eyes. Mac tried to comfort her but she was almost beyond that. Oh God, he thought, it must be the baby. Suddenly his troubles paled into insignificance beside hers. He decided to say nothing, just hold her and let her cry herself out. This was pretty much new territory for him. He had to go by instinct and instinct told him to give her time.

George had not intended for this to happen. She had been quite controlled since the doctors had told her the fatal news. It had always been on the cards. They never expected her baby to live as long as she did and it wasn't as if George hadn't been through this before. She had already had three miscarriages but somehow with Ella the prospect that she might actually be a mother at last seemed more tangible. Well, she was a mother. Ella was real. She just was born too soon and the cards were stacked against her from the start. What was worse for George was she couldn't help but blame herself, although she did wonder if she had not had all the upset from Nicky, whether she might have been able to carry her daughter another month. In the end she had been born so premature and had been so tiny. Even if she had lived she probably would have had respiratory problems all her life. It was probably for the best, the doctors had said. Given that she and Nicky were no more, maybe they had a point. No of course not. How can it ever be for the best when a young innocent life is taken? She sobbed her heart out into this strangers' warm cosy chest. What was she doing? She had absolutely no idea. She had walked around as if in a trance since yesterday.

Why should she choose this moment of all moments to break down? Poor Mac didn't deserve or need this. She must pull herself together.

Mac didn't feel poor. He felt privileged but he was on unsure ground and that always bothered him. He didn't want to say or do the wrong thing. After a very long time George, having cried her-self out, tried to get her self together and sat up again. He offered her a tissue from his bedside table and she sniffed into it. "I'm so sorry. I seem to have to keep apologising to you" she finally got out.

"No apologies necessary. I mean it," he told her.

"You're probably wondering what on earth has happened," she sniffed.

"I'm just desperately sorry for whatever it is. Is it Ella?" he asked gently not wishing to sound intrusive.

"Yes", she got out before sobbing again. He pulled her to him this time and held her very tight. It felt so comforting she didn't want to say any more and for a while they were happy in each other's arms. He was impressively strong for a sick man and he made her feel safe.

"Can you talk about it?" he eventually asked her.

"There's not much to say really. She just slipped away. She was so tiny you see. The fight for life wore her out," George explained.

"Poor little Ella," he simply said.

George sat up again to look at Mac and noticed he too had tears in his eyes. She was incredibly moved and kissed him on the lips. It felt amazing. They stared into each other's eyes unable to comprehend their sudden feelings of passion and then he kissed her back and for just a moment she felt free. Free, from all the grief, all the heartache. What was going on? He was just a stranger or was that the attraction? He knew nothing of what her life had been like for the last few months.

"I should go," she suddenly said not really wanting to.

"Don't," he said. "Not like this."

She was relieved. "Are you sure? I don't want to tire you out. You're supposed to be ill."

"Of course I'm sure," Mac answered. "I may suddenly drift off on you but it certainly won't be your company I promise. It's the morphine does that but please stay and if I do drift off and you have to go, please tell me you'll come again."

She had had to come back to the hospital again today to make arrangements with the mortuary at the hospital and she had wanted to see her daughter one more time before saying goodbye. There was the funeral to arrange now. She didn't expect to come back to the place where she had been coming every day of the last three months after today, so had taken the opportunity to call on the stranger just to, well, say goodbye to him too, she supposed, and Robert. It would have been rude not to. She was just going to let him know she wouldn't be back in anymore and to wish him luck for the future. She certainly never intended for what happened but now that it had and now that he had asked her to come and visit him, well. His son was gone. He probably needed a visitor.

"All right," she told him and he smiled at this news.

As if reading her mind he said, "I suppose you've probably had enough of this place and I have no right asking you to come back."

"No, that's all right," she answered honestly. "I kind of feel closer to Ella here. This was where she was born and where she lived and where she died. I don't hate the place and I feel a good deal lonelier at home where there's nothing of her spirit."

"Does Ella have a father?" he asked her tentatively. She had never mentioned if there was a man in her life, although there was that strange incident with Nicky, the pop star.

"She did," she answered bitterly. "I don't have anything to do with him now."

Mac didn't know whether to push it. She had already told him all he needed to know. She was free. Not that that would do him any good. A beautiful girl like this was hardly going to fall for a damaged guy like him. He shouldn't have any illusions. This was an incredibly emotional time for her and he was just in the right place at the right time. It would never develop beyond that surely. That kiss had been magical for him but she just needed a shoulder to cry on. One thing Mac was blessed with was broad-shoulders. He shouldn't give up hope though. Remember Ben. Who would have thought a woman could fall for him, he was more messed up than Mac. Well, mentally anyway but Mac was no catch physically now, was he? She probably wasn't even aware that under the blankets and below the waistline there wasn't much left of his body. How would she react when she did?

George was wondering what Mac was thinking. He had been quiet for a while. He had asked her about her position but made no more comment. What about him, she thought. "I've seen your ex-wife Mac but is there someone else in your life?" she asked.

"No," he answered immediately thrilled at the question. Was she checking him out too? "Bernice and I divorced a long time ago and I've not met anyone else. To tell you the truth I sort of thought once bitten twice shy and my job made it very easy for me not to get tied down. Bernice and I had a fairly acrimonious parting. I caught her cheating on me with the Army Padre while I was away fighting a war. I wasn't very happy about that. Then she goes and gets custody of our son. That hurt."

"Why do partners do that?" she asked him

"What?" he asked.

"Cheat. It sucks," she said.

"Is that what Ella's father did to you?" he asked incredulously. How could any man be that stupid? She was amazing.

"Nicky. His name is Nicky Darrow. He's the guitarist Robert saw the other day when I stormed off," she explained. "Nicky and I are married," she felt she owed him the truth. "We've been together for five years."

Mac was slightly in awe of this news. She was married to one of the most famous pop stars on the planet and he had felt he might have a chance. Well forget it soldier. You knew this girl was out of your league, he told himself.

George saw his face and it made her smile. "Don't worry. Being married to a pop star isn't all that it's cracked up to be, believe me."

"What went wrong?" he decided to ask.

"I suppose it wasn't all Nicky's fault," she began. "I wanted a child but wasn't able to carry one full term. We kept trying and I kept failing. It was a miserable time. In the meantime, he's going out on the stage and doing his thing. The show must go on and all that. He had to put on an act but I wasn't convinced it was just an act. I accused him of not caring. I thought perhaps it must be easier for a man to lose a child than a woman. Then when I got pregnant again the doctors are telling me to have like, permanent bed rest, a bit like the Victorians used to do. It was a bizarre life and Nicky's group was going on tour. You can probably guess the rest. Temptation got to him. He and I hadn't exactly been intimate since I found out about the pregnancy and it's there on a plate on tour. I guess he did what any red-blooded male would do. He told me it hadn't meant anything but I was inconsolable. We had a terrible row and I went into labour, too soon. Then Ella was born and of course I blamed him. I wouldn't let him see us. When he turned up at the hospital two days ago I was furious he had come. It's a tribute to this hospital that it hasn't made the front pages of the Sun newspaper, the row we had. Then what happens? While I'm rowing with him about turning up, my little girl . . ." she broke off as the tears began to roll again, "dies."

Mac held her once again gently but firmly. "That sounds like the worst kind of betrayal," he said, understanding her pain.

"You went through it too," she said. "We both got cheated on at the worst possible times in our lives. I'm having Nicks baby and you're fighting a war. Bernice and Nicky should get together. They have a lot in common."

"No I don't think so, but we do," he stated.

"Yes" she said and they fell silent in each other's arms.

CHAPTER TWENTY-THREE

"Mac, wake up." It was Ben's voice. When Mac opened his eyes he realised that his friend was at his bedside alone. Had he been dreaming? She was gone. He felt a small twinge of pain, "Are you all right mate?" Ben noticed his friend's discomfort.

"Yeah, yeah, I'm fine," Mac answered coming out of his sleep. "What day is it?"

"Tuesday mate, you're going to have to stop taking that morphine," Ben joked.

Tuesday wasn't so bad. It had been Monday when she was here last. Maybe she'll be in later. "You okay then? How's love's young dream?"

"Great. Listen mate I can't stop long. Apparently the CO's on his way over to visit you. I don't want to run into him."

"You should," Mac told his friend. "You should confront him on what's going on with your job?"

"I know but I'm not ready to find out myself yet. I'm thinking of leaving the Army," Ben added surprisingly.

"What you? Never! What will you do?" Mac was shocked. He knew things would never be the same in the Regiment now of course. He wouldn't be there for one thing and Ben had proved he could get into trouble without Mac there to watch his back, but leave? That was unexpected. This girl had certainly turned his head and he needed to check her out and make sure she was genuine.

"Never mind that now Mac, I've got to tell you what I've found out about Sian," Ben said slightly agitated.

Mac had forgotten about Sian again to his shame. He hadn't been comforted by his Uncle's communication, just confused. He sensed trouble. "Go on" he told Ben.

"Well it's not much actually but I went to see Buzz and he did his usual wizardry on the computers for us and he's found out that your sister rang your mobile from Kuala Lumpur." Buzz was ex-firm. He was permanently wheelchair bound these days courtesy of a suicide bomber in Iraq. He was a techie and loved everything cyber space. He was the one the Firm went to when being assigned one of those "deniable" ops, which the Government denied they had. It was a source of amusement to people like Mac and Ben. The Home Office denied there were any such things as deniable ops. They denied the deniable. It was a joke. "Any idea what she's doing out there?"

"No. My Uncle said she went travelling and that she's in Australia," Mac said.

"Her mobile is completely off the radar. It no longer exists. Her call to you was the last," Ben continued.

"But Uncle Pat reckons he's contacted her since. How did he do that?" Mac asked.

"Beats me Mate, unless she's got another mobile or a lap-top or something. Maybe she rang him from another phone?" Ben suggested.

"No, he definitely said he had contacted her and she had run out of money. That was all. He said he had some money transmitted to her and everything was all right," Mac recalled.

"Oh, well there you are then. Nothing to worry about," Ben said.

"I'd say there's everything to worry about," Mac told his friend. "Some thing's not right here Ben. I think Uncle Pat is lying but I don't know why."

"Could he be trying to protect you or something? Does he know you're here in hospital, by the way?" Ben asked him.

"No. I didn't get round to mentioning it so he's not protecting me for that reason," Mac replied.

"Don't you think you should Mac? He's very fond of you. He will be devastated you haven't told him," Ben scolded.

"I just can't get into that right now," Mac said. "I need to come to terms with it myself first Ben, you know how it is."

Ben knew exactly how it was. They were both so proud. "So what do you think? Is there anything else you want me to do?" he asked.

"Fancy a trip to Kuala Lumpur?" Mac asked a bit tongue in cheek.

"Where do I start? All we've got is a spot on where she made the call but now that the phones dead we've got no chance to track it?" Ben was thinking out loud. He knew if his friend wanted him to go he would but it was one hell of a long shot.

"Well, maybe you might be able to find out more there," Mac suggested. "Check the area, CCTV maybe. Hell I don't really know Ben. Have we been to Kuala Lumpur before? Why would Sian go there? It doesn't add up."

"May have gone that way round to Australia I suppose," Ben wondered. "Did she go alone?"

"Good point. I don't know. I do need to speak to Uncle Pat and face to face might make it easier to judge whether he's lying to me," Mac said.

"That's settled then. You should call him, tell him where you are and get him down here. When you find out more let me know. In the meantime I'd better beat it. Boss man is due any minute. I'll call you later." Ben made a quick exit before Mac had time to ask him about love.

CHAPTER TWENTY-FOUR

"I've been thinking Charlie," Marika told her brother. "Remember you told me about that time that man chased you off from the pontoon and scared the living daylights out of you. Well, what if it was him?"

"If what was him?" Mark interrupted her, tousling her hair.

"Marky," she was pleased to see him. "What are you doing here today?"

"Can't I come and see my brother too? Must you have him all to yourself all the time?" he teased her.

"No, I just meant, you're not down on the rota, are you?" Marika noted.

"Oh, you mean Becky's rota. I'd forgotten that. I'm just on my way home from college and thought I'd check on the boy. Can I give you a lift back?" Mark stated.

"Yes, but not yet," Marika insisted.

"No rush, when you're ready sis. How is he?" Mark asked.

"Ask him," she didn't like talking about Charlie as a third person.

"What were you talking about anyway?" he asked her instead.

"Charlie told me about an incident that happened to him and Daniel down by the Pontoon about a week before the accident. He saw this man throw a large heavy looking sack or something in the Pontoon. When the man saw him he actually chased him. He had been terrified. What if he was a murderer or something and was disposing of a body in the water and he thought Charlie might go to the police, so had him run over?"

"Marika, you're such a drama queen. You're going to make a great actress when you grow up. That's a huge leap you've just made," her brother laughed.

"But what if I'm right? We should tell the Police," she persisted.

"Tell them what, exactly. Did Charlie give you a description of this man?" Mark asked.

"Not much but Mark, they haven't got anywhere looking for a drunk driver. If this man did try to kill Charlie then he may come here," she whispered, not wanting to alarm her sleeping brother.

Mark didn't know whether to feel amused at his sister's typical dramatic spirit or actually take her seriously. "Let's speak to dad first before we go to the police," he said wisely.

"No wait," Marika was only just getting warmed up. "What about Matthew? He's been questioned by the police over a girl whose gone missing from Uni. What if the girl was in the sack and is now in the pontoon?"

"Hold on, hold on. I think you're getting a bit carried away here sis. The girl went missing from Cambridge. What makes you think she might end up here in Kent?" Mark was truly impressed.

"Well, we know he's got a car don't we? He could have driven her here," she wasn't going to be denied.

"I think you have an over active imagination that is working overtime right now sis. When we leave here we can go to the pontoon if you like and you can show me where it happened," Mark said calmly.

"We might interfere with the crime scene if we do that," she was enjoying herself now.

"It was ages ago now. Loads of people will have walked their dogs around there since," Mark reasoned.

"Say what you like Mark Havers but you will never forgive yourself if that man comes here and interferes with Charlie. He needs protection," Marika was defiant.

"Well I think he has that Marika. You're always here and when you're not, dad is, or Granddad or Nurse Booth or Grandmother. I don't think we have to worry about anyone getting at Charlie but if you're going to keep going on about this let's speak to Matty tonight and maybe he can have a word with that policewoman he's going out with," Mark told her.

"Okay." That was a good idea she told herself. She had now convinced herself she was onto something and couldn't wait to follow it up. "Let's go."

Part Two—
"Finding Sian"

CHAPTER TWENTY-FIVE

After arriving at Kuala Lumpur Ben wasted no time in hiring a self-drive car, collecting some street maps and various bits of equipment, he felt might come in useful, if he hit trouble. He hadn't been able to bring his gun in but he knew how to convert seemingly innocent looking everyday articles for weapons if necessary. He headed directly to the area Buzz had indicated as the last known contact with Sian. It was not exactly a tourist area. It was on the North side of the city and close to the docks. The area appeared to be dominated with Industrial type units and he noticed a few ladies of the night evident. It was fairly deserted and he suspected a lot of the units were closed down. The only building which looked slightly interesting was a large green coloured wooden structure on the corner of the street. He noticed this building appeared to have only one entrance and no windows whatsoever and there was a camera overlooking the door which really got his attention. The only mildly interesting vehicle parked in the vicinity was a large black people carrier with blacked out windows. It was outside the green building and he found the engine was cold. Having parked his car up a couple of streets away he had decided he would look less conspicuous on foot and less likely to get accosted by one of the Ladies. He walked right round the building hoping to hear or see something but very conscious of the camera at the same time. Eventually, he found a quiet sheltered doorway on the opposite side of the road, far enough back not to be spotted, but still able to see the green door and he waited. Ben had lost count of the many stakeouts he had done in his career, anything from lying up to his armpits in marshland to spending five days and nights curled up in a tree, so this was easy for him. He didn't even know if he was on the right track. This could be a waste of time but something in his water told him to be patient and so he waited. It was 10pm local time and he would wait until just before light, if necessary.

The girls weren't very busy tonight. He noticed two or three of them chatting. They looked twitchy. They were probably on drugs, poor things.

It was a vicious cycle. He thought about speaking to them, showing them a photograph of Sian, Mac had given him. Maybe one of them might remember seeing her there. It didn't make sense though. Sian wasn't a drug addict and she would never be that desperate for money. What had she been doing here? He decided to stay hidden.

He was rewarded a couple of hours later when the green door opened and a large built bald headed man of Eastern origin came out and held the door open for his boss. He was the archetypical bodyguard and Ben could see the bulge by his armpit where he clearly kept his firearm. His boss was a good deal smaller, dressed in a suit, and walked straight to the black car. Some of the girls ran towards them clearly hopeful for business but the bodyguard spat at them and spoke to them harshly in their language. They both got into the car and left but not before Ben had taken their photographs for future reference.

Now what? Was it safe to check out the building? He doubted it was empty. Should he speak to the girls now, see if they know what goes on inside. It didn't seem like they would be loyal to the suited man after what just happened and he had enough money on him to loosen their tongues, providing they could speak a language he understood of course. He didn't think there was likely to be any more movement from the building now somehow. Maybe he should make something happen.

He didn't get a chance. Suddenly, the green door opened again and a young man stepped outside and lit up a cigarette. He ambled towards the waterside enjoying the inhalation of tobacco. One of the girls, she looked about fourteen, walked straight up to him and they had a conversation. They appeared to know each other and when he had finished his cigarette he went with her around the back of the building. Not for the first time, Ben thought, but he didn't care. The door was open and he had an opportunity he wasn't going to miss. He moved stealthily. He had to be quick and not be seen by any of the other girls. He picked his moment well and slipped in through the slightly ajar door without arousing any attention.

The building was like a warehouse inside. It was open plan and there were few areas to hide. It was warm and dimly lit and it took him seconds to realise he wasn't alone. The young man wasn't the only work force in here.

There were at least five others, that Ben could see, and maybe more that he couldn't. More than he could handle he realised quickly and resolved to get out before the young man returned. His first target for concealment was a pinball machine. It was one of many he suddenly realised. The warehouse appeared to build gaming machines, nothing more furtive than that. He didn't quite buy it. Why no windows? Why the boss man with his own bodyguard? He realised too there was an unusual smell in this building. It was a very familiar one to him.

He was doing well, moving silently from one machine to another to try and get a better view and when he saw the sunglasses he knew he had struck gold. He and Mac had been in Oman and Mac had bought the sunglasses as a gift for his sister. He had remembered it because it was only last year and it was the first time Mac had ever admitted to having a sister. It was when they returned from the mission that Ben actually met her for the first time. Mac had taken Ben up to Liverpool to celebrate his birthday in their usual style at his Uncle Pats Casino and Sian was there. She was lovely, very Irish and full of life. They had all laughed at the present. Sian was hardly going to need sunglasses in Liverpool and living in a Casino but it was the thought that counted. He tried to get closer to the glasses, lying on a dusty table, but then the front door opened and closed again. The young man was back already. What if he locked the door? He didn't get a chance to ponder further on that one, as suddenly there was a cry from above his head. He had been spotted.

It all kicked off. Ben had the element of surprise on his side but nothing more. He grabbed the glasses and secreted them into his pocket before his first assailant reached him. He had thought about acting the drunken tourist who had got lost but this bunch, were clearly not in the mood for banter. He dodged the first attack and flung himself at the second. These guys didn't appear to be too polished fortunately. No kung-fu and all that stuff. He managed to throw one of them at three others. That made them angry but they were disorganised and he was too quick. A lot of furniture got broken and there was a good deal of shouting but in the end Ben might have escaped with just a few cuts and bruises, had one of them not decided to up the 'anti', with a firearm. Once again, Ben was on him. The gunman hadn't counted on that. No one was that stupid surely. He did get a round off but it missed its' intended target and hit the pinball machines shattering the glass frontage to reveal some sealed packages inside. There was that smell again, Ben thought.

Then Ben caught him in exactly the right place and disarmed him. Collecting the gun and grabbing a hostage he threatened the rest of the workforce as they closed in on him. They hesitated long enough for him to pull his hostage out through the door and on to the street. The fourteen-year old girl was still hanging about by the door and was knocked to the ground as they emerged. Ben had let go of his hostage as he fell over her but managed to keep the gun and quickly found his feet again. All he needed to do now was to get the hell away and he ran like the wind. He didn't immediately run towards his car. He wanted to lose his pursuers first. It took a while but eventually they gave up and went back to lick their wounds.

When Ben finally returned to his car, he was surprised to see the fourteen-year old girl standing by it. Ignoring her, he opened the door and got into the driver's seat. She got in beside him and gave him a beautiful smile. "American?" she said eagerly.

"Look, sorry love. I don't need company right now," he said reaching across her to open her door and let her out.

"Please," she looked pleadingly. "You take me with you."

"I can't," he told her.

"I can help you," she offered.

"How?" he asked, full of doubt.

"You take me with you please," she pleaded again.

"No, now get out," Ben was resolved.

"They'll kill me," she said with tears in her eyes.

"No, they won't. Why should they?" Ben asked.

"They think I helped you," she explained and it dawned on him what she meant. She would be blamed for the distraction that allowed him to get inside, which was actually true, when he thought about it.

"How old are you?" he asked her.

"Sixteen," she said.

He doubted that was true but it was good enough for now. He had to take her with him. He could find her somewhere else to live at the other end of the City. He could even turn her into the Police. He was thinking he should be going to the Police now anyway with what he had found out although he doubted the warehouse would still be there by the time they got their act together and raided it. He started the car and drove off. It was still only 4am.

He drove far enough away, back to the tourist area of the City, to park up again and get himself sorted out. He was bleeding and he needed to clean himself up a bit. He stopped by a public park with a pretty fountain in the middle. She walked with him afraid to leave his side for a minute and helped him get cleaned up. "What is that place back there?" he decided to see exactly how much she knew since her English was so good.

"You saw I think," she said simply.

"Who runs it?" he asked.

"His name is Liang Won. He is a bad man," she replied.

"Was he the man in the black car?" Ben asked her again.

"Yes but I don't think he is boss man. Boss man is like you," she said.

"What do you mean, a Westerner?" he enquired.

"Yes," she answered.

CHAPTER TWENTY-SIX

"That's it," she told him, "the house with the tower and the gold gates."

Ben had decided against going to the Police. His new companion, Lucie, had advised him against that. She said that Mr Won paid a lot of the police off and it would be difficult to find one to trust. He thought she was probably protecting her own interests, she didn't want to be handed over to them and he understood that, but there may be some truth in what she said too. Instead they had found a hotel to hole up in, one that wouldn't ask too many questions about a white man and a very young Malaysian girl sharing a room. They had got some sleep. He had been awake for over twenty-four hours and needed to recharge his batteries and work out a plan. She had been in seventh heaven with the bathroom and he had left her to it. She had tried to seduce him of course but he wasn't interested. He had Marika at home and he was missing her already. He phoned her of course and he updated Mac who was very excited with his progress. It had gone better than they could have hoped so quickly, but what did it all mean for Sian?

After nightfall they had gone out for food and then much to their surprise had found Mr Won's address was listed in the telephone directory. Sometimes it amazed Ben how simple his job was. They had driven along the esplanade up to the hills lying above the sea on the South side of the city, a long way from the Wharf, and there it was. A large mansion, ornate, detached and protected by cameras and gates. Cameras! Ben suddenly remembered the camera outside the green building. He had wanted to get his hand on the film from that. "Damn," he said aloud.

"What's wrong?" Lucie asked.

"I need to go back to the Warehouse," was the unexpected reply.

She was shocked. "How can you think of that after just about escaping with your life last time?"

"Because I left something behind," he said trying to make up his mind whether to go now.

"It will be gone," she said logically. "Whatever it is you've left, it will be gone. Everything will be gone."

He accelerated the car and headed back for the North. "I need to be sure," he simply said and she froze in her seat. He noticed her tension. "Don't worry I'll drop you off at the hotel if you like?"

"No." She didn't want to go anywhere near that Wharf again but she didn't want to be parted from this stranger either. He might be her ticket out of this hell hole. "I wait for you. Look after the car for you."

There was no more conversation and he left Lucie "looking after his car," when he parked it up about half a mile from the Wharf. He instantly noticed more traffic in the area and didn't want to get too close on wheels in case he couldn't turn round. Better to walk and check things out first. There were one or two Lorries coming up and down and sometimes the drivers would be distracted by the collection of Ladies of the Night gathering once more. He arrived at the location without attracting any attention and stood in his doorway again surveying the target. On the outside nothing appeared to have changed. He waited.

Suddenly, he spotted Lucie. What was she doing? She walked right up to the door and knocked on it waiting for an answer. Either she's been having him on or she's got a suicidal tendency, similar to his own. To his surprise, the door opened and the young man who had enjoyed her company the night before came out. He had a black eye, courtesy of Ben, and a plaster over his nose. He grabbed her harshly by the arm and pulled her inside. She screamed as he pulled her in. Now what? Thanks Lucie.

He had no choice of course. He had the gun he supposed but one gun against ten or more of theirs perhaps wasn't filling him with confidence and there is only the one way in and out which really bothered him. A good soldier always looks for an exit before he makes an entrance. On top of that the black car was outside again, which meant the twenty stone Bodyguard was there too. What was she thinking? Is she trying to distract them for him? He wished they'd had more conversation in the car now.

He was just about to break cover when Lucie was dragged out of the warehouse by two thugs and thrown into the back of the black car. The boss man and his bodyguard followed. She was kicking and screaming but to no avail. It was enough to get the attention of the other working girls though and there were quite a few tonight. They ran down the street towards them and started to hassle the men. Ben simply slipped into the warehouse amid the mayhem and saw that it was being closed down. It was a lot tidier which made it harder to conceal him-self as he moved around. There were still some workers inside engaged in packing up. What had taken them so long, Ben thought? They obviously weren't expecting immediate attention from the police just as Lucie had suggested. He followed the leads from the camera mounting above the inside of the door and clambered up some metal steps to an attic area where he found what he was looking for. He picked up as many tapes as he could carry and as many as he had time to collect before the inevitable shout rang out, as he was spotted again.

Here we go again, he thought and then it occurred to him there was a hatch in the roof. He was through it before you could say a magic spell and found him-self in the open air. He ran across the apex to the rear and leapt across onto the neighbouring warehouse building just making it by the skin of his teeth. He ran across that roof onto the next and so on, until eventually he found a building with a fire escape and found ground again.

He should just leg it now of course but he couldn't. Lucie. He couldn't just leave her at their mercy. He sprinted back to the car. She had left it open and the keys were still in it. He started it up and headed back for the wharf. It was chaos. The girls were fighting with some of the geeks and the boss man and his bodyguard had gone back into the Warehouse to find out what the shouting was in there. Lucie was locked in the car but not for long. Ben pulled his car up alongside and smashed the side passenger window with the butt of the firearm he had confiscated last time. The glass shattered and Lucie climbed out through the hole and got into his car. They drove off at high speed just avoiding a lorry turning around on the Wharf and disappeared into the night.

"You came back for me," she sounded excited.

"You're crazy," he said. "Why did you have to get involved?"

"What now?" she was elated.

"Back to Mr Wons," Ben shocked her once more.

CHAPTER TWENTY-SEVEN

"This time when I say wait here do as I ask" he instructed the girl as he parked up along the Esplanade. "Sound the horn if the black car returns, okay?"

"Okay," she said disappointed to be parted from Ben but pleased, to be given a task.

Ben circuited the property swiftly before jumping up onto an eight-foot wall on the west side. The cameras appeared to be on a set pattern. If he timed it right, he could jump over the wall and reach the cover of the trees surrounding the swimming pool before the next rotation. He was quick and moved easily. Seconds later he was on the rear patio checking for a weak spot to make his entrance. The lights were on inside. Did that mean he didn't live alone or were they on a timer? Moving silently, he climbed the down pipe from the roof line gutters up to what proved to be a bathroom window on the first floor. It easily opened under pressure. There would be alarms but not on this window. He climbed in and waited. Nothing! No noise. Quietly he opened the bathroom door and took in his bearings. There was a long landing area with several doors, all closed, leading off from it and a large spiral staircase leading downstairs. He had to pass two of these doors to reach the staircase and had to take care not to cast any shadows, in case they were occupied. He crept downstairs and checked each room in turn finding a rear door to the garden. That would be his exit if needed. It led off the kitchen. The patio doors led off the dining room and then he found the office. He rifled through the desk quickly not sure what he was looking for. All the paperwork was in a language he couldn't understand. Perhaps he should have brought Lucie in after all.

Then he saw a brown paper package in the bottom drawer. It was addressed to Mr Won and the writing was definitely Western. He looked inside and found about a dozen passports. The passports were British but the photographs inside were blank. Tut-tut, he thought. What sort of business was Mr Won running? He decided to help himself to one.

Ben noticed there were several mementoes around the room from Thailand.

Mr Won had an ornate looking paperweight, an ashtray and a photograph of himself standing outside the Paradise Hotel in Phuket. Ben knew that particular Hotel had been hit badly by the Tsunami, pity Mr Won wasn't there on holiday then, he thought.

Bless her. The car horn was loud enough, just. Time to go! He took one final look and swept through to the kitchen and the rear door. As he opened it the alarms finally did their duty. Damn. They were a lot louder than the car horn. Floodlights swept the gardens and Ben thought he heard the sound of dogs. This wasn't good. He headed for the trees, remembering to avoid the pool, and grabbed a branch. He elevated himself up and away just in time as the teeth of the guard dog snapped at his heels. Climbing the tree he practised his Tarzan act and swung from one branch to the next until he reached the wall. He was over it and running before the black car had reached the front door of the house.

CHAPTER TWENTY-EIGHT

"It took a while but I got in," Buzz woke him up to say. Ben had been exhausted when he and Lucie got back to the hotel. They had picked up a take-away, devoured it together and then he had fallen asleep on the bed fully clothed. She had curled up beside him. He had been asleep for about four hours when his phone began vibrating in his pocket.

"Got in where?" Ben was trying to focus.

"The airports computer," Buzz told him, clearly pleased with him-self.

"What?" Ben sat upright.

"Yeah, I know, I'm the man," Buzz continued boastfully. "Sian McManus landed in Kuala Lumpur on the 10th December, that's what nine days ago now."

"Okay," Ben said. "We kind of knew that didn't we Buzz?" he humoured his friend.

"Well you didn't know for sure, did you? You just had the phone call to go on," he said sounding disappointed at Ben's reaction to his brilliance.

"Yeah, but I do know. I've found Sian's sunglasses," Ben stole his thunder.

"I'm taking it she wasn't wearing them?" Buzz asked flippantly.

"No," was the sour reply.

"Well, she might need them now," he added saving the best bit to last.

"What do you mean?" Ben realised Buzz was playing him.

"She's in Thailand. She left Kuala Lumpur on the 12th, that's what seven days ago," he said enjoying him-self again.

"Thailand?" Ben asked incredulously.

"Phuket, to be exact. Isn't that the place that got flooded?" Buzz recalled.

"Let me get this straight. You're saying, or at least the airports' computer is saying, Sian McManus flew out of Kuala Lumpur, destination Phuket, seven days ago?" Ben asked.

"Of course it might not have been her," Buzz reasoned. "I'm just giving you the computer data. It could have been someone using Sian's passport and identity I suppose."

"In which case it doesn't tell us much, does it?" Ben stated.

"Maybe she's travelling the world after all," Buzz said. "Heard from Mac?"

"No. Can you check Phuket Airport before I go charging off there?" he said. "Oh and check Sian's mobile records again. Did she make any other calls, from when she landed here on the 10th, before she rang Mac? Actually, do that first."

"Okay Major. Anything else I can do for you?" Buzz was being sarcastic but Ben did have something else.

"Yes. Find out what you can on a Liang Won. He's a big man out here. What's his legitimate business, if he has one, and who are his associates," Ben said. "I'll send you a photo of him now."

"Run into trouble have you?" Buzz was almost jealous.

"Who's that?" Lucie asked him as he put his phone away.

"Just a mate," Ben responded.

"Buzz, that's a funny name isn't it?" she remarked.

"Buzz Lightyear, so called because he's light years ahead of everyone else," Ben told her.

CHAPTER TWENTY-NINE

When Ben returned to the hotel room he was carrying breakfast and a VHS recorder. Lucie had been concerned when she woke up and he was gone but he hadn't gone far. He had found the second hand electrical store down a side street in the City and paid peanuts for the machine. It wasn't exactly the state of the arc in new technology but it was perfect for his purposes. He set it up in conjunction with the Hotels tiny television, while she made the coffee to go with the buns he had bought and quickly got to work feeding in the videos he had stolen from the warehouse. They weren't easy to watch. They were on a timer motion and were very jerky and a bit blurred. He had managed to whisk away five and they seemed to be about four hours long each. Luckily there were times and dates displayed so he immediately ruled out those before the 10th December. He was left with three. He decided to leave Lucie in charge while he took a much-needed shower. He showed her the photograph of Sian and told her to call him the minute she appeared on the screen.

"Is this the girl you're looking for?" Lucie said staring hard at the photograph.

"Yes."

"Is she your sweetheart?" she asked him feeling pangs of jealousy.

"No."

"She's very pretty Ben. Do you think I'm pretty?" she asked.

She didn't give up. "I think you're very young and should probably be at school," he said walking into the shower. She started to follow him and he quickly ushered her back out and locked the bathroom door. Thank Goodness Marika cannot see him right now.

"Ben, come quick, it's her," Lucies' excited voice roused him from his daydreams of Marika. Having the water pour over his body was bliss. He hadn't realised how hectic it had all been since he arrived in this country two days ago and he just needed this moment alone with his thoughts.

It was the first time he had been parted from Marika since they met, he realised, and was surprised how hard that was. He was starting to believe he would not stay in the army if it meant long departures from her. Wow!

He turned the water off, put a towel round his lower body and opened the door. He hadn't expected what happened next and later cursed him-self for being so lax. His defences were down. The bodyguard had his arms around Lucie with his hand over her frightened mouth. Another hired hand was standing by the door with a gun pointing in his direction and Mr Won was facing him, with a sardonic smile on his face.

"Good Morning Mr Casey," Mr Won spoke first. He had done his homework. Ben had supposed it was only a question of time before someone as powerful as Mr Won had tracked him down to this seedy little hotel. He should have been ready. He had taken his finger off the pulse again and now he had to think quickly. He could flick his towel in the direction of the door and disarm the geek there. He had the gun, so he was the immediate threat. Then he could throw a few well-timed punches and he might still have enough time to grab Mr Won before the bodyguard let go of Lucie and got involved. On the other hand, he wanted to hear what Mr Won had to say first.

"You don't mind if I get some clothes on while we talk?" he asked casually moving towards the bathroom door again.

The movement made the gunman twitchy and he started to make noises and moved towards Ben. Even better, Ben thought and he couldn't resist. The towel flicked him hard in the eye and the gun was twisted from his grasp before he knew anything. Amateurs! Mr Won didn't flinch so easily, however. He looked at his bodyguard who now had a gun barrel inside the mouth of Lucie. Ben raised his hands and gun in the air as if defeated and Mr Won put his hand out for Ben to place the gun in it. As he did so Mr Won took the butt and hit his own hired hand around the face with the handle. Mr Won didn't like being shown up. "Go and get your clothes Mr Casey," he told Ben politely.

CHAPTER THIRTY

"It's your lucky day Mr Casey." Somehow it didn't feel like it. Bens' wrists were sore from the plastic flex holding them together behind his back and he was cramped into a tiny compartment below deck. "My Benefactor doesn't want you harmed it seems. When you arrive at your next destination the Captain has orders to release you but be warned Mr Casey, return at your peril."

After Mr Won left Ben felt his body lurch forward and heard the sound of a ships' engine bursting into life. He was alone in the hold. He wasted no time twisting his arms down under his feet and bringing them up in front of his body. It's one thing being tied up but a lot easier when you're hands are in front. Now he could work on the plastic flex. Rub it against whatever sharp pieces of metal he could find and there are always plenty of candidates in a ships' hold. It took him all of five minutes and by now the ship was gathering speed, obviously clear of the dock area and out in the open sea. He looked around the hold. There were large wooden crates piled high with labels that suggested they contained fruit. He doubted that was all. He checked his pockets to see if Mr Won had left him anything of value. He had no passport, no wallet, no phone and no money. All he had was the pair of sunglasses that belonged to Sian. He considered finding his way to the deck and jumping overboard. Swimming back to shore might not be too bad. The seas aren't too cold or dangerous at this time of year and he probably had about two miles to cover, which he knew he could do. On the other hand Mr Won had promised him freedom at the end of the voyage. Should he just sit it out? He had no way of knowing where he was going or how long he would actually be at sea and the more time he wasted sitting about the more concerned he would be about Sian. There was Lucie too. What had happened to her? He doubted she would be kept alive, poor child. No, for Ben, there was no choice.

He found his way to the hatch up to deck and pushed it gently to see if it was open. To his surprise, it was. He opened it about an inch and listened. It was difficult to hear much above the sound of the ocean and the ships' engines but he detected two male voices to his right. He opened the hatch a bit further and peeked out. He could see the feet of the men behind the voices. They were facing the opposite way. Perfect. Of course there may be others on board, this was a reasonable size container ship, but he had no time to pussy foot around. He opened the hatch fully and climbed out, closing it again and crouching down behind the raised engine cover. He had been lucky. These two were the only ones on the deck and they seemed engaged. Wait a minute? They were engaged all right. They were both holding a small girl and about to do something fairly distasteful to her by the looks of it. Ben picked up a wooden oar lying in the lifeboat to the starboard side and crept up behind them. The girl suddenly spotted him and ducked as the oar came crashing down across the back of one of the sailors' heads sending him sideways. As the other one turned round his stomach was met with the other end of the oar full on and he doubled up in pain. Before he could stand up again his face took a sideways swipe from the oar and he fell on top of his shipmate in a crumpled heap.

"I knew you'd save me," Lucie held out her arms but Ben grabbed her hand and pulled her away. He had no time for niceties. He pulled her sharply and practically threw her tiny frame into the lifeboat. Untying its cords, he thrust the boat into the sea and jumped into it from the deck of the ship, starting the engine immediately. Thank goodness it worked and they zipped away from the ship just quick enough to dodge the barrage of fire-power that followed them as the Captain and his mate got their act together. He knew they could chase him but by the time they got the ship turned around he would be less than a mile off the coast and they couldn't risk being spotted.

The little dinghy weaved and bobbed its way back to shore and when he felt they were safe from their pursuers he slowed the engine and let her drift in slowly to the coastline. It was daylight and he didn't want to arouse suspicion. They found a place to land and climbed ashore.

"Are you okay?" he finally asked her.

She smiled her response. "I'm okay. How come he let you live?"

"Something to do with his Benefactor I believe. Do you know who that is?"

"No, only what I said before, he Westerner," she answered. "Ben?"

"Yes Lucie."

"The girl in the photograph, I have seen her before and she was on the film you know," Lucie informed him.

"Where Lucie, where have you seen her before?" he was excited.

"It was down on the wharf. She came to the wharf in a taxi but the driver he no wait for her. She went into that building, it's on the tape. That's all I know," she told him honestly.

"Tell me again exactly," he requested.

CHAPTER THIRTY-ONE

Ben made his way to the airport on foot. It didn't take him long, he was a good runner and he'd had to leave Lucie behind for this job. He found what he needed at the airport. There was an International telephone and computer desk. He reversed the charges and Buzz obliged with the rest. Solvent again he bought himself a new mobile. He would have to be more patient for a new passport. Buzz informed him that Mr Won was known as an Import and Export businessman and originated from Thailand. He had moved to Kuala Lumpur some twenty years before and quickly risen to power. He owned several properties in the City. He exported regularly to the UK.

Outside the hotel he saw the taxi rank and had an idea. It was the ninth or the tenth driver he spoke to who appeared to remember Sian. The right bribe loosened his tongue. He had collected her from the flight from the UK on the 10th and taken her to the Hilton Hotel in the City. He had given her his card and she had called him the next day to pick her up from the Raffles Tea Rooms. He remembered her because she had an unusual accent and was travelling alone. She also tipped well. The taxi drivers all wanted to drive the Westerners around for their generous tips. When she got into his taxi she made a strange request. He had seen it happen in movies but it had never happened for real, before. A black car with blacked out windows pulled up in front and a man wearing a black suit came out of Raffles and got in. She told him to follow that car.

Sian was slightly excited and nervous he felt. They followed the car out of the City and it headed north. However, when it drove into an industrial type area near the docks he had told her he couldn't go any further. He had heard stories about that part of the town and it was virtually a no go area for the taxi men. There were all sorts of bad gangs hiding out down there, he believed and it was no place for a Western woman. When he refused to continue she got out the taxi and paid him, telling him she would call him later for a lift back. He begged her not to go any further on foot but she ignored him and he never heard from her or saw her again.

Ben got a lift with this driver to the Hilton hotel and paid him well. He hadn't really learned a great deal but he believed the driver was genuine. At the hotel he asked at Reception for Sian McManus. The Receptionist looked a bit suspicious. "Is something wrong?" he asked in his most innocent voice.

"Is Miss McManus a friend of yours Sir?" the receptionist asked a bit unsure of herself.

"Yes. She should have checked in on the 10th from the UK. I was supposed to meet up with her last week but got delayed and now I'm wondering if she is still here?" he said.

The Hotel Manager had joined the Receptionist at the desk and told her he would deal with the matter now. He invited Ben in to his office and informed him that Miss McManus had checked in but had since left. "The matter is now in the hands of the Police," he said.

"The Police! Why? What's happened?" Ben tried to sound surprised.

"I'm sorry Sir, if you're a friend but Miss McManus was only booked in here for two nights. When she didn't return we had to inform the police and hand over her luggage and passport which we keep in our safe," the Manager explained politely.

"I see. So you're telling me she didn't check out?" Ben asked him.

"No. It's not her account we were concerned about you understand," he tried to excuse his actions. "We were concerned for her safety. She spent the first night here but then wasn't seen again and she couldn't have left without her passport. So the Police took everything away. You'd better speak to them. Officer Choo was dealing with it."

Ben decided it was time to give the Police a whirl. According to Buzz her passport was used the day the hotel handed it over to the Police? That was interesting. They wouldn't know he knew that bit of information of course, time to test them.

Officer Choo was a female and quite tenacious, Ben decided quickly. She liked to ask him more questions, to his questions, which he found annoying, but he had invented a story and tried to keep to the truth as much as possible. She knew Sian had gone to Raffles and met someone there. She didn't tell him who but he knew she knew. Was it Mr Won? If Officer Choo were genuine she would know Mr Won was a bad man and be suspicious of Sian and therefore Ben. If she were bent she would want to protect Mr Won. He asked to look through Sians suitcase. There was nothing to help and so he broached the subject of her passport casually. The Officer looked puzzled at first. "The hotel gave it to my colleague," she seemed to remember. Dani," she shouted across to an officer sitting nearby. "You still got that Irish girls passport?"

Dani looked hesitant and eyed Ben up and down before answering. "You had it, not me," he said emphatically.

"No, that's not right. You made me carry the case because it's pink, I remember, so you took the passport," Officer Choo recalled.

"No," he answered sternly and got up and walked out. She went across to his desk and started rummaging without success.

"That's odd," she said. "Maybe it got sent back to the Embassy."

"Could we check?" Ben tried to sound casual. "I mean she could have left if she got it back, I suppose."

Officer Choo looked very annoyed. She had been working hard on this case and if it turned out the girl had already left the country she was going to feel foolish. She had wanted to pin something on Mr Won for a long time and this case might have led to something. She made a few phone calls, first to the Embassy and receiving no joy there, to the Airport. When she put the phone down she got up and got her hat ready to leave. "Her passport was used on a flight to Thailand on the 12th. I'm going over there to check the CCTV. Want to come?"

"Thanks." At last, he thought, some action.

At the airport he started to learn to trust Officer Choo. They checked the CCTV and eventually the moment came when Sian McManus checked through departures. "I'm guessing that isn't your Irish friend?" the Officer asked Ben, as she pressed pause on the screen. It was the face of an Asian girl and the Officer printed off a still photograph of her from the video. "Can we start again?" she asked him smartly.

So Ben told her.

"You're right to be cautious," she said when he finished his story. "Clearly my colleague decided to recycle the passport. I am afraid there is a lot of corruption in the City Police but I do promise you I want to do a good job despite them. I have been after Mr Won for a long time. I suspect he is into criminal activity. He hides behind legitimate import and export businesses but he has made a lot of money very fast and he uses that money to pay off certain police and other officials I am ashamed to admit. It's hard to pin anything on him but if you can help me?"

It was an impressive speech and Ben decided to go along with it for now. "I know he has other British passports in his possession."

"How?" she asked him surprised at his knowledge.

"You don't want to know that," he told her.

"Did Sian give them to him? I told you she met with someone at Raffles earlier, it was Mr Won. A member of staff saw her hand over a small brown-papered package and a briefcase to him. Why would she be involved in something like that?" Officer Choo asked.

"I don't know. Sian is not a criminal. I believe she didn't know what she was doing. Maybe someone asked her to do it for them and afterwards she got suspicious and decided to follow him. She probably thought she was being clever following him but then she got caught. I know she was at the Warehouse and in trouble," Ben told her.

"Why do you think Mr Won let you live?" she asked suspiciously.

Ben was pleased she was suspicious. It showed she cared and she didn't trust him any more than he could trust her. It made for a healthy relationship in his line of work. "He said his Benefactor wanted it that way. Who might that be? Have you any idea?"

"Not an Asian. Maybe it's someone who knows you," the Officer said directly. Ben didn't want to think about that.

CHAPTER THIRTY-TWO

It took another day but Officer Choo finally called Ben with the good news. She had got her warrant and her target and done so out of town away from prying eyes. The shipment was due out early in the morning but there was a serious manpower problem. She didn't know who to trust in the police department and couldn't risk the information getting back to the target. She was going to have to trust this stranger for help.

Ben had found Lucie and once again holed up in a less than glamorous hotel out west. He wasn't sure what he was going to do with her, maybe Officer Choo might help when this was over. For now he gave her the false passport he had lifted from Won's house to look after. Her eyes had widened like saucers when she saw it. It could be her ticket to a new life, if all else failed. He felt a certain responsibility to her for some reason. Maybe he was starting to grow a conscience. Love can affect you that way, apparently. Marika has a lot to answer for.

He met Officer Choo at the Wharf and they watched from a concealed area, as the Ship was loaded with the Pinball machines from the green building. Clearly Mr Won hadn't been told of Ben's escape and was still confidently and arrogantly using the same premises to operate from. He suspected that the Captain of his ship hadn't wanted to tell Mr Won how he had managed to escape for fear of reprisals probably and the police department spies weren't interested in making the big man angry either. On the other hand maybe they were calling their bluff. Ben suddenly had a bad feeling. "I think they're clean," he said.

"What?" Officer Choo was not in the mood to hear that. She was poised ready to pounce. To catch him in the act was the stuff dreams were made of.

"It's too easy" he explained.

"But how would they know?" she tried to cling on to some hope.

"You don't think your colleague might have told him about me sitting in your station?" Ben said. "There's nothing here for us."

"I can't just leave it now, I've got a warrant and everything," she was cross.

"Go ahead but I'm telling you they know, it's just too easy," he said angrily and of course she knew he was right.

"Well, what about the building?" she asked vainly.

"No, it's been cleaned up," Ben told her what she already knew.

"His house, the passports were there?" she was clasping at straws.

"Not any more. It's too late," he was convinced.

"It might not be," she tried to tell him. "What about your friend? What if she's still in there?"

"That's about as likely as Santa Claus turning up," Ben stated.

"Well we can't just give up," Oficer Choo was desperate.

"We're not going to," Ben said and walked away. "We need to approach this with lateral thinking." It wasn't something he was familiar with but he knew he was right. He was a trained soldier. He didn't usually have to do the planning. Someone else did that for him. His job was to pull the job off, usually with violence. "Let's go over again what we know."

"Your friend arrives on the 10th. She goes to the Hilton where she is booked in for two nights only. She eats in the hotel that night. She doesn't make any phone calls from the hotel but we know she had a mobile, right?" Officer Choo begins. Ben nodded and she continued, "The next day she walks to Raffles Tea Rooms where she meets Mr Won and hands him over a package and a briefcase. Ten minutes later she leaves, followed by him. He gets into his car and she follows in a taxi. She is dropped off at the wharf. She goes inside the green building and loses her sunglasses. Shortly after, she makes her last call on her mobile to her brother, asking for help."

"She wasn't wearing them," Ben said.

"What?" the Officer asked.

"Her sunglasses! She wasn't wearing them on the CCTV at the door," Ben told her, unsure whether it was relevant.

"Well, she probably took them off to go inside. What does that tell us?" the Officer wasn't following.

"I don't know. Maybe she left them for someone to find. Ignore me, I'm just thinking aloud. Go on." Ben said.

"Well, that's it really as far as she's concerned isn't it? She never returns to the hotel and we find out her passport is used by someone else. You arrive and find the building. You go inside and find pinball machines like the ones we've just seen loaded on to that ship. You believe they contain drugs inside. We've still got time to stop that ship," she said vainly.

"Were the drugs coming in or getting ready to go out?" Ben asked to no one in particular.

"They make the machines so presumably the drugs were for shipping out to England. The machines are bound for Liverpool," she answered.

"Where coincidentally Sian came from," Ben added.

"Liverpool?" she asked. "Of course, that's your connection then? Who do you know in Liverpool?"

"Sian's Uncle. He owns casinos," he replied glumly. He didn't want to think that Macs' Uncle Pat was involved in all this. Mac would be shattered. Ben knew only too well what it was to have your own family betray you and he didn't want his best mate having to experience that. Yet, everything pointed that way. He was lying to Mac about Sian. Had he got her to do his dirty work for him and when she found out the truth, then what? He must have been the one who ordered Mr Won to spare him. Would he spare his own niece?

"Sounds like you need to return to England," Officer Choo observed.

"Not yet," he said. "What if you call your boss now, tell him you have just obtained the warrant and need back up at the docks but don't let him know you're already here?"

"I don't know if I can trust him or whoever he might get to give me back up," she reasoned.

"No, but we'll know whether the warrants are worth executing by the reaction of Mr Won and his merry men down there," Ben said.

"If they carry on loading and do nothing we'll know they're clean," she realised.

"Exactly and if there's a mad panic to clear things we can hit them straight away. How long will it take for back up to arrive?" They were seriously outnumbered if they had to react and Ben wasn't happy about that.

"Not long," she said bravely and made the call.

CHAPTER THIRTY-THREE

"Look," Ben handed Officer Choo the binoculars. There were half a dozen Asian women dressed in Western clothes and carrying suitcases getting ready to board the Ship. Mr Won embraced each and every one of them before they got aboard.

"That's interesting," she said.

"I'm willing to bet those ladies have all got British passports with them," Ben suggested.

"Wait. He's taking a call on his mobile," she observed. "Get ready. I'd say he looks suitably perplexed."

Even Ben had to admit this Officer had guts. She had dropped the binoculars and raced towards the docks in record time. Mr Won was clearly expecting her, but not quite so soon. The girls were caught between the ship and the wharf and looked panicked. She called out to everyone to stand still and produced the warrant for Mr Won. He took it from her and glanced around to see if she had back up. Surely she hadn't come here alone, Mr Won thought, but he had only just received the call from the station. His bodyguard moved closer to the officer. Ben knew they would overpower her, gun or no gun, very quickly, if he didn't think of something and quick.

When she ran towards the docks he had been right after her but had diverted away behind the building, so as not to be seen. Now, he was standing in the shadows when an opportunity presented itself. One of Mr Wons' hired hands had heard the Police officer and armed himself with an Uzi from the Warehouse. As he emerged with the weapon Ben jumped him. The hand didn't know what hit him. Seconds later, Ben had the Uzi and that made him feel a whole lot better. He fired it towards the Bodyguard who was getting uncomfortably close to Officer Choo. He had shocked them all including the Officer.

"You," Mr Choo said viciously. "You're proving quite a thorn Mr Casey."

"Sorry about that," Ben said. "Now I think you'd better tell your men to take it easy Mr Won, as I can be a bit trigger-happy I'm afraid."

Mr Won believed him. He was proving a formidable opponent and he had made the mistake of underestimating him before. Besides, why not wait for the police. He had nothing to hide as far as the pinball machines were concerned and if the passports held up the police would have to let him go.

Then suddenly two limousines entered the arena. They arrived swiftly and parked between Ben and Mr Won. He no longer had the upper hand. To his dismay several heavily armed Asian men alighted the cars and surrounded Mr Won and his merry men. One of them, obviously the leader, stepped out of the car and walked towards Mr Won. This wasn't the police back-up Ben had hoped for. This was more trouble. He decided to find cover and took it behind Mr Wons' vehicle. Officer Choo was caught in the middle and had no choice but to stand still and wait. She had lost all control of the situation. There was an angry exchange between Mr Won and this new Gang Leader.

The Ship's crew had decided to arm themselves and their Captain gave the order for his men to attack and suddenly the whole area was ablaze with gunfire. Officer Choo dived for cover and Ben grabbed Mr Won and dragged him off towards his car. The girls on the gangplank were screaming and jumping into the water to escape the stray bullets flying around. It was organised chaos. The Captain had asked his crew to fight back but they didn't appear to know who the enemy were and they ended up shooting at Mr Wons' hired help, while his men fired back at them. The noise was deafening. Shortly after, the police arrived and joined in with the fracas.

Ben decided it was time to take Mr Won somewhere quieter and have a word with him, before the police did. He pushed the gangster into the back of the car and rendered him unconscious with the butt of the Uzi. He got in the drivers' seat and quickly hot-wired the car. Before long, they were driving up to Mr Wons front door. He didn't know why he had chosen to take him back there. He knew the police would come calling there too once they had sorted the docks mess up but he had bought himself a bit of time and he needed somewhere they wouldn't be disturbed by the public. He pulled the semi-conscious hapless Mr Won from the car and banged on the front door, time to see who was in the house. A servant answered the door and believing his employer was hurt set about helping the stranger get him inside and sat down in a rather splendid room. "I get doctor?" he asked the stranger.

"No, he will live," Ben answered him. "Who else is here?"

"The rest of the staff has the day off, I'm afraid," he explained almost apologetically.

"That's okay. I'll take care of him. You can go too," Ben told him.

As soon as he was left alone, Ben set about bringing his captive back to life. He filled an ice bucket sitting on the cocktail-bar, (the room was very eighties), with water from the sink behind, and threw it over Mr Won.

"What are you doing?" Mr Won was not amused. "Who are you?"

"You know who I am Mr Won," Ben said coldly. "Who are you?"

"I am a businessman and you have no right to treat me like this," he was trying to sound indignant.

"Call the police then," Ben said slightly amused.

"I can call the police. I have nothing to hide," he said defiantly.

"Oh, they'll be here soon enough. In the meantime you're going to tell me where the girl is," Ben said threateningly.

"What girl?"

"Sian McManus, you met her at Raffles several days ago and then she disappeared. What have you done with her?" Ben said.

"That's why you're here?" Mr Won mused, the penny finally dropping. "Did he send you?"

"Did who send me?" Ben asked.

"I don't know where she is. I met her at Raffles as you say. We had tea together and then I thought she went back to her country," he lied.

"Why did you meet her?" Ben asked again.

"She was acting as a courier, that's all. She had brought me something and that was a business transaction, that's all Mr Casey. So you see you're wasting your time," Mr Won tried to sound convincing.

"No, Mr Won. You're wasting my time," Ben said as he pulled up the hapless man by his lapels and stared into his face. "Do you know that I am trained in many forms of intense interrogation Mr Won? If you don't tell me the truth I am going to hurt you in ways you never believed possible. Do you understand me?"

Mr Won was terrified. It was easy to believe this stranger. He had already proved himself formidable. "I'm telling the truth," he pleaded.

"What happened when she showed up at your Warehouse?" Ben asked finding the point in Mr Wons neck, that would loosen his tongue and applying pressure. He screamed.

"Nothing," he squeaked. "She ran off when someone spotted her. I don't know why."

"Yes, and you caught her. What did you do then?" He found another pressure point, which Mr Won found even more uncomfortable than the last.

"Who is it you are working for?" he asked vainly before screaming again in pain.

"I ask the questions. Where is she?" Ben shouted at him.

"Dead, like he asked," he eventually answered.

"Who asked?" Ben tried to sound emotionless but this news was what he had dreaded.

"Your boss," Mr Won told him.

"I don't have a boss Mr Won, but you do, don't you? Say his name?"

"No, I don't have a boss either, not anymore," the hapless man said.

"What do you mean?" Ben asked.

"He had double crossed me. The girl was supposed to be a show of trust because I was beginning to doubt him, but he set me up. You saw what happened at the wharf. Those men had come to kill me for giving them false money. The girl gave me that money which I handed to them for the drugs but it was a trap. They found out the money was no good and came back to make me pay. He wants me out of the picture. I see that now. If you don't work for him come and work for me," Mr Won was clutching at straws. Pain can do that for a human being.

"So you think your Benefactor set your drug supplier against you?" Ben was trying to understand.

"Yes, and just in case we didn't kill each other, he sent you. Now the police are involved. Is it those passports? Are they going to prove my downfall Mr Casey?" Ben had eased the pressure now as Mr Won was beginning to see him as an ally.

"You need to tell me everything," and Mr Won did. He left out the bit about the girl though, preferring to keep that particular card up his sleeve.

He had just finished his story when the police arrived and Ben decided it was time to disappear for now.

CHAPTER THIRTY-FOUR

Lucie was thrilled to see him back and in one piece. "How did it go?"

"Not great," Ben told her. He was feeling a little deflated. He had come to find Sian and the news that she was dead was not what he had wanted to hear. He also had not wanted to hear all that stuff about Uncle Pat. It was inconceivable to him and he was dreading going back to tell Mac the news. In his condition there was no telling how hard he would take it. His dark thoughts were interrupted when his mobile burst into life. It was Buzz.

"She's coming back," he said.

"Who is?" Ben asked still in a daze.

"Sian is, or whoever is using her passport. She's flying to Kuala Lumpur this evening from Phuket Airport," Buzz informed him.

"What time does she arrive?" Ben was suddenly interested.

"11pm your time," Buzz told him.

Ben checked his watch. It was 10.15pm. "Thanks Buzz," he hung up not in the mood for niceties. "Fancy a trip to the airport?" he asked Lucie.

Lucie didn't need a second invitation. They waited by arrivals and Ben recognised her from the Airports' CCTV immediately. She was travelling alone and only had one suitcase. He was trusting Lucie on this one. She had her brief and as soon as he gave her the nod, moved into action. She deliberately bumped into the unsuspecting woman and grabbed her suitcase and ran off with it. Ben gave chase and they acted out a play fight in which Lucie escaped and he returned the suitcase to its' grateful owner. She was very pleased with him and offered him a reward, which of course, he rejected.

"I'm Ben," he introduced himself.

"Sian," she lied mispronouncing the name completely.

"Are you getting a taxi?" he asked. "Do you want to share mine?"

She agreed that would be a good idea. She liked the idea of a chaperone after what had just happened to her and he was quite a handsome man. She asked the driver to take her to the Esplanade. In the car they made conversation. "Been on holiday?" he asked.

"I've been to visit my family in Thailand," she said. "I don't get to see them very often and I miss them."

"Your name doesn't sound very Thai," he observed. "I thought perhaps your family were from the UK?"

"No," she hesitated. "Er, I was born in the UK but my family moved to Thailand later. What about you?"

"I'm on holiday here," he said. "Maybe you could show me around?"

She was a bit taken aback. He was very direct and she wasn't used to that in her culture. He had just rescued her belongings, however, and she owed him. He was also charming. "Okay," she agreed smiling, "But I also have to work."

"What do you do?" he asked trying to sound casual.

"I am an Accountant. It's not very interesting I suppose," she smiled.

"Why work here? I mean, if you miss your family?" he asked.

"My family are very poor Ben. We lost everything in the Tsunami, including my father," she explained.

"I'm sorry," he said genuinely. He had lost a friend in that disaster too.

"I have a good job here but it's very difficult to get visas to travel home so I don't go much," she explained.

Easier with a British passport, Ben thought. "Whom do you work for?"

"Just businessmen," she said evasively. "This is my place." They had arrived at one of the more modest houses on this stretch of road, opposite end to Mr Wons. She went to pay but Ben said he would take care of it. She liked that, not only brave but also gallant.

"How can I contact you?" he asked. "Do you have a card?"

"Er, no," she hesitated. Well, not one in the name of Sian McManus, Ben thought. "Do you want to come in for a nightcap?" she took a chance.

CHAPTER THIRTY-FIVE

While she slept Ben decided to have a nose around her house. He had not enjoyed seducing her. He had kept thinking about Marika and hoped she would forgive him. She lived alone fortunately and told him the house was rented. He found the rent book and what he suspected was her real name fairly quickly in the bureau drawer in her office. Elysia Won. He recalled the photographs of Phuket in Mr Wons' house. She might be his younger sister or daughter, although, when she had told him her father was dead he had believed her. However related to Mr Won she was, she was also his Accountant and Fixer. This could be interesting. He was ahead of the Police. He ploughed through the desk but a lot of the documents were in a language he couldn't decipher. If he saw something that might be interesting he photographed it, on his mobile. Maybe Lucie would be able to translate for him later. He hoped she had dodged any airport police and got back to their hotel all right. When he had finished he decided Officer Choo might like a handle on this connection and sent her a text from his mobile. Then he stole away silently in the night and back to Lucie.

"Take a look at these," he showed Lucie the photographs. "What are they?"

"I think this one is invoice you call it?" she suggested.

"Yes, invoice is a good word. How did you learn English?" he was curious. Clearly she had never been to school.

"I had an English man look after me once. He was good to me, like you. I learn from him," she answered.

"What happened to him?" Ben was trying to help her.

"I don't know," she said distantly. "I think it is for rent of a building maybe".

"What's the address?" he asked.

"115 Hargarot Road. I know where that is," she said triumphantly. "Do you think it's important?"

"Maybe," he said suddenly feeling very tired. His mobile bleeped and Officer Choo had sent him a text back: "What happened to you?" she wrote. Good, he thought, at least she had made it out of that mess. Maybe she'll get the medal she deserves now. He decided not to answer and got some much needed sleep.

CHAPTER THIRTY-SIX

He was up early the next morning having slept really well and anxious for Lucie to take him to Hargarot Road. "How do you know this place?" he asked her as they arrived at the large house on the back street at the North side of the City again.

"It's my patch," she replied. "We're not far from the wharf and some of these houses are owned by Madams. I used to have a Madam looking after me once but it didn't work out."

Ben wondered at her past. For someone so young, so much had already happened to her it seemed. "Is this such an address?" he asked staring at the house warily.

"Why don't you find out?" she suggested cheekily, knocking on the door and running off.

He admired her spirit. He had no idea what he was going to say as he heard the door being unlocked from the inside and opened by a well-dressed female matriarch. "Yes?" she asked in English eyeing the tall stranger up and down.

"Good Morning," he said a bit lost for words. The woman mistook his hesitance for nerves and invited him.

"First time?" she asked.

"No, not at all," he said. "I've just not been here before."

"You like it here," she said smiling. "Wait here." She sat him down in the hallway and left him alone. He noticed the décor was dark and ornate and everything he would expect from a place like this. It was not his first time, of course. He had been in brothels all over the world he was ashamed to admit but when you're a working soldier sometimes you just have to get what you can, when you can. No more, he thought privately. The Madam returned with two Asian girls. Both looked under age. He showed his disapproval. "You want more experience maybe?" she asked disappointed at his reaction. Westerners were her best customers and most of them were delighted with the younger girls. In fact, the younger, the better, with a lot of them.

"I'm looking for something a bit different," he said authoritatively. "I can pay," he flaunted a large role of notes.

"What did you have in mind?" she asked suddenly very interested in her new punter and dismissing the young girls.

"Maybe, not Asian," he suggested, chancing his arm.

"You don't like Asian girls?" she asked, looking offended.

"Of course, but today I feel like something to remind me of home. I've been feeling very homesick you see. Do you have anything like that? Because if not, I can go somewhere else," he got up to leave.

"Wait," she said panic in her voice. She didn't want to lose this punter and his big roll of money that easily. "I might be able to help you but you may have to wait a moment."

"I will wait a moment," he nodded adding, "but don't take all day."

It was about fifteen minutes. He wondered what Lucie was making of it. He hoped she would not do anything silly and give him time. Eventually the Madam came back in and ushered him through the hallway door into the back of the house and up some stairs. He felt inside his coat pocket for the firearm he had retained for insurance from his earlier adventures with Mr Won just in case she was leading him into a trap. Feeling its butt reassured him as he climbed the stairs and was shown into a candlelit bedroom. It was daylight outside but you wouldn't have known it inside this Mausoleum with its' heavy drapes blocking out all natural light. "Wait here please," she said holding out her hand for payment.

"How much?" he asked.

"Five hundred," she insisted.

"That's a lot," he objected.

"Not for what you ask," she said coldly.

He handed over half that, "The rest after, if I'm satisfied," he said. He wasn't about to be conned by a back street brothel. She accepted the money and left.

Another minute passed before the door eventually opened and there she was.

He might not have recognised her at first for she was dressed in Eastern clothes and heavily made up. She was clearly drugged and she certainly didn't recognise him. He took out the sunglasses from his pocket and handed them to her. "Hello Sian, I think these belong to you," he said gently. "Would you like to try them on and see if they fit, Cinderella?"

Part Three—
"The Fall Out"

CHAPTER THIRTY-SEVEN

"We've had snow Charlie," Marika told her brother excitedly. "I can't remember seeing it so deep, it's brilliant. I went sledging yesterday and I'm covered in bruises today. You'd absolutely love it Charlie. You'd better wake up before it all goes. It's been a really exciting week. Before the snow came the police dragged the pontoon looking for bodies. Matthew told his policewoman girlfriend about you and she persuaded her bosses to check it out. They didn't find the girl from Matties Uni in there, thank goodness, but they did find something, which has got them all interested. No one's saying, of course, but there's loads of rumours flying around as you can probably imagine. They're saying they've found drugs or guns or other bodies. It's really gruesome. What do you think? You saw it. I wish you could tell me. Now they've actually got a police officer outside your room protecting you so it must be something big after all and they think it's definitely connected to what happened to you with that black car. One of the officers is rather pretty. I think you'd fancy her for sure. I told her if she gets bored sitting outside she should come in and talk to you when we're not here. Aren't you getting bored too now Charlie? You're missing so much: Christmas, snow and now all this business. You'd be in your element. I've got tickets to see Spirit by the way. Rebecca gave them to me for Christmas and she's going with me next week. I can't wait. I'm dead excited. I bet they'll be brilliant live. The keyboard player is still my absolute favourite but I reckon they're all pretty neat. Rebecca loves the guitarist best. Dads been promoted at work. I'm not sure what that means but he was really pleased."

"Hello Marika," Nurse Booth came in to check on her patient.

"Hi. Have you spoken to the police outside Nurse?" Marika asked hoping for information. Why do adults never tell you what's going on?

"Not really," the nurse said. "Why?

"I just wondered if they told you what they found in the pontoon," Marika said fishing.

"Oh no, they haven't told me, I'm afraid. I'm sure everything will be all right Marika," the nurse answered patiently.

"Oh yes, no, I'm not worried about that, I just want to know what's going on. After all it was me who told them to look in the pontoon," the girl said.

Typical child, Nurse Booth thought. She was only interested in the gore and not appreciating the consequences. The fact that this poor little boy was having twenty-four hour protection from the police meant that he was in danger. An attempt had obviously already been made on his life but his sister just wanted to know the gory details. Children have so little concept of danger. "Well let's hope your brother wakes up and puts us all out of our misery soon Marika," she said.

CHAPTER THIRTY-EIGHT

"Why didn't you tell me before?" Uncle Pat asked his nephew.

"Well you know now Uncle Pat," Mac said.

"I was going to say I could have got you into the best hospital but I see you're already in that," his Uncle observed.

"The Army believe in looking after their own," Mac explained.

"I don't believe that. Someone's paying for this and it won't be the Army," Uncle Pat said.

"What are you saying Uncle? Is this you?" Mac suddenly realised.

His Uncle smiled and said nothing. So. He had known all along. Mac felt uncomfortable, suddenly.

"They rang me while you were being flown back in," Uncle Pat decided to fill his nephew in on some details. He wanted him to feel obliged to him. It gave him control. "You have me listed as your next of kin, don't you? Since your divorce, I suppose. I can understand that and your sons much too young to make decisions. They didn't think you were going to make it son. I told them to ship you straight here. The David Essex Clinic is the very best London can offer. I was right to. You are looking really quite well now, all things considered. You might not have survived in one of those Army run hospitals, or worse, NHS ones. At least now you will be fitted up with the best equipment."

"So, you've known all along?" Mac felt annoyed at the deception and rather stupid for not questioning it himself.

"Yes, but I couldn't get here to begin with and then, when I heard you were off the danger list at least, I thought I would wait and see how long it took you to call me and tell me yourself. I didn't think it would take you so long?" he tried to sound scolding.

Mac had been so pre-occupied he hadn't really given it a thought why he was in such an exclusive hospital. His CO had made no comment and it just hadn't occurred to Mac but now when he thought about it, it all made sense. How else would he have met George? She wouldn't bring her baby to just any old hospital either. She was married to a Pop Star for Goodness sake. How stupid was he? Now, he was in his Uncles debt and that made him very uncomfortable in the light of what might be going on in Kuala Lumpur. Not that he could believe his Uncle was involved in anything underhand. He had caught him out with a lie about his sisters' whereabouts but nothing else, at the moment. He hadn't had the opportunity to speak to Ben for some time, so he had no idea what was really going on. He decided to change the subject of his doctors. "Have you spoken to Sian?" he asked looking straight at his Uncles' face hoping to detect something.

It was his Uncles' turn to feel uncomfortable. "Yes, I told you she had her bags stolen and lost her mobile. She's got a new one now and is carrying on travelling around Australia. She was just about to go to the Outback where she said she wouldn't have a signal for a while," he added anticipating Mac's next question.

"Can I have her new number?" Mac asked anyway.

"Yes, of course. I'll let you have it before I go," he said coolly. "Who's George by the way?" Uncle Pat was a dab hand at diversion. He had found the card attached to the beautiful bouquet of flowers in Macs room.

Mac actually felt his skin blush. He had been thrilled when the flowers arrived. It had never happened to him before of course. Women don't usually buy flowers for men and he wasn't exactly in touch with his feminine side but the gesture had touched him beyond belief. He had wanted to do something special for her. He had even thought of sending her flowers but realised he didn't even know where she lived. He realised his Uncle was looking at him and knew he had to answer. "I've met someone," he said embarrassed.

"Mac you have been in the Army too long," his Uncle said shocked.

"What do you mean?" Mac asked him.

"Too much company with men," Uncle Pat explained.

"Oh no, George is a woman Uncle," Mac said laughing. It was an icebreaker and for a moment the two men were favourite uncle and nephew again and all was well with the world.

CHAPTER THIRTY-NINE

Officer Choo had the biggest coup of her career. The gangster who turned up at the wharf was a known drug supplier from a neighbouring district. He had been Mr Won's supplier but when Mr Won had paid for his last shipment with counterfeit money he had destroyed a trust between known gangsters. The Captain of the ship was part of the network. The tip-off to raid Mr Won's niece's house had given them indisputable proof of all his operations and she had put such a strong case together no amount of corruption would be able to break it now. There had been a lot of fatalities down at the wharf but the inner war had made the job of the police so much easier. In all, they had shut down one of the largest import/export drug smuggling operations the city had ever been part of and several illegal brothels. They had thwarted a business in people smuggling, illegal passports and under-age sex. It was enough work to keep the Officer tied to her desk for a whole year but she still fulfilled her last promise to the stranger who had made this all possible. She found a proper home for Lucie and got her cleaned up. She became a Surrogate Aunt to the girl and watched over her for the rest of her life. All that was left was the Western connection. She would get in touch with Interpol eventually but she would give the stranger time to make his own arrangements first.

When Ben found Sian he had hardly recognised her for the fun loving pretty Irish girl he had met before. She was heavily drugged, very pale and her body had been abused. She hadn't recognised him either but her mind was not functioning correctly. Mr Wons' greed had probably saved her life. He had been told to kill her but thought he could find a better use for her in one of his brothels where blonde girls are always popular in his country. He had also felt she might offer him some insurance if things went awry but in the end she had proved his undoing. This stupid little Irish girl had bungled in somewhere she had no business to be and as a result she had brought this stranger out of the woodwork and all hell had broken out. The Matriarch had been particularly upset when Ben had led her prize girl out of the house but when she pulled a gun on the stranger he had disarmed her quicker that she could blink. Her protection muscle had been dismissed almost as quick. He had broken her windows as he, was hurled through the glass onto the street, by the Westerner. Sian had allowed herself to be led by the hand out of the hell house and up the street where they met Lucie. She had seemed more reassured to see another girl. When they got back to the hotel it was Lucie who looked after her, cleaned her up, washed her hair and dressed her decently. Ben had stolen her passport back from the Accountants house and all he needed now was a passport of his own. Buzz came through for him and by the end of the day he and Sian were on a plane back to the UK.

CHAPTER FORTY

Marika had been dreaming. She was playing in the snow. Ben had sat behind her on a sledge and cuddled close to her body as they hurtled down the slope before crashing at the bottom. It was bliss. Then she woke up and he was there in the bed beside her. His body was as cold as if he had been in the snow but it hadn't snowed in London for years, not since she was a child. She cuddled him, so delighted he was home.

"You're back," she finally said needlessly, kissing him on the lips.

"Like a bad penny," he said.

"I was just dreaming about you," she said softly. "We were playing together in the snow and then I find you in the bed, freezing me".

"Sorry about that," he cuddled her closer. Her skin was so soft and warm. "It's cold out there tonight."

"I've missed you," she whispered in his ear.

"I've missed you," he responded honestly. They made love so tenderly then and Marika felt the same blissful feeling of her dream return. In the morning Ben brought his fiancé fresh croissants and coffee from Antonios. "I love you," she said sleepily.

"You just love my service," he teased.

"Get in, you're cold again," she pulled back the duvet and he climbed in, alongside her, still wearing his tracksuit. "Am I allowed to ask?"

"Ask what?" Ben said, deliberately obtuse.

"Where you've been? I was worried about you," Marika told him.

"I've been to Kuala Lumpur," he answered honestly. "I've brought someone home with me."

"Someone?" she was shocked.

"Yes. Her name is Sian. She's my best mate's sister and she's sleeping on the sofa in the next room," Ben calmly informed her.

"I see," Marika said. This man never ceased to surprise her. "Your best mates sister. Isn't she the one you're supposed to marry then? Should I be jealous?"

CHAPTER FORTY-ONE

"It's been a while brother, how are you doing?" Matthew sat down beside Charlie. "I've been pretty busy at Uni and just haven't been able to get home until now so please forgive me for not coming earlier. Anyhow, I've broached the idea of moving to Edinburgh Uni and I go for an interview next week, before the Easter break. If I get in I won't be back home except for holidays but that won't be any different from now really, so don't worry. I'll still come and see you during the holidays, I promise, and when you wake up and feel better you can come and visit me in Edinburgh. Bet you'd like that wouldn't you? It's a brilliant place during the Annual Festival apparently, when all the stage artists and comedians amass and put on loads of plays and shows which are dead cheap to go to. Its round about August I think, so there's a target for you now. Marika would love all that stuff too, of course. She's got the lead part in "Eliza Doolittle" at the local theatre this Season, I expect she's told you all about that. I love Uni and in some ways will be sorry to leave Cambridge as I've got a great bunch of friends but if I can get better grades at Edinburgh then I have to go for it. Dad says I'll probably have to wait another term so that I've completed a whole year before I move. He doesn't really get it but he's still being supportive, to give him his due. I'm still dating Sian, the policewoman, by the way, although, what with her shifts and my studies we don't see much of each other. Oh, did I tell you they found that girl. You know the one who went missing in Cambridge. She's okay. Apparently, a pair of druggies abducted her, hoping to get some money. Her parents are worth a bob or two. They did it on the spur of the moment and weren't very organised. It didn't take too long for Sian and her team to catch them and the girl was fine. They're even suspicious she might have been in on it. She likes a few uppers herself and knew the guys pretty well from all accounts. She's not at Uni anymore, silly girl. She threw away a chance of a good career. I think she was pretty spoilt. So that was that but then of course I told

Sian about your story and before they found the girl they decided to send police trained divers into the pontoon. Obviously they didn't find the girl but they did find something of interest. I understand, and you have to keep this to yourself, because it's not common knowledge, they found a sawn-off shotgun in a sack. That's illegal of course and they've been busy carrying out tests on the gun to see if it was ever used in a crime. So, brother, you did pretty well. I see you've still got your bodyguard outside and now they're considering moving you to a more secure hospital maybe. What would you say to that? Maybe you could go to the David Essex Clinic. That would be brill. I think Nurse Booth will be very upset to lose you though. She's got a crush on dad, Marika reckons. Have you got plenty of music to keep you going here Charlie? Looks like it. I see it's nearly all stuff by Spirit. Marika's doing, I suppose. She and Rebecca have been raving non-stop about the Spirit concert they went to last month. Never mind Charlie, when you're better I'll take you to see them too and you can come to the Rugby with me and anything else you fancy, that's a promise, okay?"

CHAPTER FORTY-TWO

Mac had found it hard to know how to react to his Uncle Pats' revelation that he was paying for him to stay in the hospital. He was angry with him and yet grateful at the same time. His pride was making him angry but this was being numbed by the realisation that the care he was receiving was so good. He knew he had more chance here of being rehabilitated into a new life than he would have in some second rate Army hospital and of course there was George. He loved her. She had been a constant companion at his bedside despite her own personal grief and every day his admiration and love grew stronger. He couldn't wait to get up and return the favour. She made him feel like he wanted to take care of her for the rest of their lives.

For George, Mac was the perfect tonic to mask her grief. The loss of her precious daughter had been devastating. With it came the realisation that her marriage to Nicky was finally over. They had been struggling for a while and she knew a lot of the problems were because of her wish to start a family. She couldn't hate him as much as she wanted to. In her heart, she felt he was totally responsible for their daughters' death but in her mind, she knew he would never have wanted it that way. They had been in love for five years and you cannot just fall out of love but she knew it was over. She would never be able to look at him and not remember Elly and he knew that too. He had his own guilty demons to deal with. He agreed to give her a divorce and even hinted at leaving the Band and moving to America to begin a new life. It was a huge decision. Spirit is the biggest Band in the world. The guys had been there, supporting both of them at the Funeral. The Press invasion made it impossible for George to say Goodbye to her daughter in the way she would have wanted but Mac said he would take her back to the Churchyard later when things had died down and they would hold their own private Ceremony. It was very sweet of him. He hadn't even met Elly. Poor Mac, he seemed to have his own worries but she found it difficult to get him to open up to her. It had taken him ages to tell her what was actually wrong with him. He was desperate she would leave him when she found out he no longer had any legs. She had been cross with him, telling him he clearly didn't know her at all, but of course, he didn't, really. All they had was a series of hospital visits at a time when her life and his had fallen apart separately. It was bizarre. Had they just fixated on each other through need? She supposed all would be revealed when he finally left hospital and she had invited him to stay with her for recuperation. It wasn't exactly a direct invitation to move in with her, she told herself. It was just that he would still need some after care and she had nothing else to do.

George had started to make plans for that day. It kept her occupied and she was grateful for that. She had moved out of the marital home even though Nicky had offered to leave. They had lived in a huge house in the London suburbs, which they had been unable to fill. She didn't want those painful reminders. He was on tour with the Band, so wasn't there anyway, but still it hadn't felt right. There was the nursery to start with. She couldn't bear to go near that room now. So, she had packed a case and found a beautiful apartment in Chelsea to rent. It was perfect for her, so different from the house, very modern with an open plan design, which would be useful for Macs wheelchair. It had a good working lift, essential of course, and even came with an underground garage. She took very little from the house with her to the flat. She wanted a new start and had even considered about the possibility of going back to work. Before she had met Nicky she had been a Vet. She had given it up to tour with him but had missed it terribly. It was another part of her own identity she had lost and wanted to get back. She had a couple of dogs, which would come with her, of course, but the flat owners were fine about that. Her pets were Dobermans, not to every ones' taste. They were fiercely protective of her. She hoped Mac liked dogs. He was going to have to make friends with these boys or risk being bitten.

When she walked in to his hospital room that day she was surprised to see his friend Ben was there. He hadn't been around for ages, which had puzzled her, but Mac had brushed it off. They both looked serious, deep in conversation, and didn't even notice her standing in the doorway to begin with. When Mac spotted her, his face completely changed and he managed a smile. "Hello Darling. You remember Ben?"

Ben stood up and embraced her. He offered the obligatory bedside chair to her and she leant over the patient and kissed him tenderly on the lips before taking it. "How are you Ben?" she asked.

"Me? I'm not so bad George, it's this bugger you've got to watch," he said smiling.

"Oh I know," she smiled at Mac. He was looking pale. "Are you in pain Darling?"

"Not of the physical kind," he answered mysteriously. "You okay?"

"Oh, you know," she said. "Have you been somewhere Ben?" It was a direct question.

"Yes," Ben responded honestly. "I've been abroad but I'm home now."

George realised she knew nothing about Macs friend. She suspected he was also in the Army. Was he Special Forces too? Robert had disclosed his father was Special and she believed him. Everything about Bens' demeanour spelt special. He appeared loaded with confidence. What has he been telling Mac to upset him? "Tell me what is wrong, Mac?" There it was again, another direct question. Ben admired that.

"It's a long story," Mac answered evasively.

"Well then you tell me Ben. Why have you come here upsetting Mac?" she said accusingly.

"No, it's not Ben's fault," Mac sprung to his friends defence. "He's brought good news in a way."

"Your face says different," she observed.

"It's just complicated," Mac answered, looking paler still.

"I'm getting the doctor," she stood up. She didn't like the look of him at all. She left and returned swiftly with a doctor who examined Mac and told her and Ben to leave the room. He came out a short time later and told them that Mac was going to need another operation and they would prepare him now. He said there was no point waiting around but if they wanted to, he suggested the Restaurant was a good place to go.

"Would you like a cup of coffee?" Ben asked. He felt sorry for her. Clearly she had feelings for his friend, which Mac hadn't told him about yet. She accepted and they sat together in the Restaurant each waiting for the other to speak. Eventually Ben said, "He'll be all right you know, he's very stubborn."

"I know," she said tearfully. "What's going on Ben? You can trust me."

"Mac has had a bit of a shock. Someone he has loved all his life, someone he would probably have trusted with his life, has betrayed him and he's hurting," Ben told her understanding his friends' pain only too well.

"Well, I know something of what that feels like," she said nodding. "It really hurts."

"Yes," Ben said and something about his eyes told her he knew and understood too.

"Is there anything I can do?" she asked, drying the tears.

"You're doing it George," Ben said wisely. "I'm not sure what's been going on with you two in my absence but I know it's been good for Mac. He was really happy until I broke the bad news. Are you two an item?"

"I've asked him to come and live with me when the hospital lets him go. I will take care of him until he finds his feet, if you excuse the pun," she said, trying to force a smile.

Ben didn't have to force his smile. It came naturally. "Wow, that's big news." He was genuinely delighted. He was in love and it felt only right his best friend should be in the same boat. After all, they did everything together. Besides, in view of Macs life, the way it was falling apart, right now, this was exactly what he needed to keep going. "I'm so pleased for you both," he added after a long pause.

"I have no idea what I'm getting into, do I?" she was cheering up.

"You'll be all right," he told her, "Just as long as you've got plenty of patience?"

They both smiled. George accepted Ben wasn't going to tell her what was going on. He was loyal and knew Mac should be the one to speak of it when he was ready. Be patient he had told her.

CHAPTER FORTY-THREE

"So how exactly did you and Ben get together?" Sian asked Marika. Ben had gone off to see her brother and fill him in. They decided she should wait before visiting her brother in case her Uncle was still there. Sian was happy to lie low. She had been through the most unbelievable adventure, the worst moments of her life, and was happy to spend time recovering, in this safe haven, her guardian angel Ben, had created for her.

Marika adored Ben. He never ceased to surprise her and she knew life was never going to be dull from now on. "We met in a Bar," she said casually making tea for Sian. "Where have you come from?"

"Kuala Lumpur," Sian said shivering.

"What?" Marika said loudly. "That's where Ben's been?"

"Yes," Sian answered. "He rescued me."

Marika noticed Sian shiver at the memory and realised she had been through a dreadful experience in Kuala Lumpur. Ben had rescued her, she told her. My hero! She handed her a mug of tea, "Here, this will make you feel better."

"I doubt it," Sian said accepting the mug. She realised she was sounding ungracious to her hostess, so added, "But it will help, thank you."

"Would you like to talk about it?" Marika asked hopefully, desperate to glean an insight into the life of Ben Casey, the man she was engaged to marry.

"Would you mind if we didn't," Sian said, disappointing her. "I'd rather hear about you and Ben and nice things."

So, Marika told Sian all about her life. She didn't mind. She loved nothing more than talking about Ben and her family and her life. Sian asked her a lot of questions about all her brothers, perhaps hoping for a date. They were all highly eligible, of course. Matthew, the eldest, was a qualified doctor. He had excelled at University, as they knew he would. He had come top in the whole country and been given an apprenticeship at the David Essex Clinic where Mac was a patient. He had girlfriends but no-one special. He worked too hard, of course, like her father.

Sir Jonathan Havers was now a Coroner for Her Majesty. He had amalgamated his law degree with his medical degree and was sought after for all the major incidents in London. He lived in the flat above and was still a bachelor. He and her mother had finally divorced after a split of about ten years but neither had remarried. Jonathan just hadn't found the right woman yet.

Then there was Mark. He was the odd one out, in a way. He had gone to Agricultural College, instead of University, and was the Manager at their Grandfathers Estate in Tunbridge Wells. Their Grandfather was a High Court Judge and Mark ran the Estate as a working farm coupled with a prestigious horse stud business. It was very successful. Mark was still a bachelor too although there were rumours that he had met someone he used to go to school with and had begun dating.

Luke was a trainee Barrister. He loved Criminal Law and was living in London working for a large company. He was making lots of money but spending it too. He liked the good things in life; posh flat, fast car, the usual trimmings. He had a proper bachelor pad and a string of glamorous girlfriends. Luke was always good for a laugh.

"And then there's Charlie," Marika said with admiration.

CHAPTER FORTY-FOUR

"Your bodyguard has disappeared Charlie," Jonathan told his son. "Have you scared him off?" When he arrived at the hospital he had been surprised to find no guard at his sons' door. His stomach had sunk to his feet at first. He thought something terrible had happened to Charlie and had been relieved beyond belief to find his son in his usual position. "You look a bit hot son, would you like a clean-up?"

"May I come in?"

Jonathan was sitting at his sons' bedside wiping the boys' face gently with a wet wipe when the most beautiful enigmatic looking woman he had ever seen interrupted his thoughts. He stopped what he was doing and stood up politely. He always had a ready smile and he flashed one towards the woman now. "I'm sorry, have we met?"

"No, is this young man Charlie Havers?" she asked.

"Yes, this is Charlie," Jonathan said with a puzzled smile.

Ann couldn't help noticing those penetrating blue eyes. They sent ripples through her body and took her completely by surprise. "My name is Ann Marshall," she held out her hand and Jonathan shook it firmly.

"Jonathan Havers," he introduced himself.

"Are you his father?" she said recognising the surname.

"Yes," he answered. He didn't know who she was or why she was here but he didn't want her to go. She was stunning. He didn't know much about female fashion but clearly she was dressed to perfection. She had a designer dress, Jimmy Choo shoes, manicured nails, perfect make-up and gorgeous hair. Who is Ann Marshall?

"How is he?" she asked with concern.

"Charlie is holding his own," he couldn't hide his pride.

"I understand he has been in a coma for several months," she said.

He loved her voice. It was deep and yet feminine, soft and yet penetrating. "Yes," he answered, "Since last July."

"That's a long time," she said sympathetically. "It must be very hard on all of you?"

"It could be worse," Jonathan said not wanting to think of the alternative.

"I'm sorry, you must be wondering what on earth I'm doing here," she realised. "Did you hear about the shotgun?"

He hadn't expected that. "The one the police found in the pontoon?" Marika will be devastated not to be here, when she hears about this, he thought.

"Yes that one. The police found out it was the same gun used in a burglary. The burglary was at my house," she hesitated.

Jonathan was intrigued. "Go on," he prompted her.

"My husband disturbed the burglar and was shot by him," she explained. "Up until now the police had not been able to find the perpetrator. All they knew was a black car was involved."

"I see," he said concerned, "Your husband?"

"Died," she said glumly.

"I'm so sorry," Jonathan said genuinely. It didn't feel enough. It was an awkward moment and he wished he had other words of comfort to offer this woman.

"It was back in July," she said feeling his discomfort. "I am getting used to it but thanks to your son I now feel I have some closure at least."

"Have they caught him?" Jonathan asked surprised.

"Yes, didn't they tell you?" Ann asked.

"Not yet. I've not been home. I did wonder why there was no police officer here. They've been protecting my son, you see. I guess he's a material witness," Jonathan stated.

"Apparently they traced the gun back to its origin and eventually it led them to the burglar. They're pretty confident they've got the right man, otherwise, they wouldn't have told me, I suppose," she informed him.

"I suppose they'll get round to filling me in," he said feeling slightly annoyed to hear this monumental news, second hand.

"They may need Charlie to identify him now, do you think?" she said gently touching the boys hand. He couldn't help but notice the tenderness she demonstrated towards his son. In other circumstances he might have felt jealous.

"I hope they've got more than that to go on," he replied, the lawyer in him coming out.

"I'm sure they have," she said gently. "Thank you Charlie for your help," she added to the patient lying in a coma in a hospital bed and then she turned to go.

"I'm so sorry for your loss," Jonathan said politely and shook her hand again.

"Thank you. I hope things work out for your boy," she said with genuine affection and then she was gone leaving Jonathan feeling lonely.

"Goodbye son," he told Charlie. "I need to check some things out. I'll be back to see you later with more news."

CHAPTER FORTY-FIVE

"How are you feeling?" Dr Matthew Havers asked Mac as he started to come round from the anaesthetic.

Mac tried to focus. For a moment he believed he was somewhere else. He had been dreaming about a desert island. It was hot and sunny with a blue sky that went on forever. There were even palm trees on this island. He had made a fire from sticks collected on the beach. He knew how to survive. And she was there. George, except he didn't know her as George. She was so beautiful, so feminine and he was going to call her Gina. It was much more fitting. Then, suddenly the sun faded and was replaced with cream coloured walls and he realised, disappointingly, he was still in hospital. He realised the doctor was expecting an answer. He wanted to know he had survived this latest set-back and was back in the land of the living, "Thirsty," he managed to croak and was instantly helped to a drink by an attentive nurse. It was only water but tasted like nectar.

"Would you like a cup of tea?" the nurse asked him when he finished the water.

Would he like a cup of tea? It was like music to his ears. He loved his brew. He was never too mighty to make it, either, for his men. They used to complain they could stand their spoons up in his tea but that's how he liked it. Ben liked it that way too. Tea was like a ritual amongst the boys from the Regiment. He couldn't remember when he had last tasted tea. Did this sudden invitation mean he was on the mend finally?

"Can I have some steak and chips to go with it?" he joked.

The young doctor smiled. He was clearly pleased his patient was improving at last. Matthew was only the junior doctor, of course. He had assisted with his operations and kept regular checks on him following the procedures. He was in awe of this patient's resilience to his injuries. He loved his job, especially when you got to see the fruits of your labours. Mac would be given some respite from the hospital soon. He was going to be allowed to go home with the beautiful woman, who had lost her baby, for a few weeks, before returning to be fitted with his artificial limbs. He would have to undergo some serious physiotherapy and had a lot of hard work ahead of him but before that he had earned some time off. It was important for his well-being to be allowed to recharge his batteries and Matthew was here to give him the good news. So why not do it over a nice cup of tea.

CHAPTER FORTY-SIX

"Well done dad, great speech," Rebecca told her father as he bent down to kiss her.

"Thank you darling. What's the food like?" he asked stealing a sausage roll from her plate. They were standing in the Church Hall where his ex-wife was hosting one of her Charity Galas and he reached for a glass of punch from the passing waiter.

"Mums in her element," Rebecca observed.

Jonathan followed her gaze and saw his ex-wife in animated conversation with the most beautiful woman he had ever seen in his life. She was dressed in a beautiful dress, which showed off her womanly curves to perfection, she had high heels and great legs. She was elegant and stylish and he was afraid he was openly drooling. Rebecca noticed his face and laughed, "I didn't think you still had feelings for mum," she joked.

"Who is that woman?" he asked ignoring his stepdaughters' jibe.

"I don't actually know," Rebecca observed. "She's rather classy for mum, isn't she?" Rebecca was the local GP in Tunbridge and was unhappily for her expected to support her mother in all her Charity endeavours. She had got to know most of her mothers' boring friends over the years but didn't recognise this lady. She looked too interesting to be one of her mothers' friends.

"I think I should just check with your mother that she was happy with my speech," he said smirking. Rebecca laughed and watched her father move in. She had seen him in action before, of course. He was now regarded as one of the most eligible bachelors England had to offer and he liked the company of beautiful women. His reputation as a bit of a Gigolo had been earned in her opinion.

"Hello Sarah," he interrupted the two women.

"Jonathan," Sarah turned to her ex-husband and offered him a peck on the cheek. "Lovely speech darling," she added. "Can I introduce you to a very old friend of mine," she said turning towards the object of Jonathans' stare. "This is Ann. Ann this is my ex," she introduced them.

Jonathan shook her hand and noticed how soft her skin felt. He flashed her, his winning smile and she noticed his startling blue eyes. "Jonathan," he said as he took her hand. "I'm sorry, have we met before?" It wasn't a line. Standing close to her he suddenly had a feeling of deja vu. Everything about her felt familiar, as if they were acting out something that had already happened.

"I knew Ann long before I ever met you," Sarah interrupted him. "We go back to our teens."

"Really?" he said surprised at this information from his ex.

Ann smiled enigmatically and allowed Sarah to explain. "Yes," Sarah continued. "You remember me telling you I was in an all-girl singing group called The Dixie Chicks, when I first ran away from home at sixteen. Ann was part of that group. We toured around and lived in each other's pockets for a couple of years but then when we split up, we never kept in touch. Well, I was hardly in a state for things like that back then. It was a whole different world," she shivered at the memory. Maybe she might have been a whole lot more interesting back then, Jonathan thought privately. He couldn't imagine that his prim and proper and oh so religious bigoted wife had ever had such a different lifestyle once. It was a bit hard to imagine this beautiful elegant woman was part of that scene too.

"Gosh," he said genuinely surprised at this news. "So, how did you meet up again?"

"We just bumped into each other last week at the Savoy," it was Ann's turn to explain. Her voice seemed so mysteriously familiar to Jonathan. It sent shivers down his spine.

"Yes," Sarah enlarged, "Another Charity Gala. It took a while before we recognised each other, didn't it?" she laughed. Well, there had obviously been some dramatic changes. "When I realised Ann was a good supporter of Charity I invited her today."

"Do you support a particular Charity, or just any?" he asked her eager to hear her voice again.

"I support victims of crime mostly," she said, "Which is why I found your speech today so interesting."

Jonathan was delighted with the praise. He was a sought after speaker at all sorts of events but his vast knowledge on both the law and medicine made him doubly popular. As Her Majesty's Coroner in the biggest City in England he was never short of interesting material.

Father Benedict swooped on Sarah and Jonathan took the opportunity to lead Ann aside and offer her a drink and some food. They walked over to the Buffet table together and Rebecca watched in fascination at their body language. He was winning her over, she could tell. But then he spoiled it. "What happened to you then?" he asked her as they selected some canapés.

"What do you mean?" she asked defensively, clearly misunderstanding the question. She thought he had sensed she had been a victim of crime once, but in fact, he was referring to her past with Sarah.

He realised he had touched upon something a bit sensitive and immediately corrected his question. "Oh, sorry," he said, "I just meant after The Dixie Chicks split up. I mean, I know that Sarah had a difficult time until she met her first husband. I suppose it's none of my business, I apologise."

Ann felt immediately embarrassed. She was too touchy by far. It was just that she wasn't used to this. Since her husband had been killed she had found it really difficult to socialise at first, especially with men. "No," she said softly. "I apologise. I didn't really have the same problems as Sarah," she explained. "I wasn't into drugs or booze really but I was just fed up with the life style. It wasn't really me. To tell you the truth, Sarah and I were thrown together, but we weren't really what you would call friends. In a different life we would never have got together, I'm sure. We didn't then and I'm not sure do, have anything in common."

He admired her honesty and felt reassured. He had nothing in common with Sarah either. "You and me both," he jested. She smiled again and that felt much better.

"Are you married?" he asked noticing her wedding ring. It was something he had taught himself to observe.

"Widowed," she replied.

"I'm sorry," he said, cross with his clumsiness. As a Coroner, he really should know better.

She sensed his discomfort and added, "It was a long time ago now," as if that made it all right.

"Where do you live?" he asked, changing the subject but grateful for her understanding.

"In town," she said, "You?"

Town was what the people who lived in London called their home. "Me too," he answered.

"Do you like this food?" they had both picked at the bland canapés. The food and the punch, a glorified winter Pimms mixture, weren't really hitting the spot for either of them.

She smiled and put down her plate on a casual table. "I like food," she said, "So, no." They both laughed at this joke. It was a friendly moment.

"Would you have dinner with me?" he tried his luck.

"What?" she asked, taken aback.

"Well, you said you like food and coincidentally so do I. Have you ever eaten at Bertorellis?" Jonathan enquired.

"No, but I've heard of it," she answered. "It has an excellent reputation."

"Can I tempt you?" he asked mischievously.

She smiled and it melted his heart, "When?"

"Tomorrow night?" he didn't want to give her time to think of an excuse.

"Oh, well, okay," she found herself agreeing much to her own surprise. She hadn't been on a date in such a long time. Not for want of offers, of course. She had just not been propositioned like this before.

"Shall I pick you up?" he asked tentatively in an attempt to get her address.

"I'll meet you there," she answered calmly. If the evening was a disaster it would be easier to end it early if she wasn't dependent on him for a lift home and of course it would spare them the embarrassment of what to do on the doorstep when they said goodnight.

He wasn't disappointed she had preferred to remain independent. He quite admired that quality in her, "Eight thirty okay?"

CHAPTER FORTY-SEVEN

She must have changed her outfit five times already. This was ridiculous. Ann was the elegant, sophisticated woman, always in control. Why had she been feeling on tender hooks all day at work? It just wasn't like her. She had confided in her colleague, Lucy, she was going out on a date and there had been great excitement. She regretted her candour immediately. Lucy had her best interests at heart, of course. She had been trying to set Ann up with a date for years but to no avail. So, who was this man, who had finally broken down her defences? She asked too many questions and Ann decided to escape and go home early to get ready. Only now, she had too much time on her hands and was getting more and more nervous. She hadn't given him her address or even her phone number but he had given her his card. Sir Jonathan Havers, H.M Coroner. It was certainly a grand title. She knew of him, of course, and in particular of his reputation. She enjoyed all the glossy magazines, Hello, Cosmopolitan, Tatler. Sir Jonathan was a regular feature. She could ring him and cancel. Think of an excuse and just forget about it. Only, she couldn't think of an excuse and part of her was excited to find out what the evening might bring.

Ann wasn't a naïve woman, far from it. The two years on the road as a teenager had been a life changing experience. When it was over she had settled for a more sedate life. Tired of the travelling, living like a gypsy and dealing with the constant mood swings of her drugged up companions, she had sought a quieter life. She wanted organisation and structure in her life again and when she met Benjamin, her first husband, it had been ideal to begin with. However, three children and a boring life of drudgery had worn her down and when the children left home, so did she. She felt like a bird that had been set free and was ready to sow her wild oats again but then she met Jud. Jud was so different from Benjy. He had been a Hollywood actor once and then a successful musician but had got involved in drugs and booze and made a mess of his life. He was over all that when she met him and she found him interesting. He was good looking too and very rich but mostly he had something you just couldn't put your finger on. She had heard stories about him. In his wild days he had been very violent particularly to his own children. He had a rage inside of him, which could flare up unexpectedly, if not kept under control. Yet, he was always so gentle with her and that's what she found so attractive, the fact that he could be a complete ogre to others but only showed her, his gentle side. It was a massive turn on. In the three years they were married she never witnessed any violence on his part and yet ironically his own life had ended in exactly that way, when he was murdered.

That was a long time ago now, Ann told herself and it was definitely time to move on. She had been stuck in a kind of void since it happened, unable to come to terms with it. When they caught the man responsible and he was locked up, it had helped. It gave her enough strength to sell their property. It had happened there and she couldn't bear to live in it anyway, so it was no hardship to up sticks and move back to the City. She even got herself a job although she hardly needed the money. An old friend had requested she help out at first. Sir David Essex had a hospital in Harley Street that was world famous. It looked after all the superstars. She knew Sir David and he asked her if she could spare some time to talk to people trying to deal with bereavement. It was a service they liked to provide at the Hospital for the odd occasions when they lost patients. She had needed counselling herself when Jud died but had quickly found meeting fellow victims gave her confidence. Before long she established herself as an Advisor in her own right. Her credentials spoke for themselves. People are always more willing to hear advice from someone who has been through the same experience. She did it as a favour for Sir David but he had wisely asked for her help as a favour to her. He knew it would be a two-way therapy and he was right. She loved going there and helping people and became much more interested in raising money for this Charity. It gave her a purpose but it had also been a welcome diversion. It had allowed her to put her own life on hold and now here she was feeling like a teenager about to go out on her first date again. How sad was that? She scolded herself. You're not going to call this date off Ann, she told herself. Get ready and get to the Restaurant on time, not too early or fashionably late, but be confident and get there on time. So she did.

It was, of course, an immense disappointment and even a slight embarrassment, when she realised she was there before him. If she hadn't paid the taxi off she might have asked for him to drive her round the block a few times, like the proverbial bride, but she was inside now and seated. At least he had reserved the table and the Head Waiter was being very attentive and apologetic. It wasn't like Sir Jonathan to be late, he had told her. He was sure there was a good reason but in the meantime would she like some bread sticks and something to drink. It felt like everyone in the Restaurant was looking at her. Who is this poor woman sitting alone in a Restaurant? Her confidence was waning quickly.

How long should she wait? She was hungry. She hadn't eaten all day because of her nerves. Should she order now? The Head Waiter returned after about fifteen minutes and confirmed there had been no call for her at the Restaurant. He didn't have her mobile number, he had had no way of contacting her, she realised how stupid that was now, but she could call him. She found her way to the Powder Room and dialled his mobile number listed on the card. She was shaking, unsure what to say. She didn't have to worry. The phone immediately diverted to an Answering service. She hung up, deciding not to leave a message and returned to the Restaurant. She felt anger overtaking her fear now and ordered a steak.

It was 9.30pm when she paid her bill and ordered a taxi. The food had been as good as it's reputation but her appetite had waned as she sat by herself watching all the other couples, surrounding her table, deep in conversation. She felt very alone. The Head Waiter was mortified but it wasn't his fault so she still gave him a good tip. When she got in the taxi she suddenly had no desire to return to her empty flat. The evening had been a disaster so far but she was all dolled up and it was a pity to waste that. She told the driver to take her to the Pub. It was a long journey and the driver was delighted to have such a good fare. On the way she called her stepson Tim and invited him for a drink. Tim had been a tower of strength when his father had died. He had not been on good terms with his father for most of his life but he had a fierce loyalty, which had never broken down. He lived near the Pub and it was the only place someone as famous as him could go for a drink without getting mobbed by millions of adoring teenage girls. Tim had inherited his fathers' talent for music and was the keyboard player for the most famous Band in the world. The Band were known simply as Spirit and Tim was its' most popular member among the female fans. He had been surprised to hear from Ann and especially for the invitation of a drink. They kept in touch regularly but he always imagined she was tucked up in bed by 10pm. He knew she had been lonely since his father had been killed but she had refused many invitations to party. He was home from the latest tour for a couple of days and accepted the invitation without hesitation. He was still wide-awake at this time of day and was intrigued to see Ann.

There was always music on at the Pub and the atmosphere was perfect if you wanted to forget all your troubles and just have a good time. Tim was good company and she found herself enjoying the evening after all. She had thought about calling the mobile again but decided against it. No one stands up Ann Marshall and gets a second chance, she told herself. It seemed this was the big fish that got away.

CHAPTER FORTY-EIGHT

Marika was delighted to see Ben waiting for her at the stage door. "Hi baby, have you come to take me home?" she kissed him.

"Yes, good show?" he asked.

"Very good," she replied grabbing her coat and hat, "Train, bus or taxi?"

"Actually, do you mind if we walk?" Ben stated.

She was surprised at this suggestion. Her flat was a good three miles from the theatre. It usually took her about ten minutes on the Underground, twenty minutes on a bus or a lot less if she went by taxi. To walk it, might take at least an hour and it was nearly 11pm. Yet, she was pleased to walk with him. For the last couple of weeks they had hardly had any time alone. He had been off doing his hero stuff and then returned with an unexpected house guest. Her flat was small and they had had little privacy. The walk would give her more time alone with the man she adored, so even though she had been dancing and performing on stage all evening, she still felt she had enough energy left for this unexpected pleasure. She would not be afraid walking the streets of London at night with him by her side. She smiled and took him by the hand, "Let's go," she said joyfully.

He loved that about her. She was always so upbeat. His cup may be half empty most of the time but hers was definitely half full. She was so vibrant and always seemed to do the right thing. She had been working all night. It was selfish of him to suggest the walk but he knew he needed to talk. It was a rare feeling for him. He was an action hero and a man of very few words but this was important. This was the rest of his life.

They turned up the collars of their coats. It was cold out tonight but it was dry. The streets were still lively with revellers but they didn't seem to notice anyone. "What's wrong?" she eventually asked, breaking the comfortable silence between them.

How did she do that, he thought? "I've got to make a call tomorrow which might change the rest of my life and I just wanted to talk it over, do you mind," he asked her sincerely. He was so not used to this.

"Of course I don't mind. Ben, the rest of your life is going to be the rest of my life, isn't it? I couldn't be happier," she said reassuring him and squeezing his hand as they walked. "Who is the call to?"

"My Commanding Officer," Ben replied feeling a little more relaxed. "He's been leaving me messages and texting me, asking me to call him, for a couple of days now. I can't leave it any longer."

"No, of course not," she replied. "What is it about?"

"The way I see it, two things might happen," he explained. "The first is I could be recalled to my Regiment. I got put on hold, so to speak, following an outcry when the press got hold of my last mission and took the high moral ground. MI6 tracked some terrorists to Mexico and I was sent to take them out. Those were my precise orders Marika, I swear, and I always follow orders." She had gasped slightly when the realisation that the man she loved was a trained killer finally hit her and he had sensed her apprehension. "It's what I do Marika," he said, almost apologetically.

"Yes," she stammered. "I guess I just never really considered it before, so, so, well, so bluntly."

"Sorry," he said, "But it's best you know now, before," he broke off.

"Ben, you're a Professional. Just like me, really. Except, well, I entertain people and you, well," she was unable to finish her sentence.

"I kill people," he finished it for her.

"Yes, but that's not all you do," she said defending him from himself. "You also save lives," she reminded him.

"Do you want to know how I became a soldier Marika?" he asked unexpectedly.

"If you want to tell me," she said not wanting to add to his anxiety.

This was not on his agenda for tonight. He had wanted to talk about the future, not the past. Yet, he felt sorry for her. This girl, that he loved so much, really had no idea who she was marrying and had better find out if she's up for it now, rather than later. "I used to have a sister. She was a couple of years older than me," he began.

Just like me, and Charlie, she thought, but these thoughts couldn't have been further from the truth. His story would be nothing like hers.

"When I was eleven years old, in fact on my eleventh birthday, she drowned herself in the local pontoon."

Marika took a sharp intake of breath and waited for him to continue. "My father had raped her and she felt too ashamed to go on living," he continued. She shivered and he held her closer. "Sorry," he said. "It's not a pretty story, shall I stop?"

"No," she said giving him a soft peck on the cheek. "I'm sorry if I seem squeamish. It's just that I care about you so much and can't bear that this happened to you."

"He kept a shotgun in a cupboard that he used for shooting rabbits. I loaded the gun and aimed it at him. I wanted to kill him. The hate was fierce inside of me Marika," he said, shivering him-self now, at the memory of that fateful day. "My mother stepped in front of him as I pulled the trigger. She was probably trying to stop me doing something she thought would ruin my life, instead, it was she, who ruined it. He lived and she died. That wasn't right. I would never let the wrong person get in the way again Marika. Those terrorists may not have been armed when we shot them but their car was loaded with explosives and arms. They were intending to blow up a Night Club full of young innocent people and we stopped them. That's the truth of the matter."

Marika suddenly remembered the incident he was referring to. It was in all the papers and on all the TV channels round about the time they first met. Yet, like all news, it was big one day and gone the next. It was confirmation that her fiancé was SAS though and she had mixed emotions about that. She was full of pride and yet amazed that the man who had stolen her heart had killed real people. It was a lot to take in. Their lives were so completely different. She had been born into a loving happy family home with wonderful siblings and all she remembered of her childhood was the fun she had, growing up. Okay, she had been devastated that her parents had divorced but her dad hadn't lived at home from very early on in her life and she had got used to that. It hadn't changed how much she loved him and the time they spent together was just made even more precious. She loved her dad to bits. Imagine having a dad you hated so much you wanted him dead. It was almost incomprehensible but in the end it just made her feel closer than ever to this man at her side. "I'm so sorry Ben," she said simply, letting him know that she still supported him.

"I was put into Youth Detention Centre until I grew up," he went on. "When I was old enough I was offered the opportunity to get out of the Centre if I joined the Army Cadets. It was perfect for me. They took me in, clothed me, fed me and trained me. It became my life Marika, until now," he looked at her affectionately and she responded with another peck.

"You said two things might happen?" she said

"What?" His train of thought had been completely side tracked. He had not expected to open up to her like this but now that he had, he suddenly felt more relaxed, more sure of himself. It had been very cathartic, somehow.

"Your phone call," she reminded him. "You said it could go two ways."

"Oh yes," he remembered the start of this conversation. "The second way, of course, is that they decide to use me as a Scapegoat."

"But that's not fair," she said indignantly.

"Life's not fair, don't you know?" Ben commented.

"No, I suppose I don't know much Ben. I cannot imagine how your life has been. What you've just told me is the saddest story I think I have ever heard or will hear, ever. It's incredible that you've survived that. There are parallels between us, believe it or not, but really we've been living light years apart. It's a miracle our lives suddenly collided when you think about it. Things always happen for a reason, my daddy used to tell me, and I believe that. I may be totally naïve, I may never be able to completely understand, but I do know I love you, with all my heart and all my being. Now, more than ever," she said reaching up to him. They had hardly noticed the journey and yet here they were at the end, standing in the doorway to the flats, holding each other so tightly and lost in their embrace.

"You can get arrested for doing that". It was Marikas' beloved fathers' voice that interrupted them finally. He was standing in the street trying to get into the flats but having his passageway blocked by the locked in couple. He was charmed to see them together like that. Obviously, he had been feeling concerned about his daughters sudden infatuation with this stranger and wanted to be assured she was making all the right decisions but he realised he was no expert on love and would never interfere. His daughter knew her own mind. That much he realised, and she was not given to making needless mistakes. He liked Ben as soon as he met him. He was certainly different from all her luvvy boyfriends but he seemed solid and mature and clearly loved his daughter very much. For that, Jonathan could forgive any failings he might have.

"Dad" she said excitedly finally turning away from her lover. "What are you doing out at this time of night?"

"Hey, I'm not a pensioner yet you know. You young people don't have the monopoly on fun. Hi Ben," he held his hand out politely to shake the young man's hand after his daughter had kissed him hello. It was always a firm handshake between the men. "Can I get inside now before I get a chill?" he joked.

"Fancy cocoa," she asked sensing that this would be a good time to offer Ben a distraction from his dark thoughts. She flashed him a look just to make sure he approved. He did. For as always, she did the right thing, where he was concerned.

"Lovely," her father replied unlocking the front door to the hallway that led to their respective flats. "You are not going to believe the evening I've had," he added as they stepped inside and Marika smiled to herself. Well, Dad, you are not going to believe my evening either, she thought to herself feeling suddenly relieved and inexplicably happy.

"Actually Dad," she said. "We've run out of milk, can we go to your flat?" she added, remembering their house guest. She didn't want Ben to have to try to explain anything else tonight. She felt he had said enough and just needed to be entertained now. She knew her father was up for that task. He was the most entertaining person she knew. Whenever she felt low or things didn't quite go as planned, she could always rely on him to lift her out of her damp spirits with a story or two.

CHAPTER FORTY-NINE

"How are you my boy?" the Judge asked his Grandson. "It's been quite a nice week for this time of year. I think that Spring may be coming at last. Mark is getting ready for the lambing. It is always your favourite time, isn't it? You and your sister love helping out with the lambs. Don't see so much of her lately though at the Farm. She's always busy with some play or other and I know she spends a lot of time visiting you. Can't be everywhere I suppose. Isn't it time you woke up and gave us all a break young man. Mark seems to be getting along well though. He's got a lot of grand ideas for the old place and your Grandmother and I just let him get on with it, so long as he doesn't bankrupt us, of course. He seems to have a handle on it though, to give him his due. He's a hard worker too. It takes a lot of pressure off of me, having him run the Farm, I must admit. Starting to feel my age somewhat lately but don't go telling the others. I expect you've heard all about the bad man who tried to run you down. He's been caught at last. It was the gun that led the police to him, the one you saw being thrown in the pontoon. Well, you didn't see a gun exactly did you, but what you saw was enough to get the police suspicious. The gun was used in a particularly nasty burglary where the house owner actually got shot and killed. So he's certainly a bad lot. They've found the car that hit you now Charlie. It was hidden away in a lock-up that this villain had the keys for. They found the keys when they raided his house to arrest him. It's been in the lock-up ever since the accident. Still had the scrapes on it and paintwork from your bike, so good evidence. I'd love to be a Judge at his Trial, let me tell you but of course that won't be allowed, conflict of interest and all that. I've had a bit of a funny Trial this week. Well, not funny ha ha. A man was accused of throwing a girl off a bridge but he insisted he was trying to help her. She was suicidal, a druggie from all accounts. It was a bit sad really. Anyway, the Jury found him not guilty, which, as far as I'm concerned was right. The Prosecution hadn't been able to come up with a motive. It should never have reached my Court. Your Grandmother wants to have a Party to celebrate our Ruby Wedding Anniversary next month but I don't like Parties much. I'll object and she will have her own way as usual. It would be a much better Party if you were there young man, so come on, wake up now."

CHAPTER FIFTY

"How's the tour going?" Ann asked her stepson over a large glass of red wine. Tim had already invited her back to his house tonight so she was going to get drunk, she had decided.

"It's been okay but you've heard Nicky has decided to leave the Band," he answered.

"Yes. Actually I've been trying to counsel him a bit over the loss of his daughter and now the break-up of his marriage," Ann said not believing she was breaching any confidence by telling Tim. In fact, she knew from her own troubles, that Tim could be a tower of strength and he had been friends with Nicky for many years, so may be able to help now.

"It's been really hard for him," Tim acknowledged. "Even harder for George, I reckon."

"She's not wanted to talk to me but I understand she may have another love interest that has been helping," Ann informed him.

Tim was quite shocked at this news. "Wow! Who is it, do you know?"

"Someone she met at the Hospital," she replied taking another sip of her wine.

"What a Doctor?" Tim asked.

"No, a patient," she said. "From what I can gather they've been propping each other up and she's going to be taking care of him, during his convalescence."

"Wow," was all Tim could say. He had no idea. In fact he had hoped for the sake of his friend and the Band, George would come to forgive Nicky and their marriage might yet be saved. This news made it seem more unlikely.

January Davies was strumming her guitar gently in the background which made conversation much more congenial at the Pub tonight. However, her amplifiers were suddenly turned off and the bell for last orders hanging over the bar was rang violently by Dave Sorenson. Dave was the lead guitarist for Spirit. He lived local to the Pub and was a regular. It was his wife that Ben had tried to chat up the same evening he met Marika. He had crashed into the Pub and sought to get every ones' attention, which he managed successfully, with his actions. The Pub's Proprietor Rees Darrow looked at him quizzically. "What's going on Dave?" he asked the gate crasher.

"You better turn on your TV," Dave said to Rees. Turning, he spotted Tim and said, "You're not going to believe this," to his fellow Band player.

Rees fiddled about at the back of the Bar and recovered the remote control for the In house television and turned it on. "Which Channel?" he asked Dave.

"Any," said Dave.

The television burst into life and there was a Newsflash being broadcast. "Yes this is the scene just a few moments ago where Nicky Darrow, a member of the Rock Band, Spirit, tried to take his own life," the News reporter was saying. The screen was showing a view of a multi-storey car park somewhere in London. The streets below were heaving with people, paramedics, fire engines, police and journalists. Rees Darrow went white. He was Nicky's father.

"It's okay Rees," Dave said seeing the Landlords tormented face. "He's alive."

"Just a few moments ago Nicky Darrow was talked down from the wall on top of this car park that you're seeing on your screens," the News reporter continued. "We understand that he had been in negotiation up there since about six o'clock this evening but has now been taken off in an ambulance by paramedics to a secret location. It is not clear what has led the popular musician to contemplate suicide. I believe drugs have been ruled out but it is understood the recent death of his baby daughter and the subsequent break-up of his five-year marriage to Georgina Darrow may have been a factor.

There has been speculation in the news lately, also, of a break up with the Band he helped to form. Spirit is currently on tour but it is thought Nicky Darrow may not now finish this tour." The speculation and news reporting rambled on while the customers at the Pub tried to take it all in.

Rees was just about to turn off the television and get everybody out of his Pub so that he could find out where his son was and go to his aid, when his wife stepped in. She could see her husband was in shock and took him aside telling him to get off and she would sort things out there. Tim and Ann offered to give him support and while Tim made a few phone calls to try and ascertain where Nicky was, Ann tried to keep Rees calm. It was difficult trying to get any information but the name of Tim Marshall was powerful and eventually he was able to find out that Nicky had been taken to the David Essex Hospital in Harley Street, the same place where his daughter had died. Ann worked there, so knew she would be able to pull strings and get them in to see Nicky and they called up a taxi and set off for London.

By the time the trio got to the Hospital it was nearly midnight. There were no press outside, which was a good sign, although it wouldn't take long for the jungle drums to roll. They wondered at the wisdom of taking a taxi. It wouldn't take the driver long to put two and two together. Inside, Ann spoke to some people and ascertained that Nicky was comfortable. They would check if he was up for any visitors. There were several police officers milling about. Rees was allowed to see his son but Ann and Tim were advised to go home. A police officer offered to take them and they decided that since they were in London they might as well stay at Ann's apartment, rather than go back to the country to Tim's house.

The Police officer was able to fill them in on a few details, on the drive to Ann's apartment. Apparently, Nicky had been spotted by a member of the public, standing on the wall, at the top of the high rise Car Park at about six o'clock that evening. The police and emergency services had rushed to the scene and the upstanding member of public, who had called it in, had already begun talking to Mr Darrow. Before a police negotiator arrived at the scene, the do-gooder had struck up a good rapport apparently and Mr Darrow had insisted that he talk only to this man. He had refused to let the police get near, threatening to jump if they tried. Eventually, after nearly four hours, Mr Darrow had climbed down and been taken off to hospital unhurt.

"It's incredible," Tim said to his stepmother when they got inside her Apartment.

She gave him a hug realising he would probably be feeling not only shattered with the news, but perhaps, a little guilty for not realising how deep Nicky's grief went. They had been playing music together in front of an audience of thousands of people, just the night before. There had been no indication of his inner turmoil then, obviously. He had kept his emotions buried. Ann felt somewhat guilty herself. She had tried to counsel him but he had turned her away. She should have been more forceful perhaps. Neither would sleep well tonight.

It was all over the newspapers the next morning of course and continually being broadcast on all the television channels. The speculation went on and on. Ann decided not to read anything or watch anything. She wanted to keep fresh when she got to work today in the hope that Nicky might agree to talk to her himself. He would be given the best psychiatric care possible, of course, and probably the matter would be taken out of her hands but she felt she owed it to him, to be available, just in case. She wondered about George and what her reaction might be.

CHAPTER FIFTY-ONE

Sian was feeling a bit better today. She had spoken to her brother on the telephone at last. She desperately wanted to go and see him but had been persuaded to wait. Mac had been so pleased to hear her voice. He had been quite an absent big brother for most of her life but she knew he had to go off and save the world. She couldn't resent it now because she knew only too well she would probably be dead if Mac hadn't sent Ben after her. That was why in times of dire trouble she had turned to him. They had both grown up believing their Uncle was as good as the Father they had lost and now they were united in their grief. She cried a lot on the telephone and she suspected so did her brother, although he would never admit it. He wasn't sure what to do next about Uncle Pat. He needed to get better before he could deal with him and so she agreed to lie low at Ben and Marika's. She was in London for the first time in her life and unable to go out and enjoy it. Life sucks.

Ben and Marika were closer than they had ever been. His sudden revelations had broken down any barriers or misgivings they might have had about their relationship. He had been able to think a lot clearer because of it. The question was, did he want to stay a soldier, if he had been given a reprieve. He had to admit part of him had hoped he would be made the scapegoat and therefore, the decision would be taken out of his hands but he knew he would end up feeling bitter and resent it for the rest of his life. In any event, he was invited back to the Barracks by his Commanding Officer, so now the decision was his and his alone. If he decided to leave he would have to find some money to buy himself out. His contract had a few more years left in it to run. The Army had invested a good deal of money in training him and with the Regiment that training was still on going. If he stayed he would have a job and money and be able to support his beautiful bride. If he left he would have to be supported by her until he could come up with something. The trouble was he had been in the

Army all his working life. What else could he do? Mac had had a few ideas about starting up their own business teaching survival skills. That was quite popular with a lot of businessmen these days and of course he could always make a lot more money as a Mercenary.

Marika did not want to influence his decision one-way or the other. She would not let herself be blamed in years to come if he made the wrong decision now. If he wanted to continue being a soldier she would go with him to live in Hereford, if necessary, or wherever they might be posted. It would mean putting her own career on hold of course but she was prepared to make that sacrifice for him. She would be constantly frightened all the time he was away on missions, but she would learn to trust in his skills. From the little she had gleaned from Sian about events in Kuala Lumpur, she realised he had many such skills.

So he had left that morning for Hereford and met with his CO as ordered. He was being invited back to re-join his Regiment and no more would be said about the events in Mexico. He knew and his CO knew that he was blameless. They discussed Macs situation and Ben told him that he didn't think Mac would be back. His CO agreed. He couldn't see Major McManus wishing to play second fiddle. Ben said that his own situation had changed too. He was getting married.

His CO was shocked at this news. He believed quite rightly that Major Casey was married to the Army. He was also delighted for Ben. He was a good man and deserved some happiness. He told Ben that he could be up for promotion. He had a mission for him in Botswana, the Kalahari Desert to be exact and after that there might be a position for him, on site, as a Trainer. He said Ben could take a day or two to make up his mind but then he needed to deploy him to Africa. Ben didn't need the time. He would go to the desert and when he returned he would get promoted. With more money he would be able to get married and the promise of a job on site, also, now had its appeal. He could keep the position warm for Mac, as he knew his friend had always hankered after being a teacher. Maybe they could work together again in the future after all and if it didn't work out he would learn extra skills to take away with him. It was a win, win situation and he couldn't wait to get home and tell Marika. He had two days left with her and he didn't want to waste a minute.

Marika had busied herself while Ben was away helping her father. It had taken her mind off what Ben might do. She had telephoned her sister Rebecca for help. Her father was supposed to have met a beautiful woman on a date last night but circumstances had prevented it and now, he didn't know how to contact her to apologise. Rebecca said she would speak to their mother and find out what she could from her about Ann Marshall. It was a name that rang a bell with Marika but she couldn't think why. As Rebecca had been at the Party where they had met, it wouldn't arouse too much suspicion with their mother if she were the one asking the questions. She told her mother that she wanted to ask Ann about doing some counselling at her practice. Rebecca had never subscribed to the idea of private medicine like her brother. She much preferred being a GP and able to help the general public instead of the privileged few. She wasn't interested in the trappings and had many debates with Matthew about the rights and wrongs of private medicine. Her mother fell for the story but didn't have a home address for Ann either and now she had mislaid her telephone number. Not much help except that she did know Ann worked part-time at the same hospital as Matthew.

"I don't believe it," Marika said to Rebecca when she told her this information.

"Small world isn't it," her sister remarked.

"Do you think Mattie knows her?" Marika asked mischievously.

"I don't know but I've a feeling you're going to find out," she said to her sister.

"Well I can certainly grill him for information about this Ann woman dad seems to have taken more than a passing fancy to. You've seen her too, what's she like?" Marika asked.

"Poor dad," Rebecca commented. "Why do you always meddle in his affairs?"

"I'm trying to help him," the younger sister said indignantly. "I don't know why, but there's something about her name that seems familiar. Did you feel you knew her?"

"Well no, not when I met her at the Party but I have found out some other very interesting information since. At least, it's going to interest you, lots," Rebecca teased.

"Ooh what?" Marika asked excitedly.

"Haven't you given any thought to her surname?" Rebecca asked.

"Marshall. You don't mean, you can't mean, she's not. She's not related in some way to Tim Marshall, the love of my life, by any chance, is she?" Marika was more animated that ever.

"I thought Ben was the love of your life," Rebecca remarked. She had heard a lot about Ben but had yet to meet him.

"He is, but you know what I mean. I've adored Tim Marshall since I was about twelve years old. You liked him too. Remember when we went to see Spirit in concert?" Marika tried to justify her outburst.

"That was a long time ago," Rebecca recalled. "Well yes, I believe she was married to Tim's father, Jud Marshall."

"Of course, that's it. I knew I'd heard her name before. Don't you remember? Her husband was killed by the same man who mowed Charlie down," Marika said triumphantly. "Dad obviously hasn't made that connection yet. Should I tell him?"

"Just tell him where she works and leave him be," Rebecca said playing the big sister.

"Just think," Marika went on, her voice full of excitement. "If dad marries her we'll be related to Tim! How cool would that be?"

"Dream on, Marika," Rebecca said as she ended the call laughing.

CHAPTER FIFTY-TWO

"Are you dreaming?" Nurse Booth asked her patient as she finished up giving him a bed bath. "You look like you're thinking of something that makes you happy. I wonder what has been going through your mind, little man, in all this time."

"Hello Nurse," Mark said as he walked into the room. "How's your patient today?"

"He's looking cheerful I think," she responded straightening out his bedclothes again. "How's the lambing going?" She felt like she knew this family inside out.

"Not bad," he said. "I've come to tell Charlie that we did lose a ewe last night and so have an orphan lamb to raise now. We have to keep it warm by the Aga in the kitchen and bottle-feed it. He'd absolutely love to do that. I don't suppose I could bring it in here for Charlie, could I?" he asked tongue in cheek.

"Well, I know that they do allow some trained animals to visit patients in hospitals now. They've realised that it does the patient the world of good but I don't think I've ever heard of lambs being brought in. All the children in the wards would love that though," the nurse mused.

"Yes. Charlie loves all animals. He's also wanted a dog but my mother would never allow one in the house. He always loved visiting his Grandmother at the Farm as we have sheep dogs and farm animals everywhere. We're expecting a foal too later this month," Mark said excitedly.

"Oh how lovely," the nurse cooed. "Well, maybe he'll be awake soon and will be able to see your foal before it gets too big." She gathered her bowl of water and towels and left.

"How was the bed bath then bro?" Mark asked like a naughty schoolboy. "Did I tell you I've got a love interest now? There used to be this girl at school. She sat a couple of desks in front of me but always ignored me.

All the boys were madly in love with her but she didn't want anything to do with such adolescent spotty schoolboys and who could blame her. She was stunning. Anyhow, I met her again recently when out exercising the horses. She's a keen rider too, turns out. She didn't recognise me at first but that was a good thing, I reckon. I like to think I've matured into a slightly more handsome devil than I was as a teenager. What do you think? She hasn't changed much at all though and is still as beautiful as ever. So, I asked her out and we've been on a few dates since and she hasn't given me the elbow yet. Matthew is dead jealous, and Luke. Here's the best bit bro; her name is Juliet Marshall. Her half-brother is none other than Marika and Rebecca's favourite pop idol, Tim Marshall. Speaking of which, did you know that the man who ran you down was also responsible for killing Jud Marshall, Tim and Juliet's father? Small world, isn't it? It was terrible what happened to her father but from all accounts he wasn't a particularly nice man himself. Used to have a hell of a temper apparently and could get quite violent sometimes. Juliet said he never actually hit her but knew that he had hit her brother on many occasions. Interesting, isn't it? Of course it's not exactly common knowledge and the press would have a field day if they knew the half of it, so better keep it to your-self for now. So, you can imagine how your sister is currently on cloud nine, Charlie. She has worked out that if I marry Juliet she will be related to Tim Marshall, the love of her life. I've told her, it's a bit early to speak of marriage. We've only just started dating but you know what she's like. Gets a bit carried away. Anyhow, I'm going to have to get back to the Farm now as it's pretty much full on while the lambs are coming. Hurry up and get well and come and help Charlie, okay. We miss you."

CHAPTER FIFTY-THREE

George felt a rising in her stomach. She was excited about today. Any moment now and the Ambulance would arrive with Mac. Dr Havers, the junior doctor who had been looking after him at the hospital, was accompanying him now, on his first journey out. He would come in, just to check everything in her Apartment was suitable for his patient and he would explain the medication she would need to take charge of. She wasn't too concerned about that responsibility. She was a Vet, which isn't quite the same thing she acknowledged, but she understood how to administer drugs and wasn't afraid of them. She had been looking forward to this ever since Mac had accepted her offer last week when the possibility of a convalescence period was suggested. She wanted to take care of him. She needed to. Her maternal instincts had kicked in wholly when Elly was born and now she had a big gap to fill. Not that she felt particularly maternal towards Mac, of course, but she did want to nurture him and help him get back to full capacity. She had other feelings towards Mac of a more animal instinct and was excited about the possibility of having more freedom to explore all that. She felt like a young girl again and all the troubles of the last few years had been wiped away. Mac was good for her.

They arrived and Dr Havers had given the thumbs up for the accommodation. There wasn't much to complain about. She had made a nice nest. He also gave her a long list of instructions about what to do and what not to do and left them to it, with the knowledge she could call him day or night, if she had any concerns. He knew he was leaving his patient in good hands and felt quite relaxed but very much the gooseberry.

Mac was impressed with her flat. It was very modern and minimalist which was helpful for someone sitting in a wheel chair. He hated the chair but it was better than lying in a bed. It felt really quite odd to be so upright. She unpacked his bag while he did a quick tour. There were two

154

bedrooms he noted but she unpacked his spare clothes into hers. He had no idea how he was going to deal with the sexual side of this relationship in his condition. Mac was a macho man and felt embarrassed at the state of his poor body. He knew he wanted to give it a try though. How could he resist her?

In actual fact when it did happen there was no awkwardness, no clumsiness and no embarrassment at all. It was surprisingly beautiful and natural when they were together. She seemed to have no qualms about his body and he adored hers. They spent a wonderful night together and woke up happy. George realised it was the first time she had felt happy since the birth of her daughter and then the moment was shattered by the phone call from Tim.

She didn't wake Mac but left him still sleeping peacefully, naked in her bed, and crept off to her study. Turning on her television in there she listened to the news, still being broadcast the following morning, and her inner peace felt shattered. "Oh Nicky, what have you done?" she asked herself.

CHAPTER FIFTY-FOUR

"Are you coming into work today?" It was Lucy on the telephone to Ann Marshall, her colleague.

"I hadn't planned on it," Ann said feeling rather hung over. She hadn't been out drinking in a long time and even though her plans to get drunk had been interrupted, she had still managed quite a few glasses of red wine before the balloon went up. In the end it had been a really late night by the time she and Tim had got back and neither had slept. He had left early, wanting to make a few phone calls and check on Nicky and she was making herself a large pot of coffee trying to get her head round the events of the last twelve hours. "Why? Do you need me?"

"No, it's okay, it's just that, well, there's been a delivery for you. How did it go last night, by the way?" Lucy asked keenly. She was Ann's friend and confidante and knew all about the date. It was a big deal, as Ann didn't go on dates, so she was dying to get the details. The delivery for her had made her even more excited.

"What?" Ann couldn't believe it but had actually forgotten all about her date and being stood up, until Lucy reminded her. "What delivery? I'm not expecting anything," she asked evading the question.

"It's a beautiful bouquet of red roses," Lucy told her excitedly. "They're absolutely magnificent and must have cost a bomb. Are they from him?" she persisted.

"Roses?" Ann was surprised. "I wasn't expecting, I mean, flowers, for me?" She had never in her life had flowers sent to her before which is amazing when you think what a beautiful sophisticated woman she was. Her first husband was far too boring for such a lavish gesture and Jud, well, maybe he might have got round to it one day, she supposed.

"Not just flowers but gorgeous red roses Ann. The date must have gone well?" Lucy was still fishing for some information.

"No, no, it didn't actually. In fact it didn't happen. Is there a card?" she said mysteriously. Lucy was shocked. She was sure Ann's date must have sent the flowers to thank her for a lovely evening. It was so romantic and now it seemed she had got it wrong and she felt heartbroken for her friend, who so deserved to be happy.

"What went wrong?" she asked searching the bouquet for a card and finding one. "There is a card, in an envelope. Shall I read it to you?"

Ann didn't know whether to go in and collect the flowers. It would give her an opportunity to check on Nicky too and see if she could help there. She decided she would and told Lucy she was on her way. Lucy would have to wait a bit longer to get the story.

As it turned out, by the time she arrived at the hospital, Nicky Darrow had checked out. He had left with his dad, just before. He had agreed to undergo psychiatric treatment. The hospital had some of the best doctors in this field but he would attend for private appointments, over a series of weeks, months, however long it took. For now, he needed to just go home with his dad and spend some-time with him. Rees Darrow would take responsibility to keep watch over his son. He made it, just before the Press arrived.

Ann had to fight her way inside and the hospital desk where Lucy worked was in turmoil. The Press couldn't get in thankfully but the telephones were ringing non-stop, reporters desperate to get some update or quote. Ann took off her coat and went to the aid of her friend. It was all hands to the pumps. She didn't have time to check on her flowers.

Eventually, a statement had been given to the Press, arranged by the Manager of Spirit. He had told them that Nicky was taking some time away from the limelight due to personal problems and would not be continuing with the Tour but they assured concerned ticket holders that the show would still go on and they would find a temporary replacement for their bass guitarist. They urged people to be patient and understanding and not to hound Mr Darrow, who clearly needed peace and quiet now, in order to recharge his batteries. They confirmed that he had spent the night in hospital but was now with his family and not available for comment.

The statement worked and the hospital telephone system went back to normal. Lucy made some tea for her and Ann and they took a break. She presented Ann with the roses and Ann was delighted when she saw them. She found the envelope and read the card. It simply said, "I'm so sorry. Please forgive me. Call me, Jonathan". She suddenly felt angry again.

She had forgotten all that, but now she remembered being stood up and picked the bouquet up and threw it in the bin. Lucy was shocked.

"What are you doing?" she cried.

"No explanation, no excuse, just sorry. Well I don't forgive him and I'm certainly not going to call him," Ann said as her friend tried to retrieve the gorgeous roses from the bin. Lucy didn't have a clue what she was talking about but if Ann didn't want the flowers then she could certainly find a home for them.

CHAPTER FIFTY-FIVE

"Will you miss me?" Ben asked his fiancé as they lay together in bed. They had just made love and were both feeling emotional.

"Not really," she joked. "Sian and I can paint the town red while you're gone."

He tickled her and whispered in her ear, "I don't care what you do as long as you're still here waiting for me when I get back."

She adored his lyrical Welsh accent and kissed him in response. "I'm going to miss you so much Ben. I wish you didn't have to go and I'm going to worry about you every minute of every day so you'd better call me sometimes. I know it won't be easy but try, please."

"When it's over we can plan a new life together. Mac might be back on his feet, or at least some feet, and we can talk about the future." He was trying to be flippant to ease the agony of parting but she was consumed with fear for what he was going off to do and what might happen. Whatever his mission was it would be dangerous and his life would be on the line again but she must trust in him. She loved him so much. It hurt.

Later, as he was ready to leave, she held him for a full five minutes before eventually she let him go. Sian had tried to make her-self inconspicuous in the flat but it wasn't easy with just the one room. She busied herself in the galley kitchen until Ben had left and then she offered her Landlady a nice cup of tea. Marika had never liked tea until she met Ben. Now, she couldn't drink enough of the stuff. The girls drank their tea and chatted and before long Marika had cheered up. She was not the moronic type. "How's your brother getting on?" she asked Sian.

"Well, from all accounts," Sian answered. "He's loving being out of hospital and he seems to be pretty smitten with George. I can't wait to meet her."

"Can't wait to meet both of them," Marika added. She had heard so much about Ben's best friend but had yet to be introduced. "Tell you what, why don't we?" she said.

"What? Go over there?" Sian asked excitedly.

"Why not?" Marika said. "I can't wait around forever for Ben to get his act together and introduce us. Your brother might have some useful information about Ben I need to know before I commit the rest of my life to him," she joked.

"Well, I can't see that it would hurt. My Uncle is back in Liverpool from all accounts and I really would love to get out of this flat for a while, no offence," Sian said. "I'll ring Dan and get their address, shall I?"

"Dan?" Marika asked surprised.

"Mac," Sian explained smiling. "The army christened him Mac. My brothers' real name is Daniel."

CHAPTER FIFTY-SIX

Jonathan sent roses to the Hospital every day hoping for a response. Surely she could forgive him, couldn't she? She must have read the papers or seen the news. She would know he had no choice but to stand her up. When she didn't respond he had been even more intrigued. He wasn't accustomed to having to run after women. Considered one of the country's most eligible bachelors, women usually fell over themselves, trying to get his attention. What was so different about this one?

When the flowers arrived for the fourth day running Ann was starting to get annoyed. Can't this man take a hint, she thought? Why is he being so persistent? Surely, he can't expect a woman like her to forgive a man who blatantly stood her up. She had not been out on a date for years and years and then when she finally plucked up the courage to go he had callously knocked all the steam out of her sails. He hadn't even offered an excuse. Not that she believed any excuse would be good enough. Okay he couldn't have rung her. She had decided not to give him her mobile telephone number. Wisely, now, as it turned out, but he could still have rung the Restaurant where they were meeting and not kept her dangling embarrassingly in front of all those other diners. The memory of it made the hackles on the back of her neck rise. What a cheek.

Just because he had found out where she worked, was she supposed to forgive him? She wondered about that. At least he had made some effort she supposed to find that out. Sarah would probably have told him, so not that difficult, except she thought he didn't like speaking to his ex-wife much. Well, all right, she would give him that. He hadn't ignored her altogether. He couldn't have got cold feet or he wouldn't be trying so hard now to win her attention again. Was she being unfair? She had this conversation with herself every morning when the bouquets arrived. She had stopped throwing them in the bins but decided to decorate her flat with them as they smelt so beautiful and it was such a novelty. Should she ring him to thank him for the flowers at least?

Jonathan decided a game of golf with his old friend David Essex was in order. He and David went back a long way. Both had been upcoming stars at the same time and now, both were knights of the realm. David was a more practised golfer than Jonathan who never seemed to get the time these days to play, but who was a natural sportsman. In the nineteenth, he broached the subject of Ann to his friend.

David's ears pricked up immediately. He was very fond of Ann. She had proved herself a valuable asset to his hospital of course but she was also a good friend. He had always felt she had had a raw deal in life and both he and his wife Angeline, longed to see her settled again with a good man. Jonathan definitely fitted the bill there, he thought. It would be a match made in heaven.

"How do you know Ann?" he asked his friend.

"I don't really," Jonathan answered. "We met at one of Sarah's Charity Bashes briefly but she seemed like a lovely lady and I would love to get to know her better."

"Oh she is lovely," David said. "Tell you what, why don't you come to dinner at ours. Angeline was only saying to me this morning as I was leaving for golf that she hadn't seen you for ages."

"That would be lovely," Jonathan said, genuinely pleased for such an invitation. He liked David and Angeline very much. They were excellent company always.

"Maybe I can get Ann to come along too," David said conspiratorially. The two men raised their glasses, "Cheers," they both said together.

Part Four—
"Missing In Action"

CHAPTER FIFTY-SEVEN

Jonathan wasn't unaccustomed to being awaken in the middle of the night. As the Junior Criminal Lawyer in the Firm, it was an occupational hazard but this wasn't work. He jumped out of bed and threw on some clothes, found his car keys and raced off to the hospital.

Nurse Booth was working the night shift. She had spent so many hours of so many days of so many shifts looking after this patient. Sometimes he gave her such small signs but she was on the ball and detected the change. She checked the boy and immediately pressed the panic alarm over his bed. He had given a faint sigh, most people wouldn't even have heard it, and then he had stopped breathing. It was a terrible shock. The crash team came in and worked on him for a full minute or more before he returned to them. They stabilised the young boy with all the machines they had at their disposal and called his parents to advise them.

When Jonathan arrived he was shocked and devastated to see Sarah was there before him, accompanied by Father Benedict, who was busy administering the last rites to his son. He had had to travel from London and had made very quick time. He would worry about the speed cameras later but Sarah and her priest only lived around the corner and so had begun the ritual. He turned to Nurse Booth, tears in his eyes, "Is he?" he couldn't say the words out loud.

"Oh no," she went over to him and touched his arm compassionately. "Your son is alive, Mr Havers. He did go away for a minute or two but we got him back."

"Will he be all right?" he hardly dare ask.

"He should be," she answered gently and then added, "for now anyway."

"So what's going on here?" he suddenly felt enraged. "What do you think you're doing?" he said to the Priest. "I want you to stop this, stop this right now and get out," he physically forced Father Benedict out of the room. Sarah was outraged.

"Jonathan," she yelled at him. "Father Benedict was only obeying my wishes. Our son died tonight. I don't want that to happen again and for it to be too late to save his soul. You must apologise to him right now."

"Our son is not dead Sarah. He's not going to die. Don't ever do anything like that again, do you hear?" Jonathan wasn't given to outbursts of anger but emotions were running high.

"Oh, you impossible man," Sarah felt indignant. "I'm divorcing you," she yelled at him as she stormed out of the room and went to find the hapless Priest.

Jonathan sat down next to Charlie and looked up at Nurse Booth, "Well, something good has come out of tonight," he smiled.

Nurse Booth returned his smile. She knew that there was no love-loss between Mr and Mrs Havers and having met her and met him she could never understand how the two of them had ever got together in the first place. Sarah didn't even bother to return.

Jonathan remained at his son's bedside keeping vigil for the rest of the night. His breathing sounded steady now. The Consultant spoke with him and reassured him that they were doing everything possible for Charlie. He praised the Nurse for reacting so quickly. It was just a blip, so little was understood about comas. They had thought that Charlie was still healing but this mishap would keep them on their toes. However, it reminded them that he wasn't out of the woods yet. They were all waiting for the boy to just wake up but this showed them that he still had his own battles to fight.

"Thank you," Jonathan said to Nurse Booth after the Consultant had left.

She smiled, "It's my job," she answered modestly.

"Yes I know but I also know how good you are at it. Charlie is very lucky to have you on his side," he told the nurse.

"He's very lucky to have such a wonderful family on his side too," Nurse Booth observed.

"Yes. We won't mention this to Marika," he said protectively and the nurse nodded. The girl was a drama queen at the best of times. "If she found out she would never go to school or leave his side."

"It's rather sweet," the nurse acknowledged. "They're obviously very close."

"My daughter knows how to love and one day will make a fantastic mother," Jonathan said. "She will be like a lioness, fiercely protective and nurturing."

"Pity the man she marries," the nurse laughed. It was nice to have some light relief. She would go home this morning after a very dramatic night. She doubted she would sleep easy.

"Where did you disappear to son?" Jonathan spoke gently to Charlie. "Don't frighten me like that again. You have to stay alive, okay?"

CHAPTER FIFTY-EIGHT

When Mac woke up he couldn't remember where he was for a minute. The bed felt really warm and comfortable and his body felt good. He saw the indentation in the pillow next to his and his mind was filled with pleasant memories of the previous night. "Gina," he called out when he realised she wasn't in the bedroom with him.

He heard footsteps but was surprised to see they were of the four-legged variety. Laurel and Hardy, the two Doberman Pinschers, Gina liked to call her boys, trotted into the bedroom and bared their teeth at the intruder. He had been introduced to them yesterday but it was hardly love at first sight. The dogs were fiercely protective of their mistress and resented the intrusion into what they considered was entirely their domain. Mac was not afraid of them however, no matter how much they bared their teeth or snarled at him. He had fought the Taliban. He had stood next to a man with a bomb strapped to his torso. Now, that was someone Mac had been afraid of. Two overgrown puppy dogs that liked to pretend they were vicious killing machines just didn't worry him at all. When he presented no fear around them they quickly lost interest and decided to tolerate the stranger in their midst. That was yesterday, however, and now the stranger was alone and looking vulnerable.

"Good dogs," he said ignoring the growls. He pulled himself up to a sitting position. "Where's your mistress then?" Since the mountain wasn't coming to Mohammed, he decided he would go to the mountain but first he had to get his chair near enough. It was just out of his reach he realised. He looked around the bedroom and saw a weapon of choice by the door. It was an umbrella with a hooked handle, just like his mother used to use. In Ireland umbrellas were part of the furniture. "Okay," he said to himself as much as to the dogs, which appeared to be licking their lips now. What was that all about? "I need you boys to help me out here. How about fetching me that umbrella," he said pointing towards it. At

168

the sound of their favourite word, "Fetch", both dogs' ears pricked up but they kept their eyes firmly on this intruder and didn't follow his finger at all. "Come on you dumb puppies," he persisted. He picked his jumper up from the bottom of the bed and threw it in the direction of the umbrella. The dogs immediately responded and ran towards the jumper getting hold of it between them and pulling it apart. "No, not my jumper," he yelled at them. Okay, maybe that wasn't such a clever idea, he thought to himself. "No," he said again and the dogs dropped the slightly shredded jumper into his hands. "Thanks but I want you to fetch," he said again and pretended to throw something towards the umbrella this time. Again they responded running towards it and sniffing around frantically trying to find what he had thrown, in vain. "Fetch," he kept saying and this time the dogs knocked over the laundry basket and had a field day with its' contents. "No, no, he scolded them and Laurel emerged with a pair of Georges' knickers on his head. Mac had to laugh much to the indignation of the dog. "You weren't called Laurel and Hardy for nothing," he said to the pair. "How can I take your growls seriously with names like that, by the way?" He tried again repeating the fetch word until the dogs finally got the message. They had put their teeth around several options before eventually settling on his weapon. "Yes, yes, that's it," he was getting as excited as them now. "Bring it here, good boys." Of course the umbrella went pretty much the same way as the jumper and got pulled apart by the pair. Their teeth easily punctured the canvas covering, meaning the umbrella would function better as a colander from now on. "I'm going to have to buy her a new umbrella," he said taking it from them gratefully.

He hooked the handle around the arm of his wheelchair and was relieved as it came towards him. "Now we're cooking," he continued talking to the dogs. They sat down panting and eagerly awaiting the next command. This stranger was great fun. He clumsily pulled himself towards the chair but as he went to sit down in it, the wheels slid away and he found himself in a heap on the floor. It might have been painful but Mac was more concerned about the dogs that had leapt on top of him thinking this was the next game. They were all over him, licking him to death. Could be worse, he thought, they could be using their teeth. By the time he brushed them off, his hair was covered in dog saliva and he must have looked a mess. Unperturbed, he had another go at getting into the chair and this time managed it. The wheels were wedged against the bed and had nowhere to go. His upper body was still strong enough to lift him, he noted, with a certain amount of satisfaction. This was going to take a lot more practice, however.

In the chair, he felt more confident. He pulled the threadbare jumper on over his naked torso and looked like a tramp. He picked up a towel that had fallen out of the laundry basket and wrapped it around his lower half. "Come on then," he said to his new eager friends. "Let's go find your mistress."

George had turned the television off and decided to telephone the hospital. She would ask for Dr Havers as she knew him pretty well now. He answered her call immediately. "Is everything all right?" he asked her anxiously, concerned for his patient.

"Oh yes, sorry, this isn't about Mac but he's great since you ask," she reassured the young doctor and immediately felt calmer as she recalled the wonderful night she had just spent with his patient. "Actually, I'm calling about my husband, Nicky Darrow."

"Oh right," Matthew said feeling relieved. It had been his idea to let Mac go home with George for a few weeks and he would feel terrible if the plan had backfired on him. "Wait a minute. Nicky Darrow is your husband?" he asked incredibly.

"Yes. Well, soon to be ex-husband actually but we're still married at this present time. I heard about last night and just wanted to know how he is. Can you tell me?" George asked the young doctor.

Matthew just hadn't made the connection. Since starting work at this hospital he was beginning to meet all sorts of celebrities. His sister would be dead jealous. "Well actually George I can't really tell you much. He's obviously not my patient but I do know he checked out this morning already. He left with his father, Rees Darrow."

"Oh, I see," George felt relieved at this news. "That's good news I suppose or did he check himself out?" Should she feel more concerned his life was in danger.

"I don't know any details I'm afraid but I think he was feeling much better although obviously his recovery will be on going. I suspect he will be looked after by his dad and receive treatment from our Psychiatric Department and maybe some Counselling, that sort of thing." Matthew said carefully. He wouldn't give out too much detail about any patient of course but he wasn't breaching any confidence here and she was his wife.

"Thank you Doctor," she said feeling altogether happier. Nicky was his fathers' responsibility now. There was nothing she could do for him.

"Call me Matthew please," he said smoothly. "By the way, did you know it was my dad that talked him down?"

"What?" she was surprised.

"My dad," he expounded proudly. "He was on his way home from work when he spotted your husband on the top of the wall on the roof of the car park. He called the police and drove up to the top and then engaged in conversation with Nicky for over three hours apparently. He got him to get down."

"Gosh," George said. "You must thank him for me and thank you."

Feeling slightly more relaxed she telephoned the Pub. She knew the number off by heart. She had always had a brilliant relationship with her father-in-law. He had supported her throughout and was genuinely sorry that their marriage had broken down. Rees was pleased to hear from her. "He's such an idiot," he told her. "Are you okay?"

"Oh, you know," she said. "I honestly had no idea Nicky was feeling suicidal Rees."

"None of us did," Rees replied. "There's no blame here George. You know Nicky. He's always been more concerned about his public persona than his true feelings. He keeps them close to his chest. He'll be all right George. We'll look after him here and see he gets the treatment he needs."

"I'm very grateful," George said genuinely.

"He's dropped out from the tour which will help. He couldn't go on getting on that stage and just pretending everything was all right, night after night. The boys in the Band have been very understanding and Tim will keep him in the loop. You just worry about yourself now George," Rees told her.

That was typical of her father-in-law. He was always on her side and she would miss him. When a marriage breaks up it isn't just the couple involved. It affects everybody's family too. She hoped she would always remain friends with Nicky's. "Do you want to speak with him?" Rees asked her suddenly.

She panicked. She hadn't thought about that. "Actually," she said after a moment's thought. "I don't think I do, dad. Do you mind?"

"That's all right," he said gently. "I just thought I'd better ask."

"It's just that I think we've exhausted everything we had to say to each other. I really don't know what to say to him anymore," she said mournfully.

"Don't beat your-self up George," he sympathised. "Like I said there's no blame here. Nicky will come through this and be all the stronger for it, I promise."

"You can tell him I called and that I'm thinking of him," she said and ended the call.

She felt tears pricking the corners of her eyes. She had no reason to feel guilty for not talking to him, but still did. Suddenly, her thoughts were interrupted. She got up from the desk intending to make some coffee when she stopped in her tracks. In the hallway was a very dishevelled man sitting in a wheelchair. He looked like he had been for a dip in the canal. His hair was wet and his jumper half hanging off his shoulders was torn. He had an old towel around his nether regions. Next to him were two very guilty looking hounds. One had a pair of her knickers on its' head and the other clearly had threads from the ripped jumper hanging from its' jaws. All three bore a conspiratorial look that said please don't be cross with me, it wasn't my fault. In seconds, her mood lightened and she burst out laughing.

"Thank you boys," she said to their hurt faces. "I needed that."

CHAPTER FIFTY-NINE

Ann was enjoying herself. She didn't get many social invitations to attend where she knew she could just relax and be amongst friends. When David, her boss, had invited her to dinner, she was delighted. She really liked David and his wife, Angeline, and knew from experience, they gave wonderful dinner parties. It had been too long since she last went to one. What's more, another colleague, Dr Justin Hayward and his lovely wife, Pamela, were also invited and had offered her a lift, which she had been pleased to accept.

She knew David was the perfect Host and there would be no feeling of being the odd one out and she didn't smell a rat. She didn't even notice that the table was set for eight and they appeared to be a party of seven. The other couple were an old friend of Angeline's, Andy Jones and his wife Jennifer. Andy was a West End Superstar. He was the star in all the best musicals and a truly lovely guy. His wife was an Equestrian and Ann had been thinking a lot lately about getting back into horse riding, something she had done as a child. The conversation flowed easily.

True to form Jonathan was the late arrival. He hadn't planned it that way of course but once again his career had gotten in the way of his social life. As the Chief Coroner for London he was constantly in demand but tonight he had stressed that he wasn't on call. When he had been contacted just as he was leaving for the Party he had cursed. In the end it hadn't taken him long to sort the problem out but it had meant he was late and he could just imagine how that would go down with Mrs Ann Marshall. He made sure his mobile phone was turned off, after that.

He couldn't believe himself but he was actually nervous about meeting her again. She had ignored all his attempts at an apology. He didn't want to embarrass his hosts and prayed she would be more susceptible to his redoubtable charms, face to face. She, actually, was in ignorance of his invitation. David had omitted to mention it, especially when the time came to sit down around the table and Jonathan still hadn't turned up. He decided that if his friend wasn't going to make it, better Ann knew nothing about the cunning plan. Angeline would have preferred to warn Ann but had been over-ruled by her husband. In any case, what she didn't know wouldn't hurt her, she supposed.

However, Jonathan did turn up and took his seat at the table opposite Ann. David introduced him to all the guests and Ann greeted him coolly. She was suddenly feeling very stupid. Was this a set-up? She gave her boss a cold stare but he just responded with a smile and opened another bottle of wine. "It's nice of you to turn up," she whispered sarcastically across the table, before adding, "this time."

Jonathan was amazed. Was there no end to this woman's hurt? "Oh come on," he said glibly. "Let it go."

She was furious. She wanted to say a whole lot more towards this arrogant, egotistical, pig but remembered where she was and held her tongue. Instead, she tried desperately to ignore any conversation with him and engaged with Justin and Andy sitting either side of her, instead.

Jonathan went to assist his host clearing the plates away in the kitchen. "It's not going well," he said, understating the obvious. "I don't know how to get through to her."

"I don't understand it," David said feeling rather amused at his friends dilemma. "Ann is usually so receptive and friendly," he added rubbing it in. "What the hec did you do to her?"

"I stood her up, for which I have profusely apologised for, over and over but she clearly doesn't accept it," Jonathan told him. "I'm not going to give up. Are these plates to go back in?"

"Yes please," David said enjoying the situation. "Maybe Jonathan, you need to accept there is one woman out there who doesn't fall for your inestimable charms."

"Don't believe it," Jonathan said joining in the banter. "Watch and learn boy."

Back at the table Ann found she couldn't take her eyes off him, despite herself. He was extremely handsome and she had to admit had style. The ease at which he mixed with the company was admirable. "How's your daughter getting on?" Andy asked him.

"Pretty good actually, thanks Andy," Jonathan replied. "She's got the lead in a small comedy in the City and seems to be enjoying herself."

"I had the pleasure of working with Marika, Jonathan's daughter," Andy explained to the others. "She was a chorus girl in the Mutiny on the Bounty and I knew then she was a star in the making. Lead part eh? Good for her. Give her my regards."

"Do you like musicals Ann?" Jonathan asked directly. The whole table were in on this conversation so she could hardly ignore him now. She would never be rude to her hosts.

"Yes I do," she replied blushing at being made to speak to him.

"Have you been to many?" he persisted.

"One or two," she answered. "I always look out for the ones you're starring in Andy," she diverted the response.

"Oh nice pass," Jonathan whispered to her. She tried not to smile.

"I love the opera," Angeline commented and began a whole new conversation about what the latest show at Covent Garden was like at her end of the table. Jonathan took advantage of the moment. Angeline was talking with Jenny, Andy and Pamela about opera and David was talking with Justin about work. He refilled Ann's glass for her and offered her the cheese platter.

"By the way, what did you think of the steak?" he asked.

"If you're talking about Bertorellis then, yes, it was very good?" she answered tersely.

"I told you, you'd like it. Fancy a re-run?" he chanced his luck.

"You must be joking," she gave him one of her sternest looks.

"Oh come on, you know I didn't want to have to stand you up but under the circumstances, surely you can find it in your heart to forgive me," he persisted.

"There can be no possible circumstances that would warrant keeping a lady waiting," she said unreasonably and rather more loudly than she intended. David stopped talking to Justin and listened in, ready to rescue the situation if he felt it required it.

"I've got it," Jonathan said suddenly, smiling.

"You certainly have," she replied crossly. "You are full of it. You were referring to arrogance, weren't you?"

"Ouch," he said enjoying the banter. This woman certainly was a challenge. "No, I meant I've just remembered where I know you from."

Ann looked a bit puzzled. "What are you talking about?"

"You remember when we met at Sarah's party, I asked you if we had ever met before?" he asked her. That party was starting to feel like a lifetime ago. She nodded still not quite understanding what he was getting at. "We had," he continued. "Something about your voice just now reminded me. It was just after your husband had been killed. You came to the hospital to meet my son. He had been involved indirectly in finding the killer. You came to thank him."

The penny suddenly dropped with Ann too. Of course! Those deep blue eyes that followed you around the room and appeared to look deep into your soul had left an impression on her back then. How could she have forgotten? He hadn't really changed, may be, a bit greyer around the gills, but still infuriatingly good looking. Her tone altered, as she felt a bit more compassion towards this man. His life hadn't always gone his way, it seemed. "Your son was in a coma," she said acknowledging his memory.

"Yes," he replied excitedly. She remembered him.

The rest of the room had been enjoying the banter between these two persons who were obviously made for each other but even they had to admit to feeling slight relief when the conversation was toned down and they seemed to have found some mutual ground. Pamela was interested in the story. "So, your husband was killed by the same man who ran over Jonathan's son?" she asked intrigued at the connection.

"Yes," Jonathan replied politely. "Charlie saw the man trying to dispose of the gun, you see," he explained.

"What and he told the police and the man tried to run him over?" Justin asked, also intrigued.

"Well, not quite. Charlie didn't tell anyone except his sister and she didn't tell us until after Charlie had been run over. He hadn't really known what he saw, I suppose. The gun was in a sack when he threw it in the pontoon and Charlie just happened to be in the wrong place at the wrong time," Jonathan explained to the whole room now. They were all listening intently.

It had been big news when Jud Marshall got shot. Andy Jones had cause not to like Jud although he had never held it against Ann. Jud had had an affair with Andy's first wife, long before he had met Ann, and the relationship had resulted in her getting pregnant by him. She gave birth to a baby girl and that girl was Juliet, Mark Havers' new girlfriend. "At least they caught him and put him away," he said.

"Shall we adjourn to the drawing room?" David decided to interject. The conversation was in danger of becoming a bit morbid and he couldn't have that at one of his dinner parties. At least Ann was starting to get along a bit better with his friend now.

"How is Charlie?" she asked him gently now, as they walked into the other room and sat down together.

CHAPTER SIXTY

"Hello darling," Ben whispered into his mobile. He was lying in a ditch in the middle of the desert, somewhere in Africa. It was night and very shortly his team would begin what they had come out there to do. It was a highly dangerous mission in a hostile country and everyone was feeling the pressure. He wasn't supposed to make calls but he wanted to hear her voice just one more time before going into combat. He might not hear it again for a long time. All phones and any form of identification had to be left behind tonight. Marika was excited to hear from him.

"Are you okay?" she whispered back. She had no idea why she did that but it seemed like the right thing to do.

"I'm good," he lied. He was freezing cold and anxious. The desert was so hot in the day but once the sun went down it was a vicious terrain. "I just wanted to hear your voice."

"That makes a change," she laughed. "Usually, you're telling me to shut up talking all the time."

"Well, I'm not tonight," he replied patiently. "Tell me what you've been up to."

"Nothing much really, just the usual. Oh but I met your best friend today and his girlfriend. She's lovely," she told him.

"You're kidding?" Why did she never cease to give him nice surprises? "You've met Mac and George? How? Where?"

"Sian and I went over to their beautiful flat in Chelsea to see them. You should see it Ben, it's gorgeous, right on the Embankment overlooking the Thames. I want to live in a flat like that one day, do you hear?"

"Wait a minute, Mac's out of hospital?" he asked incredulously.

"Yes," she answered. "My brother let him out for good behaviour. It's just for a little while Ben to help him recuperate before they work on his legs and all that. George has taken him in. How lucky is he? I love him, by the way," she added knowing Ben would be pleased with that.

"Lucky dog," he said thinking of his present plight. His best friend was lying in some posh flat in Chelsea, in the lap of luxury, with a gorgeous bird to take care of him. Life was just a little unfair sometimes.

"Are you jealous?" Marika asked him teasingly.

"Only of his soft comfortable bed," he replied turning his attention back to the love of his life. "Right now, I'd give plenty to be in yours."

"Mmm, do you want me to talk dirty to you soldier boy," she continued to tease.

"Don't get me worked up," he said. "I'm working."

"I'll be thinking about you now for the rest of the day," she told him. "Sian has moved out, by the way. I'm actually lying on our sofa again watching a weepie on the TV, as we speak."

"Where has she gone?" he asked concerned.

"She's moved in with the lovers," she answered. "It made sense really. They've got two bedrooms in their magical flat and she is Macs' sister after all."

"I hope Mac doesn't do anything stupid," he said. He knew his friend too well. Having Sian with him he would start thinking about the unfinished business with his Uncle.

"He can't Ben. He's still quite poorly really," she said reassuringly. She didn't know Mac like he did.

"I may not be able to call you again after this honey, not for a long time, I'm afraid," he said bringing the conversation back. He would have to get going in a minute and he didn't want her to be worried if things didn't go as smoothly as they hoped.

"I miss you," she said softly, tears welling in her beautiful deep blue eyes.

"I'll be home soon," he told her. "We can start looking for your dream flat then."

She knew he didn't mean it. He was just trying to appease her, keep her morale up. He is a great leader she thought. She could just imagine how the men under his command would look up to him and how he would look after every one of them. "Keep safe."

"I love you," were his last words.

CHAPTER SIXTY-ONE

"Your Grandfather is so in the doghouse," Charlie's Grandmother told him. "He stood me up. Can you believe that? He was supposed to be taking me out for our Anniversary on Thursday night. We're having a party at the Farm on Sunday, Charlie. Just Sunday lunch really but with all the family and a few friends. It's our fortieth wedding anniversary and he's supposed to buy me rubies. I'm expecting a large ruby necklace from him now at the very least after the old fool left me stranded at Bertorellis this week. Apparently he forgot he was having a meal with me privately and went straight from the Courthouse to his wretched Club. I had to eat my steak on my own. It was delicious of course but I was furious as we had tickets for the Opera afterwards. Anyhow, your father came to the rescue. I called him and he made it from work in time to accompany me to the Opera instead. He did say he could go to the Club and drag his father out but I decided I would rather have my sons company. I want your Granddad to suffer for a bit. I sometimes wonder if he isn't losing his memory you know. I suppose I should be worried really. He seems to forget lots of things lately, I've noticed. Getting old, I suppose. I'm pleased to say I don't feel old at all. Do you realise that you are nearly a year older now young man? Isn't it time you came back to the real world? What do you think about Charlie while you're lying there? I wish we had a window into your mind."

CHAPTER SIXTY-TWO

Ann was genuinely sorry when she had to leave. Dr Justin Hayward, the designated driver, was on duty early the next morning and was ready to go. He had been the only sober one at the party so must have found it amusing watching everyone else make fools of themselves. Andy, Jennifer and Jonathan were all staying on for the night, it seemed. She had been invited to stay also, by Angeline, but had thought it more prudent to leave, while she had the offer of a lift. It had been a great party and she couldn't remember when she had laughed so much. After dinner they had played silly games and she had got a little tipsy on brandy. David was a very generous host.

The conversation in the car on the way home was naturally about the party and how brilliant a cook Angeline was and what a brilliant host her husband was. Pamela was also full of praise and enthusiasm for Sir Jonathan Havers. Ann had to admit he was great company. He was charming, polite, attentive and highly amusing. Once the ice had been broken between them she had really started to relax and enjoy her-self more. When they had come to leave he had simply kissed her lightly on the cheek and whispered in her ear, "I hope to see you again Ann." That was all he said and it had sent shivers down her backbone. He didn't force himself on her anymore and she was grateful for that. She still wasn't sure if she would accept a date at this stage. She didn't want to set herself up again for a fall.

"Are you treating Nicky?" Ann asked Pamela. Pamela was the resident psychiatrist for David Essex and often worked with Ann. She would sometimes refer her patients to Ann for counselling and similarly Ann, if she felt a patient needed more professional care than she could offer, would refer them to Pamela.

"Yes," Pamela answered surprised at the sober question from her colleague. "It's going to be on going but he's doing well, at his dads."

"I noticed you were deep in conversation with Jonathan at one stage, tonight," Pamela's husband commented. "Were you asking him about his exploits on the roof?"

Ann's ears pricked up. On the roof did he just say? What was this?

"Yes," Pamela answered. "It gave me a useful insight into Nicky's state of mind at the time. They talked for nearly three hours. That's a long time. He was very brave."

"Who was?" Ann asked intrigued.

"Jonathan," Pamela answered surprised Ann had to ask.

"Why?" Ann asked again.

"Well, climbing up onto that wall for one thing. He could have fallen to his death or Nicky might have pulled him over with him. You just never know in situations like that." Pamela was full of admiration.

"Yes," her husband added smiling. "I've heard of the Coroner being called after the event but it was certainly above and beyond the call of duty being there throughout the intended suicide, wasn't it?"

"I'm sorry," Ann interrupted their joke. "Are you saying that the member of the public who saw Nicky, called the Police and then climbed up there himself to talk him down was none other than Sir Jonathan Havers?" She was in shock.

Pamela and Justin exchanged incredulous glances with each other. "Where have you been Ann?" Justin asked her.

"It's been all over the papers and broadcast on the television for the last, God knows, how long," Pamela added.

Ann was suddenly feeling unbelievably foolish. "I know," she tried to explain lamely. "I started watching the news but when I saw Nicky I rushed to the hospital. I was with Tim and his father at the time we found out. The next morning it was just so busy at work with the Press calling in all the time that I never had time to look at a paper. Then, I suppose I just didn't want to read about it or watch it. You know, when you know the person, it's very difficult to listen to speculation and gossip about them."

"So, what was all that about with Jonathan tonight?" Pamela was intrigued. It hadn't escaped her notice that her friend had been very antagonistic towards the hero at first.

"He stood me up," she said wishing the ground would swallow her up. "That night, he stood me up and I had no idea why?" She started to fumble inside her handbag.

Justin was highly amused. "Well he's not quite as arrogant as you accused him of being then. He didn't even boast about his act of heroism, it seems."

"No," Ann smiled. She knew the joke was on her but she had to take it on the chin. "He just sent me flowers by way of an apology," and all three started laughing.

She found what she was looking for in her bag. She still had it. She had no idea why she hadn't just torn it up, but there it was; his card. She took out her phone and dialled his mobile. It went straight to his messaging service, as he, true to his word, had turned it off for the evening. She waited for the recorded introduction to finish and the bleep to sound and then said, "Same time, same place, next Friday night." She hesitated before adding, "You've got my mobile number this time, in case you feel like doing something heroic on the way again." She knew her phone number would be automatically registered into his mobile, with the message.

CHAPTER SIXTY-THREE

Sian and Mac sat on the London platform waiting for the 1.30pm train to Liverpool. Mac had wanted to wait till he felt more ready, physically, but he knew it was unfinished business and he couldn't put it off any longer. He had wanted to leave Sian behind but she wouldn't hear of it. In any event he was grateful for her help. He would never have made the journey alone. He had no plan. He was just acting on automatic pilot. Neither sibling spoke much on the journey north, both lost in their own private thoughts. Sian knew it was worse for Mac. She had not had the same close relationship with her Uncle that her brother had. Uncle Pat had moved to England when she was growing up in Ireland and didn't take an interest in her future, in the same way he had done for her brother. She told herself it was because she was just a girl. Her uncle had never married and she often wondered why that was.

What she didn't know was her parentage was never in doubt. Mac's was. Uncle Pat had had a brief affair with his brother's wife not too many months before Mac came along. There had been no repeat scandal after that time. There was definitely no love-loss between Uncle Pat and their father but Sian had been too young to know anything about that. All Mac knew was his Uncle Pat was always there for him. His father worked long hours and it was shift work and he wasn't. He missed all those school sports days, prize giving events and special moments. It was Uncle Pat who cheered him on in the boxing ring, who took him to his first Gaelic football match and who congratulated him when he passed all his exams. He even bought him his first car at seventeen much to his own father's fury. It had caused quite a row, he recalled. There were lots of rows between the brothers, Mac remembered, but he didn't know the half of it. Strangely, though, his Uncle had not been at his passing out parade when he joined the Army and by then his own father was dead.

"What do you think you will do now?" Sian asked her brother making conversation.

"You mean, about the Army?" he asked.

"Yes. Will you be able to carry on, do you think, once you get your legs?"

"I don't honestly know. I have no idea how good I'll be," he answered her honestly.

"I don't really see George as an Army wife," she remarked.

"Wife? I think we have a long way to go before we get to that stage but you're probably right," he agreed with her. "What about you? Will you go back to Business College?"

"No way," she answered emphatically. "I never enjoyed it much to begin with. It was just a way to escape home."

"So, will you go home?" he asked her.

She looked at her brother coyly. "I'd hate to go home Daniel." She didn't use her brother's Army nickname. "In fact, I was kind of hoping, you might let me stay with you."

"I don't think so Sian. Much though I love you, it's Gina's flat and you don't even have a job," he said bluntly.

"I could get a job. Oh please," she pleaded.

It was hard to resist a little sister but it wasn't his call. "We'll see," was all he said and their conversation fell silent again. She seemed satisfied with that, it was better than No.

When they arrived at Liverpool she helped him down from the train with the aid of a Guardsman. He hated being crippled and depending on others but he just had to put up with it for now. They made their way to the Casino. It was nearly 6pm now and the Casino wouldn't be open for a couple more hours at least but Uncle Pat lived above. The front door was all locked up and Sian suggested they try the kitchens at the back. She had helped out at weekends when she first came over and had got to know some of the staff. One of the kitchen staff, Tony, had fancied her rotten until he found out she was the boss's niece. He had been too frightened to pursue it further. The boss was a formidable man. Uncle Pat's staff knew a different side to the man that, until lately, his nephew had had no idea.

Tony was standing out the back having a crafty cigarette. The Casino had a decent Restaurant and the kitchen staff, were always in a couple of hours before opening, to prepare. He recognised Sian immediately but although he had seen Mac before he didn't make the connection with the wheelchair. "Hey," he said to her. "Good to see you." His Scouse accent was thick.

"Hello Tony," she smiled at him. "This is my brother. We're visiting Uncle Pat. Is he in, do you know?"

"Oh yes," he said giving her a wink. "The King is in the Counting house, counting out his money," he quipped. The Office was at the back of the Casino, all on the same level.

"Can we go through this way?" she asked politely pointing to the kitchen door, which was ajar. It was always hot working in a kitchen and the staff liked ventilation.

"Sure thing. Go through. There's no one else here yet," he said taking another drag on his cigarette.

Sian pushed her brother's wheelchair through the open door and then went ahead ready to hold the kitchen swing door to the Restaurant open for him. Mac wheeled himself through the kitchen and spotting a Chef's knife lying around, surreptitiously collected it up from the shelf and concealed it into his coat pocket. He hated going into conflict without a weapon.

Uncle Pat was in his Office going through yesterday's takings. It had been a good night. Although there were CCTV monitors all over the Casino he wasn't watching the monitors. The cleaning staff had gone home and it would be a couple of hours before the Casino staff and his Doormen and bouncers arrived for work. His office door was solid metal, about six inches thick and had a coded locking system. He would have to buzz anyone in and before he did that, he would check the monitor. There would be no surprise attack here, Mac realised.

As they arrived at the door Sian asked him, "What's the plan?" She was suddenly feeling a bit scared. Uncle Pat had ordered her execution and didn't know she was still alive. What would he do? She knew Mac was more than a match for the older man normally but he wasn't in any fit state to put up a fight now. Just what were they going to do?

"Try knocking," Mac told her. There was no plan. He was still finding it hard to come to terms with. A part of him, even now, refused to believe his Uncle would betray him. There has to be a reason for what's been going on, surely.

His Uncle cursed. He hated being interrupted when he was counting. Now he would have to start all over again. He looked up from the desk and stared open mouthed at the monitor. "So," he said out loud to an empty room, "I see you've come at last." He pressed the button under his desk to release the catch on the door and buzz his visitors in. He didn't even bother moving the money.

"Dan, my boy," he stood up and went round the desk hoping to embrace his nephew but the look Mac gave him told him not to bother. "And Sian?" he added moving towards her. She backed away stumbling over a chair that was in her way. She was clearly terrified. "Back from your travels, I see. How nice." He decided to sit back down at his desk. "To what do I owe the honour?"

"You've been lying to me Uncle Pat," Mac said. He wanted to give him a chance to explain. "You told me Sian was in Australia but as you can see."

"I told you that so as not to worry you son," he said looking directly at Mac. "You shouldn't have got involved. How come you are out of hospital so quick?"

Sian stood with her back to the wall in a corner of the office, as far away from Uncle Pat as she could. "How could you do that to me?" she said to him accusingly.

He didn't even deign to look at her. She really meant nothing to him. He got up swooping his money into a bag and walked across to a corner of the room to where his safe was wall mounted. As he began to open the safe he said viciously, "You're just like your father. Always poking your nose in where it's not wanted." He hadn't lost any of his harsh Belfast accent. "You should have just done what I asked of you and then there would have been no need for any of this."

"What was the plan Uncle? Get your niece to deliver the counterfeit money because that way your Supplier would be more likely to take it on trust. What were you trying to achieve?" Mac asked.

Clearly, he couldn't bluff his way out of this one. They already knew more than was good for them, Uncle Pat realised. He shouldn't have taken pity on Mac's best friend. It doesn't pay to be sentimental. He knew Ben had saved Mac's life on many occasions but nevertheless, he was a soldier, and Pat would never have let him live in the old days. He opened the safe door and carefully placed the bag of money inside, finding his pistol, which he kept ready loaded, just in case. He picked the gun up and turned to face them. He made no show of hiding it. Sian gasped in fear and Mac felt his heart sink to his feet, wherever they were. He was bitterly disappointed. "I was trying to close the network down," Uncle Pat explained. "The idea was, when Mr Won handed his dealers the money, it would start a War. I wanted them all to kill each other so I could be rid of them. I knew I couldn't just drop out of the game. Won knows too much but I was tired of him and the business. I'm getting old Daniel and I wanted to do things by the book from now on. This Casino is legitimate. It makes a lot of money legally and I've always told you that it's yours, when you're ready. I've left it to you in my Will but I may want to opt out before then. You can't work for that thankless British Army any more. Why not come and work for me? Get a feel for the place and when you're ready you can have it all, son. I'll bow out and I won't interfere, I promise." It was a last ditch attempt by the old man to stay reconciled with his potential son. He was being genuine and hoping against hope he could lure the boy with promises of wealth. "You can be a millionaire," he continued relentlessly. "Your girlfriend, I read in the Press lately about her husband. He's a Pop star, isn't he? No doubt worth a fortune. As his ex she will be worth a fortune too. How will you cope with that son? I know you. You're too much a man to live off a woman. Take over here and you can be her equal."

He was offering up a strong argument and tempting though it sounded Mac couldn't get his head around what his Uncle had done. "Why, Uncle Pat?" he asked desperate to try and find some good in him, still. "With all the money the Casino makes, why would you need to get involved in drugs?"

"I told you," he answered his heart going out to the boy. "That was then. This is now. I needed to get started but I didn't keep the money from the drugs for myself son."

"What do you mean? Where did it go?" Mac asked.

"It was for the love of our country, boy. It was for Ireland," he replied passionately.

Sian interrupted the conversation. She had begun to understand which direction it was turning and wanted to know it all now before she died. "What did you mean Uncle, when you said I'm just like my father? Did he find out about you? Did he threaten to arrest you?" Anger was making her brave.

"Always poking his nose," he said vehemently. "He couldn't leave it. I had to put a stop to his interfering. It was for the cause, don't you see?"

Mac was horrified. He had tears in his eyes. "What are you saying? Did you plant the bomb under dad's car?" It was the ultimate betrayal. He didn't know if he could handle any more of this emotion. He felt sick to his stomach.

"In the end it backfired on me, didn't it?" his Uncle continued unfazed. "You went and joined the Army, you silly sod. I couldn't believe it when you went to work for the enemy. I thought you were smarter than that, son."

"Don't call me son," Mac was starting to choke.

"Why not?" Uncle Pat asked him cruelly. "It could be true."

Sian gasped. She didn't think this man could sink any lower. She was so angry she just reacted on instinct and picked up the heavy glass paperweight on his desk and hurled it at his head. It struck him on the side of his head and knocked him sideways. While he was off balance Mac's training suddenly kicked in and he pushed his chair towards him knocking him off his feet completely. He heaved himself out of the chair and jumped on top of his Uncle struggling to get the gun off him. His Uncle had been caught off guard and dropped it. He struggled now, trying to get the weight of his nephew off and reach the weapon. When Mac hit the ground it had hurt like stink. Pain had seared through the stumps where his legs used to be and he felt like retching. He had to overcome the feeling and keep his Uncle down. He reached in his pocket and pulled out the knife and the two men struggled to take control. They were rolling and fighting and neither could get the upper hand. Uncle Pat was older but he was a reasonably fit man. Mac was not. He was close to passing out but he couldn't let that happen. Their lives depended on his staying awake. The knife flew out of their hands too and his Uncle was gaining. He was getting on top of Mac now. "Get the gun Sian," Mac shouted at his sister who had been rooted to the spot after initiating the attack.

She followed orders immediately and managed to find the weapon under the upturned desk. She had never even been close to a gun before, let alone fire one and her hands were shaking as she pointed it towards her Uncle. "Get off him," she tried to sound assertive but was trembling inside.

They stopped struggling and Uncle Pat stood up. Mac was helpless, his hurt body spent and he remained lying on the floor, frightened for his sister. "Give the gun to me Sian," he said trying to keep her calm.

She looked at Mac and at her Uncle and kept the gun trained on him. He was moving towards her. She kept stepping backwards trying to keep the distance between them but there was nowhere else to go when her back hit the wall of the office. "Keep back," she said to him, her voice betraying her terror.

"You're not going to shoot me, little girl," Uncle Pat said condescendingly. He held out his hand, "Give the gun to me before you kill us all." He felt confident. She was clearly completely out of her comfort zone.

"Ignore him Sian, give me the gun," Mac told her but he was starting to lose conscious.

Sian looked at her brother and then, at her Uncle closing in on her menacingly, and fired the gun at point blank range.

CHAPTER SIXTY-FOUR

"I'm so frightened Dad," Marika told her father over a cup of coffee in Antonios.

"I'm sure he will be fine," Jonathan told his beautiful daughter. He was feeling so good today nothing would bring him down. He had been having a nightcap with David when the message had come through on his mobile. He had tried to ignore it out of politeness but something compelled him to look at it when his host went to find his cigars. He had nearly choked. True, they had definitely broken the glazier between them that evening, but she had given no indication when she left that she was about to forgive him any day soon. Let alone, less than an hour after leaving. He was excited and checked his diary immediately to ensure he was free Friday night. If not, he would move heaven and earth to clear his engagements. This was one date he was not going to miss, not for all the tea in China.

"But it's been over a week," Marika's voice brought him back.

"Yes, but didn't he tell you he might not be able to call for some time," Jonathan tried to reassure his daughter. It was a task he was well used to. Marika had found the perfect career. All her life she was known as the drama queen with an over active imagination that kept the entire family amused. He was always the shoulder for her to cry on, the ear for her to vent her fears and the punch bag for her when things were not going as they should. He had endless patience where his daughter was concerned.

"Yes he did," she accepted. "It's just that I know he's doing something really dangerous and what would I do dad, if something happened to him?"

"He's a professional honey. Just like you, just like me. Living dangerously is what he does and I'm certain, having got to know him, he does it well. You just have to trust him," he told her patiently.

"That's what he tells me," she accepted again. "Dad, I love him so much. I don't think I could go on if something bad happened."

Jonathan gave her a comforting cuddle which always made her feel tons better. "Nothing will happen, Princess because you and Ben are going to have that fairy-tale wedding you always dreamed about when you were a little girl and I'm going to see to that."

"Thanks Dad, I'm being a drama queen again, aren't I?" she cheered up.

"Just a smidgeon," he laughed. "But that's okay. It reassures me all is well with the world."

"You're in a good mood today," she suddenly realised.

"Am I?" he asked her teasingly.

"What's going on Dad? Has she finally forgiven you?" Marika was back in his world now.

"Seems so," he said smugly. "We've got another date."

"Wow! Don't muck this one up Dad," his youngest daughter warned him.

"That's a bit unfair," he protested. "It wasn't like I intended to stand her up."

"No, that's true. You're my hero Dad," she cuddled him again.

"Did I tell you who she is?" Jonathan asked.

"Yes Ann Marshall."

"Yes, but I only realised the other night Ann Marshall used to be married to Jud Marshall the celebrity who was killed by the man who ran over Charlie. She came to the hospital back then and I met her. I was hypnotised by her beauty even then," Jonathan recalled.

"I knew that Dad. Have you only just realised? Honestly, you're hopeless sometimes. Rebecca and I made that connection ages ago," Marika scolded him. "What's even more exciting is that she must be the step-mother to the Tim Marshall!"

"Oh who's he?" Jonathan teased his daughter. He knew only too well she had been a fan of Tim since a teenager.

"Can't wait for your Wedding Dad," she teased back. "He'll be on the Guest list surely."

"Hey, we're going on our first date," he said. "Give me a chance."

They were interrupted by the sound of Marika's mobile. She had it switched on all the time for Ben and eagerly checked to see if the call was from him. She didn't recognise the number. When she answered a police officer identified him-self to her and told her that a Sian McManus wanted to speak to her. She was taken aback but agreed to the call.

"Marika," Sian said tearfully. "I'm sorry to call you but I need help and I didn't know who else I could rely on."

"That's okay Sian," Marika said intrigued and concerned. "What's going on?"

"I'm at the main police station at Liverpool, being held in custody, so I'm only allowed one call. I've been arrested on suspicion of murder," she explained.

"What?" Marika almost shouted down the phone and people in the café all looked towards her. "What's happened? Are you all right?"

"Yes I am but poor Daniel is back in hospital up here. Can you let George know? Also, do you know a good lawyer?" Sian asked her.

"I'm sitting next to one now," Marika tried to reassure her. She knew her father wouldn't be able to help with this personally but he would certainly know someone who could.

"Is Ben back yet?" Sian asked tentatively.

"No. He's abroad still," Marika told her trying not to get all tearful again.

"Oh, it's just that he might be able to help. He has the contact of the police in Kuala Lumpur and the police here need to speak with them," Sian explained.

"I'm sorry, Sian. Ben has gone AWOL at the moment and I've no way to contact him. What about Interpol?" Marika suggested sensibly.

"Yes, good idea. I'll tell the police here," Sian said. "I've got to go now but thanks."

"Don't worry Sian. We'll get you a lawyer and George and I will come on up straight away, okay?" Marika said before the call was ended. "Keep your chin up."

"Who was that?" Jonathan asked.

"That was Sian, poor girl. She needs your help badly Dad," Marika told him.

CHAPTER SIXTY-FIVE

At the exact time Mac was going into battle with his Uncle, his best friend met one of the hardest conflicts of his life. The boys were seriously outnumbered on this one and the planning committee had completely messed up. He was not a happy bunny. With two men down they would have to back down before reaching the target. Ben hated retreating but he had to think about the welfare of his men. In any event, they would be lucky to escape at all. The desert was such a hard place to operate in. He hated it. It offered little cover and was difficult to negotiate on foot. What's more, they had hoped to rely heavily on the element of surprise but the enemy appeared to have been expecting them. Just like Uncle Pat knew his days with his son/nephew were over. There were certain parallels with the two comrades in arms. For like Mac, Ben too lost consciousness, when a stray bullet struck his helmet.

When he woke up he was lying in a very uncomfortable position. He was freezing cold, his body ached from the hard floor and it was so dark he found it hard to focus. He tried to move but found his arms and legs shackled with chains attached to the hard floor. His head was thumping and his brain in a turmoil but it didn't take him too long to realise he was in serious trouble. He heard the sound of keys unlocking a door and some light flooded into his Cell. Two men entered the room and unlocked his leg shackles. They grabbed him under his arms and sat him up. Then, they just started kicking him. It was brutal. When they were done they left him to lie in his own blood and he was back in total darkness. This started to become a routine, he realised. He had no concept of time but just as he might be drifting off to sleep back they would come and wake him from his dreams with more pain and torture.

Ben had been trained for days just like this one but when it actually happens for real, it is just terrifying. Before he met Marika he would not have been scared, he realised. He would have provoked his tormentors in the hope they would finish him off quickly and save the agony. Now, things were different. He had so much to live for. He must stay alive for her.

CHAPTER SIXTY-SIX

By the time Marika had filled in George and arranged cover for her-self at the theatre that night, her father called to say he had a brilliant criminal lawyer on the case. The girls drove up to Liverpool together. George was anxious to go to the hospital and Marika wanted to go to the police station. They decided to split up and George dropped Marika off at the station before finding her way to the hospital. She had called Dr Havers before leaving home and he had told her he would speak to doctors up there and keep her updated. True to his word he had called her whilst she was still on the road to say that Mac was comfortable. He had injured his legs but they had re-stitched his wounds and given him some serious painkillers. He was going to survive this episode but he was rapidly using up his nine lives. She would give him hell. What was he thinking? She had been at her Solicitors discussing her divorce when he and Sian had crept off. They had left her a note but she had no idea what they were intending to do.

When Marika got to the police station she found Sian was in consultation with her lawyer. She had to wait a long time before being informed about what was going on. In the end the lawyer took care of everything. Interpol had confirmed their interest in the deceased and the police were excited to have such a major criminal to investigate, albeit posthumously. When Sian had pulled the trigger, Uncle Pat had died, instantly.

Sian was released on police bail after the charge was reduced to manslaughter. It appeared on the face of it to be self-defence but the only witness was not fit to give a statement at that present time. There would most likely be a trial but Sian's lawyer was confident common sense would prevail. No jury would convict her, he assured her.

She was delighted to find Marika waiting for her and the two girls embraced. Sian had been in such shock after the shooting and had had to hold herself together all this time. She still had to find out how her brother was before she could let herself go and insisted on going directly to the hospital, following her release. The Lawyer gave them a lift.

They found their way to Macs ward and found George sitting quietly by her man's side, holding his hand and smoothing his hair gently. He had just gained consciousness again but was heavily sedated. Sian was so relieved to see him and he her. Suddenly the tears she had been holding back all day came and she sobbed in his arms. It was a touching scene between two siblings who hadn't been all that close, until recent events had changed that. George and Marika decided to leave them alone for a while and went to find something to eat.

When Sian eventually stopped crying Mac said, "Thank you sister."

"What for?" she asked him.

"Saving our lives," he said simply. "That was supposed to be my job."

"Did I do okay?" she asked.

"You did okay," he answered. The result of her actions would take a long time to sink in for both of them.

"It wasn't true you know," she said. "All that stuff about you being his son."

"No, of course not," he said. He couldn't bear to think about that now.

"And what he said about killing dad. Do you think that was true?" she asked timidly.

"I don't know Sian. It would seem likely given what we now know about him," Mac said with a sigh.

"It makes everything seem so unreal somehow," she observed. "In fact the last couple of months have felt completely surreal." She had certainly been through it.

"I know," he said trying to comfort her but beginning to fade.

"I've had a thought Dan, about what you asked me on the way up," she said more cheerfully.

It was enough to rouse him temporarily, "What about?"

"You asked me what I intend to do with the rest of my life. You can blame Uncle Pat for this. I think," she said, "I think, I might join the police force. What do you think?"

"I think your father would be very proud," he said before losing consciousness.

CHAPTER SIXTY-SEVEN

"Wake up Charlie, please wake up." Marika was having an unusual down day and she needed her brother. "I really miss you now."

"What's up misery guts?" her elder brother Matthew had joined them.

"What are comas?" she asked the boy who wanted to be the best doctor in the world.

"It's a state of unconsciousness. When people have suffered a massive trauma and need time to recover without outside influence they might drift off into a coma. It's a sort of defence mechanism that the body uses to reinvent itself," he tried to explain. He was hardly an authority yet, but one day he hoped to be, of course. To his baby sister Matthew was an authority now. "Sometimes doctors can even induce comas for patients perhaps recovering from brain damage, that sort of thing, I believe."

"Will Charlie have brain damage?" she asked him.

"We won't know that sis, not till he wakes up," Matthew told her. "It's possible I suppose. He may not be able to see, or speak or walk. He may have no memory."

"Gosh," she exclaimed. "You mean he could wake up and not know who we are?"

"It's possible," Matthew said.

"Yes, but he'll know me," she objected. "I've been talking to him all this time and telling him stories and keeping him updated with everything that's going on. I'm sure he can hear me. I sometimes see him react. He even opens his eyes occasionally, doesn't he? Nurse Booth says that's natural but even she thinks he knows what's going on. Don't you think he can hear us Mattie?"

"Who knows? Let's just wait and see, shall we?" He didn't want to think about that now. His brother Charlie was a revelation in their family. He had been so full of life, just like Marika really. The two of them were very alike and he loved them to bits. "Come on, this isn't like you. What's really up?"

"Nothing," she said. "I've had a row with my boyfriend but it's not really that. I just feel fed up and I can't really explain why."

"It'll be your hormones kicking in," he told her still trying to sound authoritative. "You're growing up Marika. How serious is it with your boyfriend?"

"Not very," she confessed. "We've only kissed now and again and held hands."

Matthew laughed. "I meant the row," he said. "But I'm very glad that's all you've done."

"I'm only thirteen," she said. "Oh I don't know. He was complaining that he doesn't see enough of me but I've got lots of stuff. There's the theatre for a start and school and Charlie," she explained.

"And they all take priority over him," he stated feeling a bit sorry for the boyfriend.

"I'm a busy person Mattie. What can I say? Anyhow, how's your love life going?" she asked him.

"Like yours probably. What with her working shifts and me going up to Edinburgh soon I don't think it will last," Matthew said philosophically.

"It must be so interesting going out with a policewoman though. Does she tell you lots of gory stories?" Marika's dramatic instinct was kicking back in.

"Not really. We don't do much talking really," Matthew said smiling.

Marika was only thirteen but she wasn't naïve. She punched him in the ribs playfully. "I hope Charlie grows up to have a nice girlfriend," she said sweetly.

"I hope Charlie grows up," Matthew said solemnly.

CHAPTER SIXTY-EIGHT

"Wake up," the tormentor told his prisoner as he threw a bucket of water over the unconscious victim. Ben spat out some blood and a tooth with it as he came round again ready to face the next beating. He was pulled roughly by two guards and placed on a chair to face the English-speaking Interrogator. Here we go, he thought to himself.

"What is your name?" the man asked him.

"Roger Rabbit," Ben told him smiling through gritted and blooded teeth. The guard to his left made him pay for that one. There goes another broken rib.

"What are you doing here?" his Interrogator ignored his first answer.

"I thought I'd check out what you've got for dinner," Ben was defiant as he prepared his body to take the next assault.

"You think you are very brave now English dog, but I promise you, you will answer my questions and you will beg me to finish you off when we're done," his Interrogator threatened.

No, I won't, Ben thought to himself and I'm not English either. I am going to stay alive no matter what. "Go ahead," he told them. "Let's see what you can do." He wanted to drift off into unconsciousness again so that he could go on with his dream about Marika. It didn't take long. A few more kicks and punches and he was there, lying on a desert island with the girl of his dreams.

Another bucket of water washed over his face and brought him back to the present with a jolt. "Wake up imbecile," he was told. They pulled him up again and sat him on the chair. His hands were in manacles connected with a thick chain about two feet long. The water had refreshed him more than he realised because as the guard to his left moved in close to slap his face Ben suddenly saw an opportunity and took it. He elbowed the guard full in his face smashing his nose and sending him reeling backwards in pain. He jumped up ready to take the guard to his right and picked up the chair and smashed it over his head. Then there was the Interrogator to take care of. He did so by looping the chain from his manacles around his neck and pulling it tight, so that the hapless man could no longer breathe. It all happened so quickly and all because the guards had made the fatal mistake of under-estimating their charge. The interrogator fell to the ground lifeless, just in time for Ben to kick the first guard who was coming at him again. The kick landed on his broken nose and he doubled over grabbing it. Ben brought the chains down on his head and he dropped to the ground like a sack of coal. The last guard who had taken the chair on his head was moaning on the ground. Ben dealt with him before he knew what the hell was going on and the moaning stopped.

He searched their bodies quickly looking for the keys to his manacles but found none. He didn't want to waste any more time looking. He needed to get out before the alarm was raised. He had absolutely no idea where he was or how many others there were. The door to the Cell had been left unlocked. He simply walked through it and on finding some stone steps that appeared to lead to some light, took them. Out in the fresh air he was relieved to see it was night and he might find cover. The light he had followed had seemed bright in comparison to his Cell, which had been in pitch darkness but it was only the moon. He realised he had been in some kind of man-made bunker, probably a relic from one of the old wars and when he got outside he moved stealthily into the shadows trying to take in his surroundings. This was not the Camp his men had planned to attack. It was more like a satellite camp. He saw only two vehicles, both Jeeps and a couple of tents. He guessed the others might be sleeping in there but he had spotted the tell-tale sign of the designated sentry having a cigarette by the vehicles. He saw the red glow before he saw the shape of the smoker. "Naughty boy," he said to himself. These guys were not exactly professional but then he supposed they had thought they had nothing to worry about. Their one prisoner was supposed to be locked up in a concrete bunker underneath the sand dunes. Wrong.

He moved silently around the sand dunes until he was behind the sentry who was just putting out his cigarette. It was good timing for a condemned man would always be given a cigarette and he certainly was condemned. He didn't even know it until the chains went around his neck and tightened.

Ben collected his AK47 rifle, the usual choice of an insurgent, pleased to feel dressed again. He checked the vehicles. There was a large canister containing fuel, nearby, and he placed it into his intended transport. He had no idea where he was but guessed he may have to travel a long distance before finding any friendly faces out in this hostile terrain. He would head south but first he had to deal with the other vehicle. He considered waking the rest of the Camp up and giving them all a bullet but couldn't be sure there wasn't another major Camp nearby who might hear. Instead he lifted the bonnet of the other Jeep and found what he was looking for to disable it permanently.

There were no keys in his Jeep but he knew how to hot-wire a vehicle. He had the rifle at the ready knowing that the sound of its' engine starting up might attract some unwanted attention and he was right. As the Jeep burst into life he put his foot to the floor and hoped for the best. He didn't turn its lights on so he had to drive blindly but that would be safer until he put some distance between him and the camp. The enemy came out of their tents carrying their rifles but saw nothing to fire at.

He just had to hope their communication network wasn't so hot. The journey was rough as the Jeep lurched and fell over the dunes at full throttle but even though his ribs were feeling the full force he wouldn't slow down. He would keep going until the Jeep either ran out of petrol or it got light.

CHAPTER SIXTY-NINE

When Ann got to the Restaurant she was ten minutes late. It was deliberate of course. In fact she had even toyed with the idea of not turning up at all but she realised that would not be in her interests and besides she was better than that. However, when she walked in and couldn't see her date immediately, she began to have second thoughts. The Head Waiter greeted her like an old friend and took her coat, asking her to follow him. He led her straight across the dining room and out through the back. "What's going on?" she asked him when they were standing in a hall area at the back.

"Please follow me," he said smiling and opened a door from the hallway. The door led into a small private room that had a table for two all set up in the middle. The first thing she couldn't help but notice as she walked in was the beautiful scented smell of flowers. They were everywhere and in all shapes and sizes. Jonathan stood up as she walked in and took a moment to take in her beauty.

"Hello Ann," he said softly. "You look stunning. Thank you for coming."

She smiled when she saw him standing before her. He was very handsome and his eyes made her feel like she was the only person there. She was, almost, except for Luigi who held out the chair for her to sit down on. She took her place and Jonathan sat back down opposite her. "Can I bring you an aperitif?" Luigi asked.

"Ann, would you like a Kir?" Jonathan suggested.

"That's a wonderful idea," she told him and Luigi left them alone. "What's all this?"

"I'm sorry. I hope you don't mind. It's just that I've had a lot of trouble with the press since the events of last week following me about and I was afraid they might turn up here and make you uncomfortable with taking pictures of the two of us. I thought we might get away with it if we had a room to ourselves and Luigi was brilliant," Jonathan explained.

"Of course I don't mind. This is lovely and the flowers are amazing," she replied. Considerate, thoughtful as well as dashing, she thought. No wonder he has been labelled the most eligible bachelor and here she was on a date. Wow!

"Well you didn't appear to like red roses so I wasn't sure which flower is your favourite. In the end I decided I better try them all," he told her.

"That's unbelievably generous of you but you're wrong. I love all flowers and I'm particularly partial to red roses now," she said. "I've been so rude and I have a big apology to make to you for not thanking you before now for the beautiful bouquets."

"It's okay, really," he said modestly. "I should be apologising to you."

"Oh, you've more than done that," she told him. "You're not going to believe it but I had no idea what had held you up last week and you never said anything."

"I see," he laughed feeling relieved she hadn't ignored his apologies for nothing. "I suppose I thought you would see for yourself and I don't really like talking about it."

She liked that about him. He wasn't prepared to blow his own trumpet at the expense of someone's suffering. It showed a generosity of spirit and a good heart. Luigi brought their Kirs and gave them the menu to study. They chose their food and he left them alone again. Ann felt she was in some kind of fairy tale.

"Cheers," he said holding his glass up. "Here's to no more misunderstandings."

"I'll drink to that," she said happily. "This was a lovely idea Jonathan, thank you."

"You're very welcome," he told her. "I'm so pleased we've finally got round to it."

"How did you find out about this place?" she asked him.

"It was from my parents, actually. My mother loves her meat and the steak here is really something to write home about. They have an apartment not far from here," he explained.

"So, they live here in London. Do you live with them?" she asked him half joking.

"No," he smiled enjoying her little joke. "I have a small flat in Putney. I really should move somewhere grander I suppose but I've been a bit lazy about it and actually the flat suits me. My daughter lives beneath, which is lovely. How about you?" he asked her.

"Yes, I have an apartment too. I like living in the City and it's convenient just now," she answered still not giving anything away about her actual address, he noted.

"My parents also have a house in the country. It's a working farm actually and one of my sons runs it," he continued.

She liked that he was an obvious family man. "Just how many children do you and Sarah have exactly?" she asked him.

"Oh well, we only have two biologically together. My daughter that lives near me and as you heard at the party, the other day, is an actress and my son that you met in hospital. Sarah has four other children but I consider them to be my own too. They were all quite young when I first got involved with Sarah and I've always had a great relationship with them. You probably know Matthew, he's a doctor at David's hospital and of course you met Rebecca at the Charity Gala. There's just Mark then who runs my parents farm and Luke who is training to be a lawyer. What about you, tell me all about Ann Marshall," he requested and so she did. She told him about Benjamin, her children, their miserable life together and about Jud. She surprised herself by really opening up to him. Ann was quite a private person and although she was the trained Counsellor who encouraged others to vent their true feelings and emotions, she was not good at following her own advice. Until now that is. Jonathan was such a good listener and he made her feel that he was really interested in everything she had to say. Conversation with him was just so easy.

"There's something else I must ask you," she said after they had enjoyed their steaks.

"Fire away," he told her. She had clearly been so open and honest with him he felt more than a little obliged to follow suit.

"You and Sarah?" she almost laughed as she asked him.

"I know, I know," he said laughing back and putting his hands up in defeat. "I don't know what happened there. Thinking back I was so young and had no idea but I have to say I have no regrets. I love my children very much and they are what is important to me now."

It was a lovely admission and she admired him for it. "Fair enough," she said. "I won't tease you anymore."

"I guess I married the wrong Dixie," he said, his blue eyes piercing her heart.

"Obviously, we've both made mistakes," she agreed with him. "I'm a lot more careful these days, and you, you're the confirmed bachelor I believe."

"I don't agree with labels," he told her earnestly. "I think we are dealt a hand of cards and it's up to us how we choose to play them. Life is not a rehearsal is it, so we're going to make mistakes along the way but we mustn't stop trying to find the perfect flush."

"So, not confirmed then?" she asked him.

"Definitely not," he said. "Let's just say I hadn't met Miss Right before but it's not stopped me looking and hoping."

Ann liked the way he composed that sentence, as if it was in the past. "I've had a lovely evening Jonathan," she told him honestly as they got ready to leave. Luigi was busy collecting all the flowers for her to take with her.

"Will you be able to manage them?" Jonathan asked her.

"Do you want to share a taxi and give me a hand?" she surprised herself by breaking her first rule.

CHAPTER SEVENTY

Ben drove all night. He didn't even know for sure if he was going the right way but instinct told him he needed to keep heading south. He had pushed the Jeep to the limit and must have put a couple of hundred miles between him and the enemy before the vehicle finally spluttered and ran out of power. It was a fuel guzzler but then it was a difficult terrain and he had thrashed it. He had already used the extra container of fuel and it was beginning to get light. He couldn't afford to be out in the open when the sun came up. Not only would he be a sitting target but, the sun could get so hot in this part of the desert he would not survive. He grabbed the rifle and the canteen of water he had been pleased to find on the back seat and ditched the Jeep still heading south, but now he was on foot.

When he felt he had put a couple of miles between him and the Jeep and sensed the heat of the sun starting to warm his aching bones, he dug himself into a sand dune and took cover. He was almost completely buried in sand and covered his head with an oil rag he had taken from the vehicle. He couldn't take his upper clothes off without tearing them as he still had his hands manacled. He had thought about trying to shoot the chain but decided it was too dangerous. It wasn't long before sleep overtook him. He was absolutely shattered.

Ben repeated this routine for days. He walked at night and buried himself in sand during the day. His canteen of water had run out ages ago despite his trying to ration himself and he was getting weaker and more dehydrated all the time. After the fourth day without food or water he was almost dead on his feet. He had to force his legs on. He couldn't give in.

Eventually, he dropped to his knees unable to go any further and just about had enough strength left to bury his self. He must have slept for four hours or so because it looked like the sun was overhead when the sound of a bell roused him. He opened his eyes and had to close them again almost immediately, stunned at the sudden brightness. He tried again, squinting this time, and saw the outline of a goat. He kept absolutely still hoping the beast wouldn't get too close and felt his finger locate the rifles trigger under his sand blanket, just in case. He heard more bells and then could see the young goat herder walking with his animals. Walking to God knows where. What were they doing out here in the middle of nowhere? Was he just dreaming? It could be a mirage, he supposed. May be he was starting to lose it already. Perhaps he had taken a wrong turn or was he closer to civilisation than he thought. He'd like to capture one of these goats and drink its milk for he was very hungry and thirsty he realised. At least that meant he was still alive.

The Herd passed by without incident. They seemed to be heading south east and dream or no dream he knew he would follow their path tonight.

CHAPTER SEVENTY-ONE

As soon as Mac was fit to travel he was transferred by ambulance down to London and ensconced back at the David Essex Hospital for further treatment. His holiday at George's Apartment had been short lived and he felt very sorry for himself. He actually felt quite depressed and desperate to see his old mate, Ben. Only his best friend could really understand about such betrayal. The last thing George needed was another man suffering from depression. She tried to stay positive and set about getting her own life in order.

The divorce would still go ahead despite Nicky's mental state and she had started the search for premises in order to set up her own Veterinary Practice. She knew she didn't have to work for money but badly needed the distraction. She hadn't given up on Mac but realised he had his own demons to fight and she couldn't help him with that. He would figure it out for himself and when he did she would still be there for him.

Nicky had asked to see her and she had agreed although she didn't know what to say. In the end, she had gone to the Pub to see him there. Her father-in-law would be around and she would enjoy seeing him again, at least. It turned out to be a good decision for once as she and Nicky actually had a good talk and aired a lot of their grievances. It was good to say all those things out loud to him, about how much he had hurt her, and she didn't hold back. She didn't know if it was wise for him to hear them but he seemed so much better. He had received a lot of therapy from Dr Pamela Hayward and was definitely getting back on track. He accepted George's abuse and took it on the chin. He told her he realised they no longer had a future together and he would not contest the divorce. He was going to go back to his original plan, which was to leave the Band and try his luck as a solo artist in America. He wanted a fresh start and she wished him luck and genuinely meant it.

Sian was still a house guest at her apartment in Chelsea. She, too, was mentally bruised but showed she clearly had a fighting spirit. Once all the truth came out about Uncle Pats illegal dealings with the drug industry and his former life with the IRA the Crown Prosecution Service in Liverpool were prepared to drop all the charges against Sian and accept the self-defence argument. They realised it wasn't in the public interest to pursue a prosecution against her. Mac had given a statement in her favour of course and the gun belonged to their Uncle. This meant that Sian could pursue her sudden change of career to join the Police Force. She would no longer have a criminal record, and was just the news she needed to help her recover.

Marika went to visit Mac in hospital. She hadn't heard from Ben in over a fortnight now and felt desperate. She sensed something was wrong and needed to talk about it with someone who would understand. It was just the tonic Mac needed to stop him feeling sorry for him-self and ruminating over his own troubles. He had lost touch with the Army. His CO hadn't visited for some time and he couldn't throw any light on where Ben might be but he knew a man who could. He had plenty of friends in the Regiment and it would only take a couple of phone calls to find out. What he found out knocked him completely off track. He realised he had to start getting better if he was to help his friend out of this one and help him, he would.

He telephoned Buzz and then set about arranging physiotherapy in preparation for his artificial limbs. He was a man on a mission once more.

CHAPTER SEVENTY-TWO

"Hi Charlie," Daniel said sheepishly to his once best friend. "It's me, Dan. How are you doing? I'm sorry I haven't been for ages and ages. I started my new school and made new friends and somehow what with mum not wanting me to come while that man was still wanted by police, I just kind of forgot about you. That sounds horrible, doesn't it? It wasn't like that though, I promise. It's just, well life goes on Charlie, for the rest of us anyway. When are you going to join this world again? I can't believe you haven't woken up. Do you realise it's almost a year now? Anyhow, my new best friend turned out to be a dork. I told him all our secrets and he went and told everyone else and then these other boys all went to our camp and ruined it. It's all broken up now Charlie and no good. I punched him and he told on me to his mother. She told my mother and I ended up getting grounded for a week. Anyhow, while I was grounded I started thinking about you and how you would never betray me and I realised I'd been an idiot. Do you remember that time I went scrumping apples, from Mrs Brown's garden and you tried to stop me. Then she came out and I ran off and she caught you instead. She gave you a right telling off and you never told her that it was me. I was hiding behind the fence with the apples. You were dead loyal and I thought we should stay best friends forever. I'm sorry Charlie. I hope when you wake up you will forgive me but I don't care what mum says I'm going to keep coming now until you're better. She won't mind so much now that man has been caught and is in prison I guess. That was quite a big deal round here and it's all thanks to you he got caught. I heard my parents talking about it. It was in the papers and on the television and everything coz the man he shot was dead famous apparently. Well done Major. You're going to be so gutted you missed out on that excitement. This boy, James, I thought was my friend had some great computer games but it wasn't as much fun playing with them as it used to be playing with you. I really miss you Charlie and your fantastic imagination."

Part Five—
Coming Home

CHAPTER SEVENTY-THREE

Ben had changed his direction hoping to catch up with that goat herder again. This time he wouldn't hesitate. He would kill a goat and steal the herders' water. He couldn't afford to be sentimental or worry about getting caught any more. He was just too weak. Something in him was driving him on, stopping him from giving up. The temptation to just lie down and not get up again was very strong. He was beginning to lose his mind. He had forgotten who he was or why he was in the desert in the first place and whilst he knew in his heart there was a strong reason to get through this he couldn't remember what it was. As he stomped across the dunes his legs were beginning to feel like dead weights. He dropped the rifle unable to carry it any more. The manacles around his wrists were cutting into his skin and his ribs were still so sore. Suddenly, he thought he could see some lights in the distance but couldn't be sure it wasn't just his mind playing tricks on him. In any case, it was just before dawn and his body finally gave up. He collapsed, paralysed to the spot where he fell. He entered into a state of unconsciousness and never saw the sun get up less than an hour later.

CHAPTER SEVENTY-FOUR

Buzz had some good news for Mac. "I think I may have an idea where he is," he told his old friend and colleague.

"Go on," Mac told him, pleased his luck may be changing at last.

"I've heard on the vine that the Americans discovered some satellite camps surrounding the main camp, which our boys had targeted."

"How did you hear that?" Buzz never ceased to amaze Mac.

"You don't want to know. Let's just say I know how to infiltrate certain networks. We know where our boys were heading and that Ben got taken down just outside of that camp. Supposing, he was still alive and taken prisoner to one of the satellite camps. Apparently they were just old war time concrete bunkers buried in the desert," Buzz explained.

"That's a big suppose," Mac said not convinced.

"Ah, but I heard that when the Americans visited one of those bunkers they found four dead insurgents. Three bodies were found inside the bunker where there was evidence of a prisoner being held," Buzz told him joyfully. "Another body was found outside. All four had been killed manually, if you follow my meaning."

Mac was suddenly convinced after all. "Do you think Ben broke out?"

"Well somebody did, I reckon, and that somebody would have to be well trained in the art of self-defence and manual combat. Sound like Ben?" Buzz was feeling very pleased with himself and it showed on his face.

"Okay, let's just say, for the sake of argument, it was Ben. He made a break for it. This camp is in the middle of the Kalahari desert, right?" Mac started to reason. "Where would he go and how would he survive?"

"I can't answer that Mac. You know him better than anyone. What do you reckon?" Buzz asked him.

"Okay. South Africa is to the south and east. He would want to avoid Zimbabwe. He's got Namibia to the west and potentially more desert." Mac tried to remember his geography.

"South Africa then?" Buzz reasoned.

"Would he be on foot?" Mac was asking himself, as much as Buzz, trying to figure out his friends tactics.

"They found a defunct vehicle at the camp and tyre tracks," Buzz remembered.

"Good. He took a vehicle then and demobilised the other one. Let's say he got a couple of hundred miles under his belt before having to start walking," Mac was calculating.

"How long has he been missing?" Buzz asked him. He knew the answer but was joining in with Mac trying to help his reasoning.

"It's been ten days but we don't know how long he was held for, do we?" Mac realised.

"I don't think it could have been too long if he had the strength left to overcome three guards," Buzz said in admiration. "Let's just suppose he's been out in the desert and on foot for about seven days. He could be almost home if he kept his course and travelled by night."

"So many ifs and supposes," Mac said unhappily. "We need a search party somewhere around the edge of the desert and South African border. Know anyone with a helicopter who might help?"

"What about the Regiment? Aren't they still out looking for him?" Buzz asked even though he knew the answer to that one. Of course they would be concerned and would never exactly, give up, until they found his body but they still had a job to do and the target was still outstanding. The Americans must have been asked to do a swoop of the camps for them while they pressed on with their mission. Mac knew the CO would know as much as them but his hands would be tied until the mission was over and he didn't think his friend could last that long. Mac didn't answer and Buzz then said, "There's Jezzer."

Jezzer was a mercenary. He was ex-job. He had become disillusioned after a mission had gone disastrously wrong and he had lost his best mate. Mac knew how he felt. He was always a bit of a rebel. He had developed quite a drink problem following a particularly harrowing operation and the army had "let him go". He had been drummed out and reacted by becoming a mercenary. He had made a good living at first but his drinking had caused problems wherever he went. Eventually he had settled in

South Africa and was apparently running a flying school although he still liked his alcohol. He found the restrictions out there were more forgiving clearly.

"He will want paying of course," Buzz said.

"I'll find the money," Mac had made his decision. Jezzer might be high risk but right now he was all they had.

"I'll get back to you," Buzz said, delighted to be doing something positive finally, even if it was clutching at straws.

CHAPTER SEVENTY-FIVE

Ann was walking on cloud nine. She had been in such a good mood since the date with Jonathan. It was a marked difference from the last time. When the taxi had arrived at her address, Jonathan had kept the driver waiting while he assisted her with the flowers. She had invited him in but he had given her a gentle kiss on the lips before saying, "Goodnight." She had been disappointed and relieved all in the same moment. Her hormones were racing. There was no doubt she fancied him and even just the light kiss had left her lips reeling for more, but on the other hand, common sense told her not to rush things. She had been on her own a long time and it was a big step to take. She needed to know she was ready and she loved that he got that and respected it.

He telephoned her the next day to tell her he had enjoyed himself and to thank her for her company and suggested they might like to do it again sometime. She had tried to sound casual but had been delighted at the suggestion. "You said you like going to the theatre at David's, I remember," he said. "Would you like to see my daughters play at the Review theatre sometime?"

"Yes, I would," she had replied excitedly.

"It's only a small back street theatre in London but it's a good show. A comedy. Do you like comedies?" he asked her.

"Yes, of course," she answered. "I hope you haven't seen it too many times already?"

"Well no, just a few," he replied laughing. "I won't spoil the punch lines for you though, I promise."

"Okay," she said, "When?"

"I can probably get tickets most nights," he admitted. "It's one of the perks of being related to the main star. How would Friday suit?"

So they had their second date and things were definitely looking up.

CHAPTER SEVENTY-SIX

There was no doubt Ben would have fried where he lay if the brothers had not found him. He was so close to his goal it would have been a tragedy. The lights he saw were indeed at the end of the road. He had travelled nearly four hundred miles across desert, half of it on foot and without provisions. It was a miracle he was still alive. The boys were not supposed to leave the township compound but they had been in trouble at school and decided not to go in that day. Their game of soldiers had often over spilled from their secret little hut on the edge of the desert as they loved to hide behind the dunes and attack one another. They had spotted what looked like a bundle of clothes in the distance but it was much further away than they had first thought. Had they realised the desert plays such tricks on your eyes they might not have gone to investigate but once they started to, they had to go on. When they found there was a body, inside the clothes, they had hesitated before approaching too close. Eventually curiosity had gotten the better of them and they had moved in and poked and prodded the mound.

They were lucky Ben was out of it or they might not have survived his response.

"He's got chains on his hands," the younger boy said to his brother. "Is he an escaped prisoner?"

"There are no prisons near here," his brother told him.

"Then, why has he got chains?" asked the younger boy.

"I don't know. Is he dead?" Umbabo was the elder boy, by one year.

"I think so," Mimbabo replied. "What shall we do?"

"We'd better go," his brother said. "We're not supposed to be here."

"But we can't just leave him?" Mimbabo said disappointed at his brothers' reaction.

"Let's check his clothes. See if he's got anything on him," Umbabo suggested and began checking the soldier's body. His fumbling was enough to rouse the unconscious Ben. He grabbed the boy's arm tightly making him jump out of his skin. Mimbabo jumped back in fright while Ben held on to Umbabo.

Realising it was just a boy he released his grip on his arm and said, "Water." The boy stared at him open mouthed not understanding. "Water," he repeated, barely able to speak through parched lips.

"What's he saying?" Mimbabo asked his brother in his own native language. Umbabo moved away from the stranger, grateful to be released.

"Waahhter," he tried to imitate the strangers' word.

"Yes," Ben said when he heard, nodding towards the boys, "Water."

Both boys realised that this stranger was in no position to hurt them and were fascinated with him. He was speaking a strange language that they didn't understand but it was exciting. "What does that mean?" Mimbabo said to his brother.

"I think it could be his name," his brother suggested and turned to the stranger pointing at himself saying "Umbabo."

His brother joined in, "Mimbabo."

They both pointed to Ben and said together, "Waahhter?"

It was the most frustrating moment Ben had ever experienced. "No," he whispered hardly able to speak. "No. I'm Ben, you Mimbabo, you Umbabo."

"Ahh, Ben," Umbabo said enjoying himself.

"Yes," Ben said, "and I need water please," he smacked his lips together and tried to show he was thirsty. He imitated someone drinking wishing he had Marika's talent for acting.

The boys looked puzzled but then the penny dropped. Umbabo had a bottle of water in his school bag, back at their hut and raced back across the sand, to fetch it. He was back in no time and offered the water to the stranger. Ben was thrilled and took it eagerly from him, guzzling the entire bottle straight off. Both boys smiled. They had obviously done the right thing. When he had finished Ben looked at the two boys who were both smiling back at him and wondered if he wasn't hallucinating. "Where am I?" he asked them futilely as they clearly didn't understand English.

"Waahhter?" Umbabo asked him again.

Ben nodded and looked around him. He could vaguely see the outline of the wooden hut where the boy had ran to, to get the water. It looked like he had found civilisation at last. Whether it was friendly or hostile remained to be seen but these boys were certainly not the enemy. He tried to get up but it was difficult with his hands chained and his body so weak. The boys helped him and he gave them his best smile. He started to walk towards their hut and they walked with him, half propping him up. "Is this your house?" he asked again unable to communicate. He could speak some Arabic and small smatterings of Swahili but their chatter didn't seem to equate to those languages.

They helped him to reach the hut and he went inside but was disappointed to find nothing in there. It had obviously once been a home but was now deserted but it did offer him shelter from the sun, at least. He sat down on the sandy floor leaning against the wooden wall. Mimbabo picked up his satchel and found his water, which he gladly handed to the stranger. Ben drank it greedily, just as he had the first bottle. The boy also pulled out his school lunch box and offered Ben its' contents. He was very happy when he saw the fruit and piece of bread and patted the boy to show his appreciation. Again, he ate the food greedily, but after, felt decidedly groggy. His head was raging with pain. He had taken a hit to the head before capture and had suffered many blows whilst a prisoner. The dehydration was the final straw and it felt like his brains were about to explode inside his head. He had to shut his eyes, the brightness of the sun, even inside the building, was blinding. He quickly fell asleep and the boys sat with him until it was time to go home. They would tell no-one of course as they should have been at school but Ben would be their secret and tomorrow they would return with more "waahhter" and food.

CHAPTER SEVENTY-SEVEN

"Hey Charlie, it's me, Luke." Luke was on hospital duty tonight and had come straight from school. He had brought his brother a comic and would read him the stories from it if he ran out of conversation. "Schools crap as usual," he said. Unlike his elder brother Matthew, Luke was not a worker. He was just as ambitious but wanted to get there the easy route if possible.

"You've missed a year now brother, you lucky dog. You better hurry up or I won't be there any longer to look after you. I've got a secret Charlie and you're not to tell anyone but I know you'll love it. I've got a cat. Whatever you do don't tell mum, you know how she's dead against any animals. It's a stray and came into our garden about a week ago, miaowing for food. It was ever so thin and its' coat was all dirty and ragged so I gave it some milk from the kitchen when mum wasn't looking. It lapped it up and was all round me purring and rubbing its' body up against my legs, poor thing. It didn't have a collar or anything and as it didn't look like anyone had been feeding it or looking after it, I decided to keep it. I made it a bed from a blanket I stole from the airing cupboard and put it inside the garden shed where we keep our bikes. Mum never goes in there and there's a hole at the back just big enough for the cat to come and go. I think it's a girl cat but I'm not exactly sure. I've called it Georgie, which covers it either way, I reckon. He or she is really friendly and loves to sit on my lap. When mum goes to her exercise class or whatever I let Georgie come in the house. Marika knows all about it, of course, and she adores Georgie just like me. I've sworn her to secrecy though, so she probably hasn't told you but I think I can trust you. I know you've always wanted a pet and mum is really mean not to let us have one. Hopefully, you can meet Georgie when you come home and you can help me sneak food and milk outside for her. It's not too difficult fortunately as you know how mum never knows what's going on.

That's a pretty good secret, isn't it? Anyhow, would you like to know what Dennis the Menace is up to, these days?" He took the comic out and began reading.

CHAPTER SEVENTY-EIGHT

It seemed like a real stroke of luck for Ben that the boys had found him just in time to stop him frying in the heat of the sun but in fact another five minutes might have seen a different rescue altogether. Jezzer flew over the exact spot where he lay just an hour later, on his way to the desert. He searched as far as he dare and fuel would allow but of course was just too late. He tried in vain again the next day widening his search and again the day after but the news wasn't good for Mac and Buzz.

Mac, feeling encouraged by Buzz's visit had bucked himself up completely. He told Dr Havers he wanted to begin physiotherapy and cut down on some of the heavy drugs he was on. He started to work hard for his recovery and realised he owed Gina an apology. After a few days of intense recuperation he sent her a text asking her to please pay him a visit.

George had busied her-self with sorting out her life and had been quite glad of the respite. However, when the text arrived, she was delighted and responded immediately. She was shocked to see the change in her man. He was sitting up on his bed looking altogether brighter and they exchanged a tender kiss. "Thank you for coming Gina," he told her. "I've been a right a**e, I'm so sorry."

"It's not your fault," she told him tenderly. "You've been through hell, I know that and I didn't blame you. I just thought it best to let you work it out yourself. I'm sorry too."

"Things are going to get better now," he told her positively. "I promise."

"No promises necessary," she said. "I just want you home again."

"I've been doing a lot of physiotherapy work and have tried my new legs," he informed her. "I can't walk very well and certainly not unaided just now but I'll get there. It will take time I realise but I'm on a bit of a tight schedule."

George was thrilled to hear he had already tried his artificial limbs and was working towards being able to walk again. She hadn't expected anything so drastic for ages yet. She didn't want him to run before he could walk though and warned him about being impatient. "Why don't you just come home again first and spend time recuperating. Your respite was interrupted last time," she said. "I don't want you overdoing things again."

"Instead of going home, how are you fixed to go away for a few days with me?" he asked her unexpectedly.

"Go away," she said shocked. "You mean take a holiday?"

"Sort of," he replied mysteriously. "Have you ever been to Africa?"

"What are you up to now?" she asked him suspiciously. "Mac, you know what happened last time you tried to go off on a mission before you were ready. Please tell me you're not thinking of doing something stupid again."

"Well, it is a sort of mission," he said sheepishly. "Only this time I'll have you with me to keep a check on me. You can make sure I don't do anything stupid."

"You are doing, even thinking about it," she told him.

"You haven't answered my question," he said cheekily, hoping to win her over.

"I went to Kenya once on a safari. It was wonderful to see the animals in the wild. I'm guessing we're not heading for Kenya though," she replied.

"South Africa has safari parks," he suggested. "We may just need to do another kind of safari first."

Suddenly, George remembered that Ben had gone off to Africa and that Marika was tearing her hair out because she hadn't heard from him in a couple of weeks or so. "Has this something to do with Ben, by any chance," she asked, letting him know she was on to him.

He smiled, "Yes, everything."

CHAPTER SEVENTY-NINE

Mimbabo and Umbabo were excited. They told no one back at home and conspired to steal more food and water for their secret friend. They would have to go to school the next day but could visit him on the way home. They often played for a couple of hours before going home and their parents wouldn't question it. They couldn't wait for the school bell to go and raced all the way to their hut eagerly anticipating meeting up with their special friend. Ben, refreshed by the water, they had given him the previous day, had dropped into a deep sleep. His head had been thumping and sleep was a welcome respite. He awoke, just as the brothers arrived and cursed because he still felt unable to move. He was relieved to see it was just the boys and they had come alone. Did this mean they hadn't told on him? He had no idea whether their families would be hostile or not and didn't feel ready to find out. He needed more time to recover and hiding out in this hut was perfect, especially if they kept up the supplies of food and water for him.

The boys were as delighted as he was, to see their friend had stayed in their hut. They offered him the food and water and he showed his appreciation with a big smile and a pat to their heads. They were thrilled. It was good to help this man and to do it in secret was exciting. They chatted away to him but he still couldn't work out what they were trying to say. Umbabo had also thought to bring some medicine for the man who looked very ill. He had stolen some towelling to clean up his wounds and some of the spirit drink that his father liked so much. His brother had been shocked when he produced the small bottle of whisky from his school bag and offered it to Ben. "If dad finds it missing you will be beaten every day for a month," he told his brother, but was secretly proud. Neither boy liked their dad drinking the spirit. He always seemed to get in a bad mood after. They hoped that wouldn't happen to their friend.

In fact, their friend didn't drink it. He poured some of it onto the towelling and rubbed it against his wounds, squirming as it stung. They looked open mouthed at him and especially when he lifted his shirt and they saw so many bruises across his body. "Can you get me an axe?" he asked them drawing the shape of an axe on the sandy floor, after finishing cleaning up his wounds.

They looked at the drawing and looked puzzled. He showed them the chain between his manacles and how much the manacles were cutting his wrists, which he had to try to soak with the whisky soaked towelling, so they might understand what he needed the axe for. Mimbabo seemed to get it and nodded. He would steal the hatchet from the woodshed behind their school tomorrow and bring it to Ben. He tried to ask Ben why he had the chains and manacles but conversation was difficult. It was like playing a game of charades but the boys were obviously enjoying themselves and so Ben humoured them and tried to mime back. In the end, they began to understand one another with their mimes and the brothers were very happy with this. Ben was glad. He needed to keep them on his side, at least until he was stronger.

He just couldn't be sure if he had made it to safe ground or not. He believed he had been heading for South Africa and if the boys were speaking Afrikaans then he'd probably arrived but it was a chance he couldn't afford to take. Not yet anyway. Maybe in a couple of days when hopefully his strength returned, he could take more risks, but he knew he was in no position to defend him-self now, if the shit hit the fan. He had come too far, not to throw it all away. He couldn't actually remember what he should be afraid of, but instinct told him not to trust anyone. It was his survival skills kicking in.

CHAPTER EIGHTY

"Did you enjoy it?" Marika asked Ann after being introduced to her, by her father, backstage.

"I loved it," Ann admitted honestly. She couldn't remember when she had laughed so much. The play was a farce and somewhat predictable in parts but nevertheless so beautifully acted it couldn't fail to make one laugh.

"You're not just saying that?" Marika checked.

"Darling, stop fishing for compliments," her father scolded her. "Ann said she loved it, now come on, get your coat and I'll take you two beautiful ladies for a drink."

Marika didn't need a second invitation. She had been pretty low this past week and welcomed the chance to go out with her beloved dad and his new girlfriend. She had coped the first week Ben had not been in touch and the second had been a bit fraught but now she was sick with worry. It was a testament to her fine acting skills that she could still go out every evening and put on a good show.

They walked across to the Pub opposite, which was packed with other Theatregoers, but without her make-up Marika was able to mingle unnoticed. While Jonathan got the drinks in, she sat with Ann and set about grilling her. She had introduced Ben to her father and he had passed the test with flying colours. Now it was the turn of Ann to past the test with Marika. "I understand you live in London," she said to Ann.

"Yes, Knightsbridge," Ann responded.

That's a posh address, Marika noted. "So do you go to lots of shows?"

"I try to but lately I haven't seen many," Ann answered her honestly. "I would never go alone and a lot of my friends have partners. I understand you live just below your father?" Ann turned the tables.

"Yes, it's great actually. We're very close, as you probably realise," she said, not really meaning it to sound like a warning.

"That's nice," Ann said quietly. "I know most of your family now."

"Really," Marika asked, annoyed she was one of the last to meet Ann.

"Yes, well, I work at the David Essex Hospital where your brother Matthew is a doctor and I met your sister Rebecca at the same time I met your father."

Ann started to explain.

"Oh yes and of course you know my mother from way back," Marika remembered. "What was she like back then?"

"Very different from all accounts," Ann informed her. "We were both very young, of course."

"I hear she was a bit of a disaster," Marika was enjoying this. There was no love-loss between her mother and her and it was exciting to meet someone who might be able to offer some scandal.

Jonathan returned with their drinks and Ann decided to nip that conversation in the bud. She had no desire to spread tittle-tattle. "Let's just say she has changed a lot."

"Who has?" Jonathan asked trying to catch up on the conversation.

"We were talking about mother," Marika told him. "Cheers dad."

"Oh please, let's change the subject," Jonathan said. "Have you heard from Ben?"

Marikas' ebullient mood changed immediately. "No Dad and I am really worried. I think Mac is too, but he is going to try and find out from his work for me, if there's any news."

Jonathan explained to Ann that Ben had gone off to do his duty. "Marikas' boyfriend is best friends with one of your patients at the hospital, Mac is it?"

"That's what Ben calls him. I don't actually know his real name would you believe," Marika said. "They were in the Army together until Mac got blown up and lost his legs," she informed Ann.

"I think I know whom you mean," Ann said recalling the handsome soldier that Nicky Darrow's wife George, had taken up with. "He's very brave."

"So's my Ben," Marika stated. "That's what worries me."

"I'm sure he'll be fine," her father offered her comfort. "He looks to me like someone who knows what they're about."

"So Ann," Marika decided to change the subject this time. "Do you have children?"

"Yes," Ann answered. It was not a subject she liked to talk about but it would be rude not to say anything. "I have three children by my first marriage and some step-children from my second."

Luckily for her it was her stepchildren that Marika was most interested in. There was no doubt Ann had a much better relationship with Jud's children than with her own. It was actually one stepchild, in particular, Marika was keen to hear about and Jonathan realising where she was going smiled inwardly. "Do you see much of your stepchildren?" she asked.

"When I can," Ann replied. "They are all grown-ups now and have their own busy lives so it's not as often as we might like."

"I have to tell you," Marika decided to come clean. "I have been a massive fan of Tim Marshall for like only all my life."

"Yes," Ann said not surprised at all. "You and the entire female population of this country I think".

"Is he big-headed about that?" Marika asked not really wanting to know if he was. She would hate to be disillusioned after all these years.

"Tim?" Ann answered smiling, "No, not at all. He really is as lovely on the inside, as he is, on the out."

Marika was so happy to hear this.

CHAPTER EIGHTY-ONE

The two young African boys kept up their secret for several days and Bens' health improved all the time. He was physically on the mend but his mind was still very confused. He could remember nothing about who he was or where he came from or indeed how he had got into this mess. The axe had broken the chain between his arms but he had been unable to free his wrists from the manacles. Still, it was a start. He was actually starting to have better communication with Umbabo and Mimbabo. Drawing and miming were the main medium but the odd words were beginning to stick. Noticing how he appeared to squint so much whenever daylight was allowed into the hut, Umbabo had stolen his mothers' sunglasses for Ben. She hardly ever wore them so hopefully would not realise they were missing for a while. Ben had been touched by the boys' sensitivity and the glasses certainly helped his headaches. There was something about the glasses too that rang a bell in his head. He felt there was a connection somewhere in his past to ladies sunglasses but couldn't think what. What he was trying to remember were the sunglasses left behind by Sian, in Kuala Lumpur, before she was abducted, but that memory was buried in his brain for now.

Ben was sitting cross-legged on the floor of the hut, enjoying some bread and fruit, brought to him by the brothers. They had been to school and eaten their own meal at home before coming out to see him tonight. It was just beginning to get dark and they would have to go home soon. Suddenly, Ben heard a sound that he recognised. It was the sound of gunfire. Both boys stood up in terror. "Rekelo," Umbabo said to his younger brother. "Quick, we must get home before they find us."

His brother was rooted to the spot and unable to move for fear. "What's going on?" Ben asked them.

"Rekelo are here and if they catch us they will take us away. We have to get home and hide," Umbabo said excitedly.

Unfortunately, Ben couldn't understand what he was saying. He put his glasses on and went to open the door of the hut to see for him-self what was happening. Both boys shouted at him and grabbed his arms trying to prevent him from going outside. "No, mister, you mustn't go out. Rekelo will shoot you. They are bad men." Umbabo pleaded with him.

"Rekelo?" Ben asked them puzzled.

"Yes, yes," Mimbabo shouted at him. "We have to stay here now and hide. It's too late to get home. They will catch us," he told his brother.

"Rekelo," Ben asked again, "Bad men?"

"Yes, bad," Umbabo told him, "Very bad."

Ben put his arm around both boys and led them to the corner of the hut and sat them down. He put his blanket that they had stolen for him, around them both and put his finger to his lips. "Be quiet and stay here," he told them hoping they would get the message. They were too frightened to move even when he went outside and closed the door on them.

Ben instinctively knew how to approach the scene without being seen. He saw a Jeep had pulled up in the middle of the township. The township was nothing but a collection of huts, much like the one he was hiding in, but it was home to about forty or fifty Africans. One of the "Rekelo" was standing in the Jeep and firing a rifle into the air. He was clearly drunk and enjoying himself putting the fear of God into the villagers. There were three other likely candidates of "Rekelo" who were on the ground and grabbing at any villagers who came within range. Then, Ben saw them enter a hut and pull out a woman. She was screaming and they were laughing at her and pushing her between them. Ben didn't like the look of it. He had seen scenes like this before but he couldn't remember where. He saw the woman's husband come out of their home and try to protest but he was dealt with by one of the men, who pistol-whipped him. Ben wondered why the rest of the village didn't come out to help but realised they were probably powerless against guns. He needed to make the "Rekelo" just as powerless and targeted the trigger-happy drunk in the Jeep.

Getting himself around the other side, so that the Jeep was between him and the men on the ground, he sprung up from behind the hapless drunk and pulled him backwards out of the vehicle. They both disappeared from the view of the other three, who were intent on stripping the woman. There was a great deal of screaming and shouting going on and no one heard what followed. He quickly silenced the drunk permanently and retrieved his rifle. The other three never knew what hit them but in seconds the woman was freed and the men were all wounded. Ben, quickly stripped them all of their guns, and held the rifle on them. He had no idea what he should do now but slowly the villagers began to appear, one by one, from their huts where they had been hiding. They had all been watching in awe. The sudden silence had also brought Umbabo and Mimbabo out of hiding and they couldn't believe their eyes. "Rekelo" were beaten.

Their female victim stood up and dressed herself and then she picked up a lump of wood and began beating one of the injured men with it. Her husband, his face dripping with blood, joined in and then the rest of the villagers were all at it. Ben just stood and watched keeping the rifle on them. It looked like he didn't have to worry about what to do with the men. He thought about getting into their Jeep and just driving away but the two young boys came over to him and hugged his legs in gratitude.

Then a tall African man dressed in white approached and told Ben, in English, to fire a bullet in the air. Ben obliged and the mugging stopped. The villagers all turned to hear what their leader was going to say. "Good People, don't do this," he said in Afrikaans. "Let them go. They can try to get home on foot. We will keep their weapons and vehicle. You are better than them."

Clearly this man was the wise chief. Ben didn't understand what he had said but could guess by the reaction of his followers. The injured men were kicked out. They might make it home or they might all bleed to death or be caught by some wild animals but their fate would be in their own hands and not at the hands of the villagers. It was the right thing to do.

"We owe you a debt of gratitude," he said in good English to Ben. "Umbabo, Mimbabo, who is this man?" he said to the boys in Afrikaans.

The boys looked a bit sheepish but were also immensely proud. "This is Ben, Okebe," they told their leader. "He's our friend."

Okebe smiled at them and patted them on their heads. "Good boys."

"Who were those men?" Ben asked Okebe, pleased to have someone he could communicate with, at last.

"We call them Rekelo. The enemy," he told Ben. "Thank you Ben. They terrorise this village and we are powerless against their fire power. Nearly every week they come to rape our women and steal our children. The villagers here have lived in terror of them, for quite a while. We have no police here to help and when we try to get out, to let other people know, they kill us. We have Rekelo on one side and the desert on the other. We have been unable to escape."

"I see," Ben said understanding their plight. Caught between the devil and the deep blue sea for he knew no one would wish to escape via the desert.

"How many of them are there?"

Okebe nodded. The stranger understood well. "Yes, Ben, there are more, of course, and they will be back for revenge."

"Perhaps you shouldn't have let those three go?" Ben told him. He was made of more ruthless stuff. "Have I started a war for you?"

"I am afraid so, but we are grateful nevertheless," Okebe answered. "It couldn't go on. Now we are more even. You took their guns?"

"Yes and there's this Jeep. One of you could take it and get help?" Ben suggested.

"No one here could drive it," Okebe told him. The stranger hadn't quite comprehended their poverty in this part of the world. The village had no vehicles or need of them.

"I can go, if you like," Ben offered although in his heart he felt his expertise, would be better used on the ground, defending the village.

"Who are you?" Okebe asked unable to understand where this stranger had come from. "How did you get here?"

"I came from the north," Ben pointed to the desert on their doorstep. "These boys," he pointed to Umbabo and Mimbabo, "helped me. Now it's my turn.

I'll go and get you help but you need to tell me where I should go."

CHAPTER EIGHTY-TWO

When Mac and George landed in Pretoria they both felt well enough to head straight for Jezzers' address. George had splashed out and treated them to first class on the aeroplane. The flight had been at night and they had both slept well. Mac was wearing his new legs but unable to walk without sticks. They hired a car at the airport, which George drove, leaving Mac free to navigate. They arrived at the broken down homestead that was Jezzers retreat just before lunch. Their host was flat out lying down on the couch on his veranda, hung over from the night before. He never even heard them arrive.

"Sorry about the greeting," Mac apologised to George. They had travelled first class but were now about to slum it. George looked around. The house inside was dirty and unkempt as she half expected but there was hope. The scenery was stunning.

Mac roused his old friend who wanted to welcome them both with a drink but they persuaded him to try some coffee. George obliged by making it and managing to find some clean cups. She even found some food, which would suffice for their lunch. Jezzer was very impressed. He made a few complimentary comments and Mac shot him a warning stare to back off.

After lunch the two men studied the map of the area and Jezzer showed him where he had searched. There was some other news from Buzz. He had heard that the Americans had located an abandoned Jeep, which had belonged to the Insurgents, in the desert. There were no tracks, it was too late for that but it gave them an indication of the direction Ben had been travelling in and also how far he would have had to walk.

Jezzer was sober enough to take them both up in his helicopter that afternoon and for a special treat for George he gave her a good look at the amazing scenery around Pretoria before venturing towards the desert. They returned that evening disappointed with the search but invigorated by the trip. George was beginning to realise that being married to a pop star had nothing on dating an ex-vet, when it came to excitement.

CHAPTER EIGHTY-THREE

Mrs Ann Marshall was really enjoying her courtship with Sir Jonathan Havers. He was such a gentleman and sometimes when he looked at her it just took her breath away. That week he had telephoned her to make a very interesting proposition. "What are your plans this weekend?" he had asked her.

"I don't think I have any yet," she answered intrigued.

"I've been invited to a dinner and dance type function at a medical convention on Saturday night and I would love it if you would accompany me," he said.

"Saturday night?" she checked, knowing she really had nothing else on.

"Yes, do you like dancing Ann?" he asked.

She adored dancing but seldom ever got the chance. It wasn't something she would ever do on her own. "Yes," she replied trying to sound nonchalant.

"Your boss, Sir David Essex and Lady Angeline will be there," he said trying to persuade her.

She didn't need persuading, of course, but was trying to sound non-committal for effect. "That will be nice," she responded quietly, hiding her excitement.

"There's just one snag," he told her.

Here we go, she thought, but what could possibly spoil an evening wining, dining and dancing with Jonathan. "What?" she had to ask.

"It's in Paris," he told her managing to sound concerned but secretly smiling.

"I don't really see that as a snag," she said, thrilled now.

"Oh good," he said. "Then you'll come?"

"Try and stop me," she told him, unable to hide her excitement finally.

"Okay, well I'll book the Eurostar. We can go straight from London on Saturday morning and be having lunch overlooking the Seine," he said.

"We will have to stay overnight, is that all right?"

"Of course," she replied. "Could we do some sightseeing on Sunday before coming home, do you think?"

"Certainly," he answered pleased with her reaction. "Have you been before?"

""I've been to Paris before, yes," she told him. "I've seen Notre Dame and climbed the Eiffel Tower, but I'd love to visit the Louvres, if we've got the time."

"Good," he said. "That's settled then. I'll book us a couple of rooms at the same hotel where the convention is being held. It'll be easier to stay there and I believe it's quite stunning. Is that all right?"

"Lovely," she said. "I'll trust your judgement. There's just one thing."

"Name it," he told her.

"One room should be enough," came the unexpected answer.

CHAPTER EIGHTY-FOUR

"Well Charlie, I survived," Judge Havers told his Grandson. "Your Grandmothers finally forgiven me for standing her up on the night of our fortieth wedding anniversary. We had a good family party at the farmhouse at the weekend and I gave her the rubies. The way to a woman's heart, eh, son? How are you now? I think you may have a bit more colour. Did you know you're being fought over at the moment? Your mother, bless her, wants to move you to a private clinic in London. Your father doesn't think it's a good idea. He says there is nothing any doctor can do to help. You will recover when you're good and ready but you know what a snob your mother is. She thinks you should be in a private clinic and believe me if I thought it would help I would pay for it myself but I am in agreement with your father over this one. Your father doesn't want to move you because he says your nurse here is one of the best and because we can all visit you a lot easier. If you're in London it won't bother me, or your Grandmother, of course, but your father is worried about Marika. She comes in nearly every day after school I understand, and Luke and Mark and the others. Your friend Daniel has been coming too, again. Your father doesn't think it right to take that away from them but your mother is putting up a fight. In the end, she may have the final say, so I think young man you'd better settle this thing now and wake up. Okay, that's my lecture over now let me tell you about my week in court. Now let me see. Oh yes, this week we had a trial. The defendants were a gang of hoodlums who had been terrorising this housing estate in the east end of London. It was a bit like the day of the Kray brothers. You wouldn't remember them but this family were actually foreign nationals and they called themselves, The Re, er Re, Ke something. Oh I can't remember the exact name now. My memory isn't what it used to be. It's an African word apparently, meaning, "The Enemy". They were just overgrown bullies and the police put together an undercover operation to flush them out. None of the victims would testify against them. Too frightened of reprisals and one can't blame them really so the undercover cop did the trick. It worked well and I'm pleased to say the Jury came to the right decision. I try to remain neutral as you know but nothing gets my goat more than the little man being bullied. Did you just smile Charlie?"

CHAPTER EIGHTY-FIVE

Mac wanted to be careful he didn't leave George out. When Jezzer announced he had some private work the next day, he decided to take George into the countryside in the farms Jeep. Jezzer had given him a rifle to take with him and briefed him on the trouble spots to avoid first. He would, of course, head North-west towards Botswana, just in case.

George was keen to see as many wild animals as she could and she wasn't disappointed when they unexpectedly came across a herd of wildebeest. She had her camera ready. After the herd had passed, Mac opened the flask of coffee for them and she gave him an affectionate kiss. "Thank you for this Mac," she told him. "I know how anxious you are to find Ben."

"I think he can look after himself for one more day," Mac told her, pleased that she was enjoying herself. If anyone deserved to, she did.

As they sipped their coffee, they suddenly heard the sound of a gunshot in the distance. "What's that?" George asked alarmed.

"Could be hunters I suppose," Mac answered trying to identify the fire power.

"Oh, I hope they're not shooting at these beautiful animals Mac. It's so unfair."

"Do you want to go and see?" he offered.

"Won't that be dangerous?" she wavered. "I mean Jezzer said to keep away from trouble."

"I know sweetheart," Mac answered. "But maybe you can help the animals?"

George knew it was a daft idea. What could she do? Yet, her heart told her she must try, even if her head told her no. She nodded at Mac, finished her coffee and they set off towards the direction of the gunshot they had heard.

CHAPTER EIGHTY-SIX

In the end Ben realised he couldn't just drive off and leave the villagers to it. He would have to pass through the place where the Rekelo hung out and then it was another fifty miles or so before he would reach any kind of town that might have a policeman. It would take too long and he feared for their safety. He had started this war and it was down to him to finish it. He asked Okebe to find him a villager who he could teach to drive the Jeep. It shouldn't take long to pick it up and it wasn't like the driver would have to worry about other traffic or road signs. He would just have to start the vehicle, work the throttle, brakes and the clutch. With the help of Okebe's translation it took him about half an hour to get the chosen man on the road. He would drive to the outskirts of the Rekelo camp site and wait until dark or they were drunk, before trying to get through. It was highly dangerous but the man was prepared to try. He was very brave.

In the meantime Ben would teach other men how to use the guns he had confiscated. He also organised a work group to reinforce the schoolhouse. It was the biggest building in the village and capable of sheltering all the children and women if necessary. Some of the older men set about making spears, which Ben found rather amusing. It was like preparing for the attack of the Zulu in reverse, he thought. Much to his relief, a native was able to remove the manacles around his wrists, finally. Okebes wife mixed him up a potion to put on his cuts. He had no idea what was in it but it worked a treat.

The day passed without incident. Perhaps the three hapless members of the gang had yet to make it home or had died en route. They could only hope.

He organised a night watchman and enjoyed a hearty meal with Okebe and his wife before settling down for the night. As he lay down trying to sleep he tried to remember something about his past. He had remembered his name was Ben. He had done so without thinking, but for some reason he couldn't recall anything else. It was very frustrating. Sometimes flashes of memories popped into his head, like the sunglasses. He could visualise them but where they came from was still a mystery. Then there was the girls face.

She was beautiful, dark hair, fair skin and the bluest of blue eyes. He could see her so clearly in his head but had no idea who she was.

CHAPTER EIGHTY-SEVEN

Ann and Jonathan had arrived in Paris at lunchtime as planned and enjoyed a typically French meal at a tiny riverside café. In the afternoon, Jonathan had to attend the medical conference and Ann decided to stay at the hotel and rest. The Hotel was extremely grand and their room was more like a suite, it was so large. She enjoyed a luxurious bath before getting into her best dress. When Jonathan returned to the room he just had time to shower and change. He looked magnificent in his dinner jacket and she was very proud to accompany him down to the ballroom. They were pleased to be seated close to David and Angeline Essex for the meal, which was typically drawn out over several courses. It was fabulous food though and Ann was enjoying the conversation at the table. When everything was cleared away they had taken to the dance floor and Ann danced all night. She had a number of requests but was delighted to end up with her partner for the last half hour of slow waltzes. She had drunk too much, she realised, and felt quite dizzy on dancing but when she rested her head on Jonathan's shoulder as they moved slowly to the music, she felt relaxed and so very happy.

When the evening was finally over and everyone had said their goodbyes the couple made their way back to their suite. David and Angeline would be leaving early the next morning as they needed to get home and so they had taken their leave before the end. Jonathan and Ann were among the last to leave the dance floor, content to just smooch together. When they got to their room, the smooching continued.

The following day the happy couple had breakfast in their room before setting off to visit the Louvres. Ann was walking on air. She had had a truly magical night and didn't want the weekend to end. She was happier than she had ever been in her life. The touch of culture was followed up with a short river trip and then they caught the train home.

By the time they reached London, Ann realised that she had fallen in love. When they arrived back at her flat she didn't want him to go home and let him know. He would get up early in the morning to collect his clothes from his flat for work. For now, he didn't want the weekend to end either.

CHAPTER EIGHTY-EIGHT

The firing Mac and George had heard had come from a rifle being held by a member of the Rekelo. He had been sent out to try and find his four friends who hadn't returned from a nights pillaging at the village by the desert. He found them but so had a pack of wild dogs, which were enjoying their remains. He had shot at them to scare them off and managed to injure one. He felt sick when he saw his friends but there was enough left of them to realise it wasn't the dogs who had killed them. They had bullet wounds. It didn't make sense. He collected one of the corpses and drove with it back to camp to show the others.

When Mac and George arrived at the scene they saw the two remaining corpses first. Mac told George to remain in the Jeep while he checked them out but as soon as she saw the injured dog she got out to check if she could do anything for it. Luckily for her it was unconscious and she was able to pick it up in a blanket and carry it back to the Jeep where she stemmed the bleeding from the animals' abdomen. Mac realised that the men had been shot before being mauled and there was nothing he could do for them. He saw the tracks of another vehicle heading off towards the rocks to the west.

"I need to get this dog somewhere I can operate and remove the bullet," she told Mac, ignoring the dead men.

"I suggest we get out of here and quick," Mac told her and they climbed aboard the Jeep and took off for home but not before Mac made a mental note of their location. He had a feeling he would be coming back here, and soon, but he would bring Jezzer next time, and George would have to stay behind and look after the dog.

CHAPTER EIGHTY-NINE

"I'm so cross with Mummy, Charlie," Marika told her brother. "She's going to have you moved to London to a private hospital and I won't be allowed to visit you until the weekends. I hate her and I've told her so. I can't bear not seeing you all week. It's so unfair. Dad has tried everything to reason with her but she's doing it to spite him, I reckon. They're getting a divorce now at last. Apparently Dad really upset her last time she was here with Father Benedict and that's probably why she's being so mean now. I wish you would just wake up Charlie and come home. We all miss you so much. Did Luke tell you about George the cat? She found out about that too and got rid of it. He used to let it into the house when she went out but she came home early one day and caught him. She went up the wall, poor Luke. George got taken to an animal shelter. When I grow up I'm going to rescue all those poor animals in those shelters and have them live with me. I bet you will too. I'd love a dog. Mark is so lucky as he has all those dogs on the farm. I'm really glad Daniel has been coming to see you too, lately. When you move to London he won't be able to visit at all I don't suppose, as his parents aren't really happy about it. He told me about your camp. I'm really sorry I didn't manage to keep it going for you but you can build another one. I hope when Dad gets his divorce he can meet someone really nice and get married again. He deserves to have a good woman look after him. I'll probably look after him when I grow up if he doesn't find anyone. Do you think he would like that? I'm not sure I'm ever going to get married. Ben and I had another row and I think he's going to chuck me soon."

"Hello Marika," Nurse Booth entered the room. "How are you today?"

"I'm just dandy nurse. It's everyone else who isn't," Marika said. "What do you think about my mother getting Charlie moved?"

"I shall miss him and all of your visits too," Nurse Booth admitted honestly.

"We've got to stop her," Marika said coming to a decision. She was going to fight her mother and win.

CHAPTER NINETY

As soon as George had got back to the homestead, she set about working on the dog. Mac was impressed to see her in action. She made up a sterile environment and set about removing the bullet and cleaning the wound. She didn't have her vets bag with her, of course, but improvised with what she could find in Jezzer's kitchen. The main worry was not having the necessary drugs to keep the animal sedated. It was very dangerous. If it woke up it could attack her and do her serious damage and for that reason Mac remained in the room with her, while she worked, holding the pistol Jezzer had provided. Luckily, the animal must have sensed the danger and stayed unconscious until the operation was completed. Then, they found a cage to house the animal.

"I will need to keep it sedated for a couple of days to give it time to heal," she told Mac. "Have you any idea where the nearest drug store is?"

Jezzer returned before Mac had time to respond and settled that. He would head back into town and get what she ordered, and probably visit the local hostelry while he was at it. Before he left, Mac told him about the corpses and said that he wanted to head back there tomorrow with his help. Jezzer was suddenly excited. Maybe he would give the hostelry a miss. A bit of action, like the old days, was the tonic he really needed.

Later that evening Mac told George what he was planning to do. She would have to remain to look after the dog. She was concerned for him but knew she had to learn to trust. Looking after the dog had exhilarated her. "Being a vet in England is one thing," she told him. "Looking after the care of wild animals is quite another."

"Would you fancy it full time?" he asked her.

"I'm not sure Mac. I'd never considered it before. What do you think?"

"I think you should take your time deciding," he answered wisely. Maybe when this is over we can take some time touring, visit some safari parks and you can talk to some of the vets out here. You would have to learn a whole new ball game, I suspect."

"Oh yes," she replied pleased with his response. He could be so positive where she was concerned. She wished he could be more positive about himself. "Wild animals are a whole new ball game that's for sure. I don't know much about them but I know the basics. It would certainly be challenging."

"A whole new start too?" he suggested. If she wanted to move out here and do her thing, which had impressed him enormously, he would support her. He didn't really have a job or home to go back to and maybe the change of scenery would do them both good. He wasn't against trying.

She was encouraged with his attitude. "I won't do anything without you Mac. It's got to be right for both of us. Also, there's Robert to consider."

Mac was delighted she had added that last bit. "Robert would love it out here but let's wait and see what happens. In the meantime I still have one more job to do. You'll be all right here alone?"

"I'll be fine but it's you I worry about," she told him affectionately. "Don't forget you haven't been out of hospital five minutes. What did we say about learning to walk before you run?"

"I'll be careful," he told her. "It's just that I've got a real funny feeling about those dead men. I think I'm about to find Ben."

CHAPTER NINETY-ONE

The scout had returned to camp with the corpse and his comrades had all been incensed. How could this happen? If it was the fault of the villagers, they would go there tonight and take revenge but first they needed some refreshment to get over the shock.

Whilst they were busy fortifying themselves with spirit the young volunteer driver from the village managed to sneak past without being spotted. He didn't know how to work the lights on the vehicle, which was probably a good thing. He had to drive slowly as he couldn't see that far in front of him but as soon as he felt he had got past the camp he put his foot down again on the throttle as Ben had taught him and hoped for the best. Unhappily he had only gone a mile or so when the vehicle drove straight into a ditch. He was ejected from the Jeep as it dipped its' front wheels into the ditch and landed some distance away, alive but unconscious. He would be lucky to survive the night.

In the early hours of the morning the Rekelo decided to visit the village. There were at least a dozen drunken men all carrying a weapon of some description. They piled into their two remaining Jeeps and drove off firing guns in the air as they went.

Ben had suspected there would be a night attack. He had taken the precaution of having the natives dig a large ditch across the only roadway into their village. They had found brushwood and leaves to cover up the holes. It might hinder the attack. Ben would position himself by the ditch ready to pick off the enemy if they fell.

It worked a treat. Just as their hope of help being reached, by the young man in the Jeep, had been thwarted by the hole in the ground, so too was the hope of the Rekelo, to drive right in and take what they wanted, also thwarted. The gunfire had alerted Ben and the Villagers to expect imminent attack and they braced themselves. Ben was anxious not to lose a single man on his team. He insisted most should lay hidden, except for him-self and two hand-picked men with the other guns

The Rekelo had driven into the village many times before and never met any resistance. So when the first Jeep arrived, carrying six passengers, the driver paid no heed to the brushwood and drove straight into it at full speed. The front wheels of the Jeep fell into the ditch at such an angle that the passengers, mostly drunk and not holding on, had all been thrown out.

Ben told his two comrades to cover him as he leapt forward to tidy up the fallen enemy. The first man he reached was dazed slightly from his fall but just about to get up when his head met the butt of Ben's rifle. The second was unconscious already, as his head had struck a rock, as he landed. Two others were getting to their feet but had lost their rifles and they were no match for the tall stranger bearing down on them.

The second Jeeps' driver had taken evasive action and managed to pull over just in time. Its' occupants, suddenly sobering up, jumped out with their guns and began firing at whatever moved. Ben's comrades decided to shoot at them to divert their gunfire from their friend. They weren't even close with their shots but it was good enough to keep the attention towards them. They had a pretty good cover and it was a particularly dark night.

Ben had failed to reach the final two from the Jeep who had taken to their feet and retreated back towards their gang but he had managed to retrieve several more weapons found lying about. He re-joined his comrades behind cover and checked the extra guns. All were more or less fully loaded which was good news. They might be able to hold the Rekelo at bay for now.

The Rekelo were in shock. They had found some cover just outside the boundaries of the village and decided to hole up there and take stock of the situation. They had no idea what was going on. The village was a soft touch. How had they managed to get weapons and enough courage to fight back? There were only eight of them and many more of the villagers but this had never mattered before because they had held all the cards. Now, this was different. They needed to think.

Suddenly, after all the excitement, it was deathly quiet. Everyone was waiting to see what would happen next. Ben told both of his back-up men to check on the women and children and let them know not to break cover until he said so. He asked them to stay with their families now and let them keep the guns they had. He still had four spare rifles to play with. He didn't think the enemy had gone, of course, but he could see these men were out of their depth. He didn't want the responsibility of worrying about them when the next attack came. The Rekelo had been caught out tonight but there would be no element of surprise next time around. It was obvious the villagers wanted to help him but they weren't soldiers and not cut out for this work. For some reason, he was. He couldn't explain why but he instinctively seemed to know what to do and the fight had set his adrenalin racing. He wanted to protect these people and so was prepared to take on the final eight by himself if necessary.

Before they went the village soldiers collected the two unconscious men and carted them off. The other two Ben had dealt with, would be no trouble. Ben's eyesight at night was far better than during the daylight. He had spent so long crossing the desert at night that his eyes were far more used to it. It was a distinct advantage now. He could see every movement for quite some distance. If the enemy tried to get in closer he would know.

The enemy, in fact, were licking their wounds, stunned by the events. They didn't know what to do and there was no clear leader to guide them. Some wanted to just storm in, others wanted to go home. In the end, they decided to wait until light and then they would be able to see exactly what they were up against.

CHAPTER NINETY-TWO

"Are you busy tonight darling?" Ann asked her lover, as he was about to leave for work.

"Well, I was thinking I should really go back and check on my flat and see if Marika is all right. She still hasn't heard from Ben," Jonathan replied.

"Will you collect the rest of your clothes?" she asked him hopefully.

"I can do, if you're sure you're ready," he said smiling.

"I want to cook you something special for supper tonight," she told him mysteriously. Since they had been dating they nearly always went out for dinner. There had been so many engagements and functions to attend and she had been to a few of his family dinners. It was lovely but tonight she felt like a change. She was actually a really good cook but he didn't know that yet.

"That sounds like an offer I can't refuse," he told her giving her a kiss. "What time would you like me back?"

"Of course you must see if Marika is okay first but if you could be home about 9pm, would that be okay?" she asked.

"Oh easily, Marika will be off to the theatre so I'll try and catch her early," he responded. "Make it 8pm if you like?"

"Excellent," she kissed him back and he left for work. She had the day off so had all day to prepare. It was going to be a special supper. She had already checked his diary and knew he wasn't on call tonight for once, so they should have no interruptions. She got dressed and hit the shops.

Jonathan was too happy sometimes to be doing the job he did, he told himself. He found he was starting to walk around with a permanent smile on his face and that didn't look good when dealing with the bereaved. Sir David Essex had made him a proposition after golf last week and he had been brooding about it ever since. He would discuss it with Ann tonight. She was so sensible and his decision should include her now, he felt. They were, after all, a couple. The newspapers and magazines had started to come to terms with it. They had been seen out together so often that it was looking likely that the country's most eligible bachelor might finally be taken.

After work he called on his daughter. He was relieved to find that she was in a slightly more upbeat mood, than the last time he saw her. It certainly did not suit Marika to be in low spirits and it was something her family were unaccustomed to dealing with. It was usually her cheering them all up,

"Have you had news?" he asked her hopefully.

"No, not from Ben," she told him. "However, you know his friend Mac?"

"Yes," Jonathan answered.

"He's gone out to Africa to find him," she said positively.

"How's he going to do that?" Jonathan asked astonished.

"I don't know but I trust him dad," she said. "I think he will find Ben and bring him home."

It seemed an awful long shot to Jonathan but who was he to rain on her parade. If it gave her comfort for now then that was good enough. She went off to work happily and he picked up some more stuff from his flat and went home to Ann.

Ann had cooked the most incredible meal. It was all his favourite things. He guessed he must have told her that at some time but he couldn't remember. He was just so touched that she had gone to so much trouble. She had candles on the table and the wine was just perfect. There was soft music playing in the background and he was wondering what he had done to be so well treated. He was going to talk to her about his proposed change of career. David had told him that he wanted a new figurehead for his Hospital as he had been advised to take a back seat. David's health had not been in good shape for a while, too much work and stress and it was time he listened to his own advice. He wanted Jonathan to be that figurehead. Jonathan had once trained as a doctor as well as a lawyer. He was more than qualified to take over the running of such a prestigious position and he felt flattered and tempted by the offer.

However, as he prepared to broach the subject with Ann, she made him a completely different offer, which totally threw him off track. She brought in the coffee, together with some home-made Chinese cookies. She offered him one, which as he opened it a piece of paper fell out. He was going to ignore it but she asked him to read his proverb. He opened the paper and she had written in ink clearly the words, "Will you marry me?"

Jonathan looked at her open mouthed. It was a complete surprise. He had fallen in love with her when they had been in Paris but he knew how fragile she was with relationships and had not wanted to push her. He had felt a certain amount of guilt about staying in her Apartment but she seemed to encourage him. This was just incredible. He had actually fantasised about proposing to her but had thought that was probably way off in the future. He didn't know if he had earned her trust yet. Here was his answer, and she was waiting for his.

Ann started to feel a slight rise of panic in the pit of her stomach. She had wavered over doing this tonight, all day. What if he turned her down? Where would that leave them? Was she ready for another marriage? Her last two had not ended well. Whether it was the wine or just the headiness she felt whenever she was around him but somehow she had found the courage. Why doesn't he say anything? She felt sick.

"Ann," he said softly, those gorgeous blue eyes looking deep into hers. "I'd be honoured."

CHAPTER NINETY-THREE

Mac and Jezzer left before dawn the next morning. Mac was anxious to go and they felt it would be light enough by the time they reached their intended destination. They had studied the map last night and realised the bodies had been found fairly close to the border with Botswana and the Kalahari Desert. Jezzer knew of only one settlement up there.

They drove straight to the spot but there were no remains of any bodies left to identify. "The hyenas and scavengers have done their work," Jezzer told Mac. It was a horrid thought but all animals have to eat he supposed. They looked around the area on foot and Jezzer picked up some trail, which they followed in his Jeep. It wasn't long before they came across another Jeep, which had clearly had a misunderstanding with a ditch. The young driver had survived the night by staying awake but when he heard the sound of their engine approaching, he tried to find cover, in case it was The Rekelo, but there was none. He looked terrified as the two white men drove up to him and held up his arms in defeat. "Do you need help?" Jezzer asked him in Afrikaans.

The young man's face lit up with huge white teeth as he realised he wasn't going to be killed. "I crashed my Jeep," he explained excitedly to Jezzer. "I am trying to get help for my village. The Rekelo are very bad men. They are going to attack and kill the women and children," he chattered away in his native language. Mac watched on, unable to comprehend.

"Where is your village?" Jezzer asked him.

The young man pointed and both Mac and Jezzer knew where he meant from the map they had studied. "Please can you help us?" he continued. "I am supposed to get police but I can't drive and now my Jeep is crashed."

"Hop in," Jezzer told him and the young man gladly climbed aboard. "Show us your village and we will help."

"No, I can't go back. I have to get the police," he said suddenly not so happy to be taken home having got so far. "If you go there you will have to pass through the Rekelo Camp and it's very dangerous. There are many bad men."

"Is that what you did?" Jezzer asked him. "Drove through their camp?"

"Yes," he said. "I waited until night and they had got drunk but its daylight now and they will see us."

"Not if they've already gone to attack your village they won't," Jezzer told him and started to drive off towards the camp. "How many of them are there?"

"Not so many men, maybe ten or twelve but they have guns and we have nothing," the young man explained, "Except for the stranger. He took a gun from them and killed one of them."

"Did you say stranger?" Jezzer said intrigued. "What stranger?"

"His name is Ben. He is white like you and he came from the desert," was the welcome reply. Jezzer, immediately translated for Mac who looked delighted. When the young man saw them both smile he smiled too although he was terrified to be going back through the Rekelo camp.

As it turned out, the Camp was indeed deserted and they passed through without incident. Before long they could hear gunfire and Jezzer put his foot down. "Sounds like Ben needs us," Jezzer said.

Mac took hold of their rifles in readiness, checking they were fully loaded and said, "Hang on mate, the cavalry are coming."

CHAPTER NINETY-FOUR

"Get as many from your class as you can," Marika told Daniel. "We'll storm the hospital tonight after school. It's Friday so if necessary we can stay all weekend."

The two friends were back conspiring and Daniel was delighted. He had not only missed Charlie but he had also missed Marika. She had got all grown up and started going out with boyfriends and hadn't had time for their games but tonight they would be together again fighting for their cause.

The children arrived just in time. Charlie was due to be transferred to London that evening and Nurse Booth was getting him ready for his journey. There was great concern about moving him at such a delicate stage but Mrs Havers had been determined to win. She had not, however, figured on even more determination from her youngest daughter, to make sure she lost.

Marika, Daniel, Luke and three of their friends walked into Charlies room and barricaded themselves inside along with Nurse Booth who had been captured. The other friends would wait outside and prevent anyone getting near the door. "What's going on?" Nurse Booth asked her, in surprise.

"Don't worry Nurse," Marika said. "We're here Charlie and we're going to keep you here."

"Marika, you can't do this," Nurse Booth said gently, slightly amused.

"I'm really glad you're here Nurse," Marika told her. "We're not going to let anyone else in but you can see my brother is comfortable, can't you?"

"The ambulance is coming at 6 o'clock to take him to the private clinic in London," Nurse Booth told the children. "I'm just getting him ready. Your mother has ordered it Marika. I don't think you can stop it."

"We can if they can't get in," Marika said defiantly.

"Yes and we're not going to let them in," Daniel said emphatically.

"I shall do the negotiating if they try to force us out," Luke told them all. He was practising for the future when he hoped to be a lawyer.

"They'll call Security and you won't be a match for them," Nurse Booth tried to explain.

"Oh yes we will," Marika said and the children sat down in front of the door they had locked with a heavy chain and padlock Daniel had stolen from his dads' workshop. On the other side of the door, more and more children began to arrive and sit down in front of it. Some had made placards, which read, "We shall not be moved." It was a touching campaign and beautifully organised by the young Major Marika.

The Hospital Staff were soon alerted to what was going on and some were in total agreement with the children, as was Nurse Booth. When the ambulance arrived and was told of the situation, they rang their bosses, who in turn rang Sarah Havers. She was furious and telephoned Jonathan immediately. "Sort your daughter out."

"What has OUR daughter done now?" he asked annoyed at her attitude.

"She's only gone and barricaded herself and some other kids in Charlie's room stopping the paramedics from moving him tonight," Sarah complained.

Jonathan was shocked and amused, "She's done what?"

"Get yourself to the hospital and sort her out," Sarah ordered him.

"Sorry," he said smiling to himself. God bless her ingenuity. "No can do, not tonight, I'm afraid. I'm busy."

"Well, you'll have to be un busy," she told him furiously. "This is costing money. If they can't move him tonight they'll have to come back and I'll be charged."

"It wouldn't cost you anything if you let him stay where he is," Jonathan told her. "I told you the children would be unhappy about it and it's not like it's going to help Charlie."

"Well, they can't stay there, forever," she said ignoring him. "You will have to get them moved tomorrow, if not tonight."

"I may be busy tomorrow too," Jonathan said.

"I can always get Security to move them," she warned him. "Some of the children might end up getting hurt and I'm sure you wouldn't like that."

"Doesn't this just tell you something Sarah?" he asked his soon to be ex-wife.

"Yes, you've helped raise a cheeky spoilt girl," she replied clearly not impressed.

"Okay," he said sighing. "I'll call in later and speak to them."

CHAPTER NINETY-FIVE

The Rekelo had waited for light and could finally see what they were up against. It didn't look that much. They had the weapons and should be able to overpower the one man left standing between them and the village, as far as they could see. The firing began.

Ben knew he could hold them off from his position providing they didn't all attack him at once. He fired some warning shots back hoping to keep them at bay but they were in no mood for prevaricating any longer. Their problem was they didn't really have a leader and no plan of action for this event. They would use brute force and ignorance and that's exactly what Ben would struggle with. He might pick one or two of them off but they would soon overrun him. They decided to charge.

The one at the front went down quickly and his friend just behind was next. However, the next two had split and were circling around hoping to attack Ben from different directions. Ben knew he was in trouble but he would fight to the end.

He managed to pick another Rekelo off before one behind him started shooting and a stray bullet caught his leg. He reeled round and shot the assailant but there was another to his other side and more coming towards him. He was done for.

If there had been a bugle boy he would have been playing at that moment, as the Jeep, driven by Jezzer at full speed came tearing up the road and braked hard behind the enemy. Jezzer told the village boy to keep his head down and Mac began firing, taking out two surprised Rekelo men who had turned towards him, shock written all over their faces. Jezzer jumped out and went after the one he could see off to the left. He shot him just as he had Ben in his sights. The last one panicked and tried to run off but Mac got him in the leg. As he went down, the villagers who had started to appear, afraid for their friend, ran around him with their spears, shouting and singing. It must have been a frightening sight for the hapless Rekelo man.

Just as suddenly as the firing began, it stopped and Jezzer checked around to make sure there were no rogue Rekelo men hiding in the village. Mac managed to get down from the Jeep using his rifle as a walking stick and went across to Ben, who was trying to get up. His leg had taken a slug but he was alive, thanks to these two white men. "Well, nice of you to join me," Mac told his best friend meaning that they both had bad legs now.

"On the contrary," Ben told him, "Nice of you to join me."

Mac went to embrace him but something in his face told him not to. "What happened to you Ben?"

Ben looked surprised on hearing this stranger say his name. "You know me?" he asked.

"Of course I do mate," Mac said wondering what game his friend was playing. "I know I may look a bit different standing upright on these plastic legs but even you can't be that blind, are you? Mind you, wearing those pretty sunglasses, maybe you are," Mac said laughing.

"I should know you, shouldn't I?" Ben said.

Mac was beginning to get the picture. This was no game. It certainly explained a lot though. "Ben, it's me, Mac, your best friend. I came all the way from England to find you. You've been missing for a few weeks and Marika has been going mad."

The name Marika seemed to ring a bell in Ben's head. Was that the girl he kept seeing in his dreams, the one with the beautiful blue eyes? Umbabo and Mimbabo came running over and nearly knocked Ben over as they embraced him. "You did it Ben, you did it," they were saying excitedly.

"Whooa, take it easy boys," Jezzer told them in their native language. He had checked everywhere was clear and let the women and children out of the school building. All the villagers were crowding round ready to pay homage. "I think we need to get your leg looked at," Jezzer told Ben.

Okebe came forward to thank the soldiers who had freed his village and told them they should stay and let the village thank them properly with a festival.

However, Jezzer told him they had to go, as Ben needed to see a doctor. He helped Ben into the Jeep after he had said his goodbyes and they headed off for home. Jezzer wasn't about to take Ben to see a doctor. There would be too much to explain. He could take the bullet out if it was still in there and he had a feeling George would know what to do to clean the wound, so he drove home.

Mac called George on the way and told her to prepare. Ben was very quiet on the journey. He was trying to understand and remember but he was feeling desperately tired from his efforts over the last twenty-four hours and his body was still racked with pain. He was going to need a lot of tender loving care and Mac knew just the person to give it to him. He phoned Marika in England, after speaking to George. She was beside herself with excitement and set about arranging a stand-in at the theatre so that she could catch the next plane out.

When they got back to Jezzer's homestead, George was waiting with some coffee. Jezzer gave up a bottle of his best whisky that he kept hidden for emergencies, for Ben. Mac was impressed and started to believe there was hope for Jezzer after all. Their visit had seemed to invigorate him. George cleaned up Ben's wounds. The bullet had passed right through.

"Would you like me to shave you?" George asked him. "You might recognise yourself a bit better when you look in the mirror then."

There was no doubt Ben needed a good clean up and she was desperate to get his clothes off and washed. In fact, they were probably past washing. Mac could lend him some more. Ben let her take care of him and help to restore him to a human being again. He took a few grateful swigs of the whisky before falling asleep on his first comfortable bed in a long time.

Marika had taken an overnight flight and was there by 8 o'clock the next morning. She was so excited but Mac had to put her in the picture before she woke Ben. It was quite a shock. "What happened to him?" she asked.

"Haven't been able to find out," Mac told her. "My guess is, he was taken capture in Botswana but somehow managed to escape. There is evidence that he has taken some beatings," he warned her. "Then, I think, he must have walked hundreds of miles across desert until he arrived at the village where we found him. He probably suffered dehydration and maybe that has contributed to his apparent amnesia. He only seems to know his name. He clearly didn't recognise me but at least trusted me enough to come here. George has taken care of his wounds, he also got shot in the leg yesterday during the fighting, but it's not too serious. I think you need to work your magic on him now, Marika."

"He needs to get home," Marika said. "We can get him checked out at the David Essex Hospital."

"All in good time," Mac said. "I think you are going to need some patience."

"I'm not really known for my patience but I'll try," she told him. "Can I see him now?"

George took her through to his room and left her. Ben was still asleep which was, a good thing. He had a lot of healing to do and clearly he felt secure in his surroundings, finally. Marika climbed on the bed next to the man she loved more than anything, put her arm around his poor beaten body and slept too. She also felt secure for the first time, since he had left her.

CHAPTER NINETY-SIX

Jonathan arrived at the hospital just as the ambulance from the London clinic was leaving empty handed. Marika had clearly won this particular battle. He raced inside to give her the good news and was surprised to see so many of her friends staging a sit-in outside Charlie's room. It was impressive.

"You can all go home kids and get some sleep," he told them. "The enemy have gone."

The children all cheered and stood up ready to go, one of them banging on the door, in order to alert their leader. Marika recognised her father and ordered Daniel to unlock the door. "What's going on?" she asked her troops.

"We've won," was the answer and everyone was jumping up for joy. "Victory," they chanted.

"Yes, well done everybody but I think you better celebrate outside," Jonathan told them. "Don't forget this is a hospital."

"Yes," Marika said taking up his mantle. "Well done everyone. Go home and I'll text you if you're needed again."

Jonathan noticed his daughter didn't look as jubilant as the rest. Perhaps she realised they had won the battle but were unlikely to win the war. Gradually the children left congratulating one another as they went, including Daniel who knew his parents would be anxious. "Are you okay?" Jonathan asked Luke and Marika when the rest had gone.

Luke was happy enough. "I loved that, the little people beating the big," he said. "I don't just want to be a big shot lawyer now dad, I want to fight for the underdog."

Jonathan smiled and shook Luke's hand. "Marika?" he asked his daughter who was unusually quiet considering she had organised the battle.

"It's not over though, is it dad?" she said with tears in her eyes.

Jonathan put his arm around her to comfort her. "I know sweetheart," he told her softly. "You did pretty good though, don't you think? You should be proud." Suddenly, he became aware of another person in the room. "Oh Nurse Booth, had you been taken hostage?"

"Yes," she told him smiling. "I didn't mind."

Jonathan felt a little embarrassed. "I'm so sorry," he apologised. "Are you all right?"

"Yes," she said turning from checking her patient. "And so is your son."

All three Havers stared open-mouthed as Nurse Booth stepped away from the bed to reveal Charlie with his eyes open. Jonathan moved in closer. "Charlie," he said to his youngest son trying hard to keep his emotions in check. His son was indeed awake and he smiled back at his father. It was the most amazing moment for the family who had all waited so long. Marika was just rooted to the spot and Luke with her.

"I'll just go and get the doctor," Nurse Booth said and touched both of her patients' siblings gently on their shoulders before leaving the room.

"Dad," Marika eventually said.

He turned to Luke and Marika and beckoned them forward. "Come and say hello to your brother," he urged them.

"Charlie?" Marika said with the tears now rolling down her cheeks.

"What's wrong?" the patient asked his big sister. When he spoke for the first time no one could believe it. For Jonathan he knew it meant the boy was at least recognising them, he didn't have amnesia and he wasn't blind or dumb. It was just incredible.

"Where have you been?" Marika asked him, almost telling him off.

"I think I've been in the future," Charlie answered mysteriously.

"What do you mean?" Luke asked him.

Before the conversation could go any further his doctor arrived and the family were ushered out. Jonathan took his children up to the canteen. They were starving having come straight from school and full of excitement and questions. "We should let the others know," Marika said, thoughtful as ever.

"In good time," Jonathan told her cautiously. "Let's wait and see what the doctors have to say first." He was still anxious that there might yet be problems. It had been almost a year since the accident now. Next week was Charlie's twelfth birthday and he hadn't even celebrated his eleventh.

"Matthew and Rebecca are coming home from University tonight," Marika said. "I can text them dad and tell them to come straight here. Please."

"I'll text Mark," Luke offered.

Jonathan saw the doctor outside the canteen motioning to him. "Okay," he told the children. "You do that and stay here. Eat your food. I'm just going to find out what's happening, okay?"

He left them and the doctor told him they were delighted his son had woken up. They had more tests to carry out but the good news was Charlie was responding well to conversation. The bad news was his brain wasn't sending the right messages to his spinal column and he appeared to be paralysed from the neck down. This was devastating news for Jonathan and yet he couldn't help but feel elated his son was compos mentis, at least. There was hope, of course, things would change in the future and for now they would just rejoice in this miracle.

He collected his children from the canteen and they went back down to see Charlie who was looking brighter by the minute. He had been given a drink and smiled as soon as he saw them. Marika didn't hold back this time. She ran across to the bed and hugged her brother. "I've been talking to you for ages, did you know?" she asked him.

"You've always talked at me," he laughed. They all enjoyed the joke.

"No, I mean could you hear me?" Marika really wanted to know if all her hard work had paid off.

"I don't always listen, sis, you know that," Charlie answered. The truth was he didn't really know.

"She's been telling you all about her love life," Luke teased. He was amused that his little sister had a boyfriend.

"No I haven't," she objected. "Besides I think Ben has chucked me."

"Oh never mind sis," Charlie told her. "When you grow up you're going to meet the man of your dreams, fall in love and live happily ever after."

"Of course I am," she said not realising her brother really meant it.

"You too dad," Charlie diverted his attention to his father who had been looking on.

"What's that son?" he asked tears started to prick his eyes now.

"You're going to meet someone and fall in love too," Charlie told him with an air of authority.

"What's all this love stuff?" Luke asked.

"Just what I know," Charlie said.

"What about me then?" Luke asked.

"Hadn't got that far bruv, sorry," Charlie explained. "You're going to be a lawyer though and earn lots of money. Matthew is going to be a brilliant surgeon and Rebecca a GP. Mark will be happy working on Granddads farm, although he will change things there."

Marika looked at her father. Mark had dropped out of school and started studying at Agricultural College. It was in readiness to take over his Grandfathers Estate but this had happened after Charlie's accident. It had never been discussed before. Her father just shrugged. He didn't know if Charlie had heard this whilst in a coma or it was just a guess but he did sound so positive. It was a mystery.

"Will I marry Tim Marshall then?" Marika decided to test her brother. "After all, he is the man of my dreams."

"No, sorry, it's not going to be him but you will meet him at Dads' Wedding," Charlie announced.

"Oh Charlie, I've really missed you," Marika admitted. "I always loved your stories. You would make them up and I would act them." Everyone in the room laughed. It was a truly happy time but Jonathan knew there would be trials ahead. For now, they would just enjoy the moment.

The End